Praise for *The Loved Ones*

"Hughes' prose is elusive, allusive, artful, intriguing . . . It's as though Mickey Spillane sneaked into Virginia Woolf's study to add some dialogue . . . there are marvels to behold."
—*New York Times Book Review*

"The elliptical narrative—rich in sensory detail . . . is a demanding read that rewards patience."
—*New York Times*

"Bracing . . . Hughes is preternaturally alert to subtleties of appearance, gesture, and sensory detail."
—*New Yorker*

"This portrait of a New England family, hiding its despair over the death of Lily's younger brother (and yet fighting to hold it together) is masterful; Hughes glides in and out of her characters' heads, sometimes within the span of a paragraph. But the larger issues she explores, about the emotional cost of striving for glamour and beauty, make for the same kind of stylized, nostalgic pleasures as an episode of *Mad Men*. Sexy, immersive and lushly written. Read with a sundress on—and a pair of Wayfarers."
—Oprah.com

"Mary-Beth Hughes's body of work casts a dreamy, hypnotic effect, even while slyly exposing the risks and rewards of love and its devastations among the upper class. Edith Wharton and Henry James own the mansion housing this slant of prose, all style and substance, and Hughes moves ever closer to such mastery with . . . *The Loved Ones*."
—*Elle*

NO LONGER PROPERTY
of the
Anacortes Public Library

"Emotionally raw but ultimately elegant . . . Like Jean Rhys, Hughes gives her reader only the barest of warnings before dropping them headlong into frenzy . . . Hughes brings the reader so close to each member of the Devlin family that when the faces come into view, we know the characters so well that their physical attributes seem beside the point . . . [a] brutal, lush, brittle tour of the upper echelons of midcentury family hell . . . The novel shares its nightmarish domestic sensibility with Penelope Mortimer's *The Pumpkin Eater* and its unsettling tone of constantly moving targets with the fiction of Renata Adler, but despite its 1970s setting and luxe-louche vibe, Hughes's novel is archly contemporary in aim and style."   —*Bookforum*

"A patchwork of present and past, stitched together so seamlessly . . . Hughes's novel is tender and sympathetic . . . gorgeous precision of nearly every sentence."   —*Publishers Weekly*

"Mary-Beth Hughes is a quietly devastating writer, reminiscent of Evan S. Connell and James Salter in her delicate almost surgical ability to peel back the thin skin of normal life and to lay bare our painful truths, contradictions, the stains of grief and betrayal. *The Loved Ones* is a beautiful haunting novel of a time, place and the Devlin family."   —A. M. Homes

"An extraordinarily assured performance delivered in the quiet confidence and high style of a master of the form. The astonishing compression in the sentences quivers with that elusive quality of timeless art. Hughes's psychological acuity and unerring instincts as a dramatist combine with her tough-but-tender take on humanity to produce a work that will be read as long as any of us are alive—and far longer, if there is justice."   —Matthew Thomas

NO LONGER PROPERTY
of the
Johnston Public Library

"Compulsively readable, *The Loved Ones* is a beautiful book about the mystery of family, the suspense of growing up, and the ways in which women—young and old—make their peace with the world around them. Written with clockwork precision, Hughes's portrait of the Devlins's glamorous world—cosmetics fortunes! Baccarat tables! The Dorchester Hotel!—is a shimmering background for the dramas created by their conflicting desires, their colliding egos and their money. The story's women—Jean, a gorgeous, classy bombshell and Lily her confused, yearning, and loveable daughter—are both lost and found in this sea of privilege and desire."

—Susan Cheever

"Mary-Beth Hughes is a gorgeous writer. For years her masterly short stories have been passed among readers with an adoration and fervor that borders on religious. With *The Loved Ones*, the secret is out: the story of perfect swinging sixties scions Nick and Jean Devlin, their sprite of a daughter Lily, and their mourned boy Cubbie, delves deeply beyond surfaces and eras, into the people we wish to be and the people we unfortunately are. Sly and immersive, sensual and wise, *The Loved Ones* firmly places Hughes alongside Paula Fox and Alice Munro." —Charles Bock

"A book about leave-taking is inevitably a book about returning. In Mary-Beth Hughes's new novel, departures of all kinds—by air, by ocean, by illness, by alienation, by death—lead the characters to circle one another as though in an entranced dance, looking for a safe place of arrival, hoping, perhaps, that their losses would feel less unbearable there. Hughes is a master of understatement, and deftly captures the subtle undercurrent of family life and the danger from the ever-changing world in the 1970s." —Yiyun Li

"In Mary-Beth Hughes's electric novel *The Loved Ones,* sexual currents surge as a bruised but glamorous couple strive to go on 'making life gorgeous' after the death of their young son. Underhanded transactions and self-serving characters threaten these ambitions, and the privileged life in New York and London, late sixties, is not without its costs. Hughes writes with stunning economy: fully realized characters are made with a stroke in this most seductive, irresistible fiction."

—Christine Schutt

THE
LOVED ONES

THE
LOVED ONES

Mary-Beth Hughes

Grove Press
New York

Copyright © 2015 by Mary-Beth Hughes

All rights reserved. No part of this book may be reproduced in any form
or by any electronic or mechanical means, including information storage
and retrieval systems, without permission in writing from the publisher,
except by a reviewer, who may quote brief passages in a review. Scanning,
uploading, and electronic distribution of this book or the facilitation of
such without the permission of the publisher is prohibited. Please purchase
only authorized electronic editions, and do not participate in or encourage
electronic piracy of copyrighted materials. Your support of the author's
rights is appreciated. Any member of educational institutions wishing to
photocopy part or all of the work for classroom use, or anthology, should
send inquiries to Grove Atlantic, 154 West 14th Street, New York, NY 10011
or permissions@groveatlantic.com.

First published by Grove Atlantic, June 2015

Published simultaneously in Canada
Printed in the United States of America

FIRST PAPERBACK EDITION

ISBN 978-0-8021-2498-2
eISBN 978-0-8021-9159-5

Grove Press
an imprint of Grove Atlantic
154 West 14th Street
New York, NY 10011

Distributed by Publishers Group West

groveatlantic.com

16 17 18 19   10 9 8 7 6 5 4 3 2 1

for Ethel Blossom
love always

THE
LOVED ONES

Part I

Part I

Winter 1969

1

O nly a flurry. A thin blanket of white, something to take the gray mounds of snow and make them new. It began at dawn and fell over the blighted grass and the frozen river turning everything beautiful for a moment. Jean Devlin started her car, the Valiant wagon she used for errands. Soon the car was warm enough to drive and Jean made the reverse up the steep curve, then backed into the roadside pull-off where most delivery drivers chickened out and parked. They'd rather hand carry a refrigerator than make the plunge, but Jean could do it blindfolded.

Actually everyone gave up and parked here; it was true. Over the years she'd widened the pull-off to something almost stately with a stone wall framing a pretty stone stair that zigzagged under the spruce trees. She'd made those steps walkable. No matron climbing down for a house tour would tumble off her sling-backs and sue. Every summer for the last five Jean's quiet little Cape had made the designer's showcase. The star, the best of the best, her father crowed. Jean idled on the ridgetop and watched the snow sift down through the branches and thought of him, her father studying her face, so like his own, assessing. You never have to be anyone else he liked to say. Just tell them who you are.

I'm Clyde Boll's daughter! she'd shout when tiny and he'd find her a silver dollar. Then she was nineteen years old and he was giving her a wedding gift. He'd just won Gooseneck Cove, and on this day they were taking a closer look.

Her father, stiff-legged even then, shoved aside the goldenrod grown thick in the trace of a gravel drive. She lifted her skirt high so she wouldn't spoil her sundress. They sidestepped down and stood in an open patch of long wet grass. Blue spruce and birches made a wide-open circle, like the property was an amphitheater set to watch the drama of the river. The house was rotted up to the caved-in roof. Crows screeched from the trees at their intrusion and a water rat slid out through a broken window into a break in the cattails. Jean screamed and her father pulled her close to his chest. Don't be daft, Jeanie. It's a mouse.

A stench like something dead and decaying canceled the wet soft piney air. But she could still feel it on her skin, and she turned to see what the blue needles did, shivering, reflected in the water. What she'd make of all this. What a talent she had. Everyone said so. Then they climbed back up the ridge, Jean stepping like a deer, on the lookout for garter snakes.

Today, Jean would speak to Dr. Crabtree about some kind of sedation for the dog. Nick had laughed at her idea. She's not *that* bad! he said. But how would he know. Now a sweet sickening aroma filled up the car. Between the house and the cage the miniature poodle had somehow rolled in manure.

One year, she told Nick. She'd give him the year.

That's all he needed. That's what he'd said at Thanksgiving. That's all he was asking for. One year with her in London making things gorgeous, and then they'd see. Because how can we keep this going? he said. And finally she was willing to wonder that herself.

Even so, she looked at her gray shingle house tucked into the ridge overlooking the best stretch of the river for miles and felt she belonged only here. Fifteen years since her father's poker crony gave up the tiny cove on the Navesink River. And what Jean had done with it.

But how could they keep going. Other people wondered and some had the nerve to say so aloud. Today, no doubt, Mimi Crabtree would be at the door of the barn, narrating her very limited understanding of Jean's situation.

Oh! Jean could hear her say, as if she'd already arrived. Oh! How's that handsome Nick Devlin making out on Carnaby Street?

Making out. Something her daughter Lily liked to say. Something for children. Making out. Kissing on the sly. All kissing felt like that to her now. Underground and unexpected.

Someone had the wit to clear the house after the dinner Thanksgiving Day. She never quite knew whom to credit. But the candles were still guttering on the table and the sideboard when Lionel and his latest wife, Kitty, Jean's stepmother, Doris, and her father, Clyde, Lily, and even Perry the poodle went off for a ride in Lionel's limousine and never came back. Jean had on an apron with a recipe for cornbread stenciled on the bib. Nick found her by the sink and leaned into the counter, took a cigarette from her pack on the sill, but didn't light it. Need help? he said.

Not yours, she'd said. A little late for that. Even now it seemed harsh. Then she said it again. Not from you. The next thing she knew, he'd left the room, left her there with her apron and her hands already sudsy. How sick and foolish she felt all of a sudden. Her apron someone else's holiday costume. She untied it and left it on the counter and followed him then, out through the dining room past the bayberry candles Doris insisted on, all letting out the strange spiced scent. She thought he might be in Cubbie's old room, and wanted him to be there, but of course he wasn't. He'd already talked to her about that long ago. If Cubbie were in there, I'd never be anyplace else. No, of course not. She hadn't kept it up either. About a year ago, she'd put everything in a storage room in the attic. They'd understood at least that much together.

So now it was a sewing and craft room, or something like that. A place for a housekeeper—if she could ever tolerate someone working in the house again—to have a cup of coffee undisturbed. Or a room that had no use. And that was another reason to go to London. A year to reconsider this place, how to make their life work here again.

She took the curved front stair, the pride of the house, the one thing fully intact when they found it, and walked away from the main bedrooms to the one designated all their own, a small blue room with French doors opening over a rooftop balcony where the bend of the river came closest to the house. They'd chosen this room as newlyweds, and let the grander rooms be used in other ways.

He was sitting on the desk chair, struggling with his shoes. She sat on the edge of the bed. Soon he would be forty and he was beginning again. That's what his brother Lionel said. All brand-new.

And where she'd said to Lionel, who was so sure of everything, where does that leave me?

At some point Nick reached for her in a way she almost remembers, and that the French door was ajar, though it was cold enough for frost to spark the glass panes. Her skin was cold from that air, and his hands felt hard under her thighs, holding her up, catching her weight as if her whole body could be suspended in the air for a while, and for a moment it was. Though the ache of it the next morning kept them apart from each other. She'd been in the air, then her spine juddered fast, and then her bed felt as cold as concrete and he was asleep enough to be gone. It was the kind of thing she couldn't remember even as it was happening; there was too much of that lately.

Luckily for Jean, Mimi Crabtree was focused on the Kennedys today. You look just like Joan in that coat, said Mimi, holding the door wide, a glass insert into the traditional door. They'd done a good job here; just the site and the hand-rubbed red planks of the converted barn had stolen every last client from the old vet Carter Smyth on Front Street.

Blond all over, said Mimi, nodding approval. A phrase Jean found mildly repulsive. But she smiled, and placed her cheeriest self somewhere on the damp floor between them. Yes, she laughed. And don't believe the ugly rumors. I've never even met a brunette.

Our secret, said Mimi, and waved toward her mouth, a ghost of gesture they'd made in school.

Jean gave the complicit smile, then sighed. But, seriously. I'm at the end of my R-O-P-E. I can't say the word. Imaginary objects are the worst. Jean closed her eyes and gave a joking shiver.

Jean Devlin was an extraordinary-looking woman. Mimi Crabtree could see it today, what everyone went on about. She hadn't always thought so, and she didn't agree that tragedy made people any deeper or better. Usually not, if she were honest. But who wanted honesty? Most wanted a blond looking lost in her polar bear coat.

What are we going to do with this bad boy? Mimi whispered to the cage.

God, please tell me you have some ideas.

Mimi thought for a minute. You know. Maybe I do.

But wait. Don't we need the doctor? Jean laughed. I mean I'm willing to try anything. Believe me.

No, we need to talk to my sister. How do you think Perry would like Vermont?

Vermont?

Northeast Kingdom, up just past Burlington.

Vermont? said Jean. She felt herself go still, as if something had confused her, then she remembered to smile. What an idea.

My sister has a big farm, makes this place look like the toy it is. She's got a world of dogs and cats, all kinds. Perry would fit right in.

Perry in Vermont?

Why not? A buzzer rang on the big switchboard phone behind the check-in counter. Hold on a minute while I get that. She tucked herself in behind the artfully rough panels and picked up the receiver. Everything okay, sweet love?

Such a voice, Jean thought. What kind of a woman talks to her husband that way, at work no less. She sounds like a human Tootsie Roll.

She's right here, said Mimi. No, we're fine. Fine, she said again. Then: Don't worry. She hung up the phone and beamed at Jean. He says don't worry about a thing.

8

He knows about Vermont?

He trusts me.

Jean looked down at the small poodle looking up at her through the grille at the top of the cage. Perry was curled around the gray-pink matted rabbit toy that Lily put in the cage so he'd never be scared when traveling. It was Lily's squashed companion from nearly the day she was born until age four. All drool and grime when Jean had finally pried it away and put it up on a high shelf, against her better judgment. But Doris and Nick and even Lionel had all weighed in on this. So she added a blue gingham bow to match Lily's new big-girl bedspread and the rabbit had stayed. Until years later, when Lily identified the mangled fluff as the antidote to all of Perry's problems, which of course it wasn't.

He loves that rabbit, whispered Jean.

He can take it with him, said Mimi. Why not.

Jean wondered why people were always so ready to solve all her problems. Mimi Crabtree needed a hobby. Let's start with the sedative, Jean said at last. And I'll think about Vermont.

Do you want to leave him overnight?

Sure. Why not.

The tiny airport at Teterboro closed every time a teaspoon of snow fell on the silly red awning that covered the entry to the passenger lounge, and JFK was worse. Already a half inch had come down in the last ten minutes. Mimi waved now, arms wrapped tight around the unfortunate Fair Isle sweater she wore which emphasized the heavy high lift of her shoulders, the black and white all wrong. She looked like a spindly legged spider hovering in the gray light of the doorway.

Jean turned over the engine and waited. There was no point navigating the steep downhill through the orchard until the Valiant was ready. Waving Mimi, smiling waving Mimi. Suddenly Jean rolled down her window and gave a sweet wave back; she called out a warm good-bye and thanks. She might never need to see that woman again, and realized she was actually giving the Vermont idea a chance. Mimi, finally satisfied, retreated and closed the glass door.

Jean could almost hear the telephone in her kitchen ringing from here. Lionel calling with the contingency plan. What they would all do for Christmas if Nick didn't make it across the ocean tonight. And almost in response, a knotted pear-shaped fist seemed to clench with a hard ache just behind her pubic bone. She released the emergency brake and let the car glide like a sled around the graceful curves through the apple trees, slowly, while she caught her breath, the pain that sharp and then muted again. At least Mimi Crabtree was gone. She caught herself being superstitious. In a long marriage, Mimi Crabtree had produced only one underachiever still struggling his way out of the slower eighth grade. Russell Jr. left back in kindergarten, almost unheard of, because he couldn't grasp the basic shapes that would one day become letters. That Cubbie and even Lily were reading on their own in kindergarten was just a fact. Just the way things were.

Jean eased to a stop at the end of the drive and felt the rare peace of being alone. Not a soul on the road in either direction. The snow was no longer swirling; now one of those determined showers fell all around her and muffled the thick tracks some big vehicle with chains had made not so long ago. The ache in her belly subsided completely, like a big fish that had swum thickly to the surface, then away. It was well hidden now. She was not pregnant. She'd already been through that dashed hope and it had landed her overnight in Riverview for a quick D and C. Nothing to it. But she'd asked for and received a total anesthesia.

She'd been told at the Philadelphia children's hospital that the very best thing she could do was have another baby. Have another child right away. There was lip service paid to the theme of impossible to replace, but the emphasis was: new baby. As aggressive and idiotic as they had all seemed to her at the time, Jean could barely understand or bear to think about why it hadn't happened yet. One day about a year ago, she'd made the terrible mistake of bringing it up with Doris who was, after all, the closest thing she had to a mother. Doris had said something ludicrous about god's time or god's plan, god's notion that was so enraging, that Jean had called her something horrible out loud: Christ, you're a stupid piece of shit.

When did you start talking that way Doris wanted to know, as if that were all that mattered. Her father had laughed. Just once, but he did laugh, and it had clarified a great deal about where Jean still stood with him.

The road was beginning to look bad, but if she gave up now, it almost guaranteed a lost Christmas. She'd be curled in the big plaid chair nursing a Dewar's watching Lily open a patchwork velvet miniskirt from a boutique on the King's Road. Already too small. No, she would proceed as long as possible with the plans they'd made. She put on her left blinker, though at the moment it seemed as if she were the only driver out in the county. She'd skip the usual coffee with Doris, just drop off Lily's overnight bag then beg a last-minute hair appointment. Who knew? Maybe she could get one.

Jean made the slow wide turn back onto River Road, empty and hushed, and angled the tires into the ruts left behind. The Valiant wobbled left then right. A truck maybe, something with a broader chassis. She felt herself upright in the seat, her chest coming close to the steering wheel, and took a breath. She'd be fine. But, my god, the snow had come down so fast!

Now she was on the steep hill that hugged the back of the golf club, slowly, her engine grinding out the ascent and then louder still on the downhill, with a whine to suggest it was at some breaking point. But that was impossible: she was going twenty miles per hour. The scene lay out around her; the sudden open valley all the way to the water looked like something perfect. She said out loud, Pretty! As if Lily were in the car and needed to be distracted.

The heat blast made her gloves, the whole car smell like bacon. She rolled down her window but that fogged her windshield. A jolt of panic shot through her spine when she couldn't see. She downshifted again, wiping the condensation with her hand, taking that deep slow breath she'd been taught, thinking grateful, I am grateful for the chance; she'd been taught that, too.

All the talk about summer on the shore but this was the time most beautiful, the grays and mauves and violets, the green cast in the snow that no one saw but her, and of course, Lionel. Bottle her, he always said. She'd forced herself not to think of these compliments with melting fondness. He was a scoundrel; that's what her stepmother would remark if she knew the half of it. But Doris flirted with Lionel. Gave him the full wattle, Jean told Lionel. You're getting the works, Jean laughed. She's really turning on the lights.

Yes, I see. Wicked girl, he'd called her and smiled. Very wicked, he'd said as if appraising something hidden and precious.

Two weeks ago her latest errand for Lionel had made Nick laugh. His best good laugh played out long across the overseas cables. She listened and felt happy she could still do that. Tell a story and make him laugh.

Lionel had called too early one morning and begged her to get on the train. The most recent Katherine was locked in the bedroom and couldn't or wouldn't come out. I've tried everything. Believe me. He took a deep breath. He'd tell her everything, but she cut him off.

Oh, I believe you, she'd said and then waited out the sulky silence on the other end. Lionel preferred to persuade at length.

Please come, he said, finally. Could you come right now?

Her arrangements were easily made. Lily was spending the night at Margaret Foley's. Jean could leave food and some newspaper on the floor for Perry in the basement, close off the good part of the house, and go.

She boarded the train in Red Bank with the last wave of commuters. You have me for an hour, she'd said. But ringing the door, just past ten on Sixty-Second Street, she knew her day was lost. She already heard herself calling Doris to arrange for her to check in with Lily around dinnertime. The Foleys couldn't always be counted on.

She drew back from the door and looked up at the brownstone facade, freshly pointed, all the window trim painted a subtle unexpected gray green. So Lionel—something to catch your eye and keep you looking to figure it out. Feeble blue Christmas lights twinkling off-rhythm in daylight. This must be Kitty's hand at work. How did he find them. All of Lionel's wives were named Katherine. But only the first, the loveliest and the sanest, had used the full title. The rest—only four! said Lionel plaintively—were Kates and Kokos and now, the most infantile, Kitty. The latest Mrs. Lionel Devlin was barely out of her teens. Is she out? Doris had asked, all earnest fact-finding, and Nick and Jean had roared with laughter. Maybe not, dearest, said Nick. Very possibly not.

How does a grown man meet a girl that young? Doris wanted to know. Jean took an exasperated breath, and Nick answered, Luck, dear. Someone's luck, anyway, we're not sure yet who's the fortunate one. But I think it may be Lionel. She's very sweet, this Kitty.

Oh, come on, said Jean, incredulous. She's embryonic.

A quality most don't appreciate right away, said Nick, and Jean gave him her slyest smile.

Lionel appeared at the front door in his uniform black silk kimono, belted with a hideous necktie, something in a zigzag horizontal knit. And sure enough, her eye went there, to the hangman's knot he'd affected in the brown flame stitch. She smiled up at him. You're a wonder.

No, you! How did you get here so quickly? I adore you. Come in.

He scanned the sidewalk behind her, happily, as if there might be some other pleasant surprises, and then sighed and stood back; the waft of some new scent caught her as she skirted by him. He took up the doorframe, yet assumed the posture of allowing her entry. Such an old-dog trick, he made her laugh. Look at you! she said.

His hair, usually a careful bell from crown to nape, was a nest of wet ringlets. Silver, black, beige, even green-looking damp tangles, cheeks bright pink, and teeth brushed, just, and he was saturated, completely saturated with a cologne that smelled of grapefruit rind. She barely made it past him and wondered why it never made Nick jealous—Lionel knocking her half silly with a greeting.

He's only practicing, said Nick when she asked him. But she wasn't so sure.

Practicing hard, then, she'd said.

He listened. What would you like me to say?

She shook her head. As if she'd started something stupid. He's a silly man, your brother, she said. But silly wasn't what she meant at all.

14

Lionel gave the door a pat when closed as if commending a faithful servant, odd the ways he got her to watch him. Thank god you're here, he said. We are desperate.

You are always desperate, she laughed at him and shrugged off her jacket. Where is this nightmare unfolding?

It's not funny, Jean.

No, of course not.

She's in the upper flat and won't come down. It's been days.

Days?

Day, then.

All right, she said, dropping her jacket on the red lacquer chair, all right. Have you had any breakfast?

Of course not. Lionel tugged at his knot, pulled in his belly.

Well, you're emaciated I can see. She put a fond hand toward his wet hair. Go find a brush. I'll put the coffee on.

What about Kitty?

Kitty next.

She went on to the kitchen and untangled the cord from inside the percolator, found coffee and corn toasties and Aquavit in the freezer. Even if the toasties were a thousand years old, just the scent of them would calm everyone down. Lionel reappeared in gray flannel trousers, red cashmere turtleneck, and black velvet slippers with a coat of arms embroidered in gold thread. His hair combed straight back from his forehead, his face soap shiny, fingertips pink from the scrub brush.

Much improved, she said. All right, I'll root out the girl.

You're an angel. Really, he said. You are. His eyes held her gaze then he jimmied a mug out of the dishwasher. That look he always gave her. Jean climbed up the interior stair to the upper duplex. What was that look. Longing, admiration, even love, lust, respect, something like awe, tenderness. Always something rich and good she wasn't getting much of elsewhere. But sometimes the eyes were just big and dark and blank. Today, for instance, he'd used the same attentive watchfulness to rinse the dirty cup.

Jean reached the top floor, tucked in her loose blouse, knocked shave-and-a-haircut on the bedroom door. Kitty? Sweetheart, it's Jean. Will you let me in?

The door opened a tiny crack. That didn't take much; she'd have Kitty downstairs before the toasties were defrosted.

She pushed the door gently and entered the dark, dank-smelling room. Some sweetish, moldy smell seemed to be coming off the sheets of the rumpled bed. Opaque drapes were drawn and a yellow seam of light between each pair shone bright like strips of neon. Kitty was curled on the floor. A suitcase, a very small apple-green one, like a child's overnight case, was stuffed with blue jeans and embroidered tops.

It's no use, Jean. It's really over, said Kitty. It's like a death this time. There's no changing it. I've tried everything.

She put her head inside the green suitcase and sobbed, very muffled sobs, but her shoulders shook under the peasant blouse she wore, a wispy blue and identical to the one she'd given Lily last birthday. Jean looked at the pantomime unfolding on Lionel's very good carpet. She imagined Kitty had unlocked the door then rushed into her fetal position beside the suitcase. Kitty's narrow shoulders quivered.

Jean lowered herself down, slowly, as if Kitty might be startled into a bite like Perry. Come on, she whispered, and arranged her tweed skirt close to her hips and thighs, in case Lionel decided to sneak in on them. Shh, she said and draped a very light, very tenta-tive arm around Kitty's waist. Sweetheart, hush now, really, now.

Kitty cried harder. But soon she pulled her head out of the suit-case and dropped her face into Jean's lap, which was alarming, and for a moment Jean suspended her hand's caress, then she remembered what to say: There's nothing here that can't be fixed. Nothing.

She stroked the fragile head under the thin blond hair. The skull felt light, as if Kitty's bones were thinner than other heads she'd held. Both her children had been born with hard thick heads she'd thought would protect them. She felt the thin bone under the too fine, too light hair. The weeping girl who meant well but had foolishly married Lionel. What can be so terrible? Jean crooned a little; she heard herself sounding like a cartoon character. Hmm? What's so awful as all this.

Then of course she got the answer, a baby on the way. Lionel's inability to keep his prick in his trousers.

But surely, Jean started to say. But she was a prude. She was a cartoon prude; she felt Lionel's prick was out of her range of operation. Sort of, she thought and laughed, and Kitty looked up confused. You're married, darling heart. Aren't you?

Yes, yes, but Lionel doesn't even know what married means. Kitty, sweetest, you're pregnant now.

Kitty sat up and blinked. The same wide-eyed deep blank look that Lionel gave her. And Jean made the exact same gesture. Pushed back the light fluffy hair as if to get more of that look, whatever it was. You are having a baby, said Jean. Imagine how beautiful that baby will be. Imagine. My goodness.

She pulled Kitty into an embrace now, very light, better, much better than the collapse, and she felt the warmth of Kitty nestle into the curve of her lap, the tender softness of her slender arms hold-ing Jean's own. What a pretty picture they would make if Lionel came this moment.

How about a nice bath, said Jean. I always loved baths when I was pregnant. I'd feel the baby and I were doing the same thing, just floating.

That's disgusting.

Try it.

She'd drawn the bath and changed the sheets and found clean clothes in the piles on the floor. She'd opened the drapes and for a while, the windows. By the time Kitty was tottering down the stairs smelling of lemon verbena there were voices in the kitchen. Kitty snuggled right into the depths of Lionel's turtleneck. Heaven, he said into the top of her head. The man leaning against the counter said, You're the rescuer I hear. He shook his head as if she'd done something wrong.

Here you go. He lifted a strawberry-shaped cup from Kitty's counter-top mug tree and poured the coffee Jean had made.

Lionel was speaking into Kitty's hair, and Jean could feel the comfort of that and Kitty's resistance, both at the same time like a shiver. Irving Slater, said Lionel. Meet Jean Devlin, breathtaking sister-in-law.

The first thing she noticed was that his mouth looked clean. It had sharp lines, and big-looking teeth, and dimples. It looked like a mouth that made good choices. Not like Lionel's open-ended banquet, his soft full mouth pressed to the passing parade. Irving Slater had a discerning mouth. She smiled at him. Now that Nick was becoming the great connoisseur of faces, maybe she could play this game, too.

She took a sip and said, Marvelous.

You're modest.

Oh! she said and now Kitty was laughing, too. This was all very funny. She'd done her job; now she could catch the 1:15 out of Penn Station and be home again as if nothing had happened.

* * *

Just thinking about Lionel made her smile and Jean felt the wheels find traction on the straightaway like another compliment delivered with his usual ease. She was fine and soon the snow would be over for good. December twentieth and everyone predicted an early spring. She really was okay, but once she made it over the bridge to Doris's house she'd wait out the snow after all and drive home only when the roads were sanded and clear.

2

Sister Charitina felt along the length of the microphone for the switch with her thick fingers and a clutch of eighth-grade boys laughed so uncontrollably they had to be sequestered in the milk room. Finally young Sister Mary Claire found a faulty connection in the tangle of cords and a great electric shriek rolled from the speakers silencing the room. Lily Devlin was already listening, Margaret Foley, too. They settled in to the folding chairs the eighth graders had been called in early to unstack and arrange.

Now the entire school had filed in behind them and Sister Charitina kept her lips a narrow line. Waiting. Lily took a breath and could smell the starch in the overwarm room; the nuns' vast handkerchiefs pulled from beneath the black folds and pressed along hot foreheads. One way or another, the atmosphere of the old building was beyond regulation for the Sisters of Mercy. It was either stifling or chilled to the bone, but that was the least of their worries today.

One hundred and forty-eight children, ages four to thirteen, trapped! wailed Sister Agnes when Father's infallible secretary called to say the roads were already a danger.

There were always the canned goods. At St. Thomas Aquinas, in the convent, an entire room had been fitted out with shelves to accommodate the nearly two thousand cans of green beans, yams, and stew the children had delivered to school when President Kennedy was still alive and the sisters could depend on reliable information from the government. Now the cans sat, a stay against an unnamable disaster.

Charitina felt it possible that some small variation on disaster had arrived today. Certainly a test. But she could keep them all in line. She didn't envy Dymphna over at Star of the Sea with the high schoolers. St. Tom's stopped at the first edge of adolescence and she never failed, never once failed, to be grateful. Still, there were challenges.

Lily Devlin for instance. She was becoming a queer one and wasn't that predictable. Taken up this year with Margaret Foley like her life depended on it. Like her life depended on it, she heard herself say out loud at the dinner table not long ago, and only Mary Claire, still so unsure of herself, had the courage to reply. And maybe it does? All the others were quick to agree with Charitina, and their constant agreement was pleasant and her due and only occasionally wearing. Charitina felt that Lily Devlin needed to be taken down a peg or two. We've spoiled her, Charitina said. Killed her with kindness, said Josephine. Too much of a good thing, said Agnes, and Charitina turned her benevolent gaze back to Mary Claire at the end of the table. She was all for well-reasoned dissent. Her brothers were both Jesuits after all. But Mary Claire nodded and said, It's a terrible thing. I mean what happened.

We know that, dear, said Charitina and suppressed the sigh she knew would injure. We know.

Outside the *scrape, scrape* of Teedle's snow shovel made a slow ugly beat. The swirling gray filled in the mesh glass doors and Teedle's long back could be seen bending like a beetle inching along the path he made from the auditorium to Father Mulroney's door. She could imagine Mae Manon in the rectory cloakroom brushing Father's cashmere coat. Sniffing the maroon wool scarf that brought out the kind blue of his eyes, just a dash of lavender she'd put in a sachet to keep away the moths, but would the scent betray itself and overwhelm?

Mae lined the galoshes and the gloves by the carved oak chair and waited. They were all used to waiting for Father and pleased to do it. It gave life a nice structure. Unlike Monsignor Reese who wouldn't, couldn't, leave them alone. There was such a thing as too much benevolence. He'd been sent to the missions in Paraguay where the language barrier would make his constant earnest smiling less oppressive. Mae Manon had shared this observation with Sister Charitina and to her pleased surprise, Sister had agreed with a wink. That wink still played in her mind from time to time—two women unafraid to see what was right in front of them. But the thing in front of her now was the hole she'd failed to notice earlier. Father's good cashmere coat punctured in the lapel. No doubt some pin he'd been forced to wear and had pulled off immediately, she didn't blame him, but shivered that she hadn't noticed earlier and now what. He'd be disheveled just when he needed to be at his most commanding. Charitina would know just who to blame.

Charitina came down from the stage and paced the front row of eighth graders. Lily Devlin was slumping again. Her round pink knees on full view, chafed above the mismatched knee socks half sliding down her calves. At least she wasn't shaving her legs yet as so many of the eighth-grade girls were making it their business to do. She had only so much jurisdiction. She couldn't force the use of deodorants either, though there had been one sad intervention on poor Ruth Le Baron.

Then there was the whole business of tampons. They'd decided after a nearly unbearable meeting with Father Mulroney to cancel sex education altogether. Father made a joke that even now, thinking about it, stopped her thoughts. The tampon as precursor to married life. She remembered his smiling sip from the Waterford tumbler, the pretty spectrum of amber playing in the facets. Mae Manon had made an admirable fire. The scent of pine sap, warmed and crackling, filling the study. Here is where Father Mulroney conducted his summit talks—his joke—with Charitina. Monsignor Reese had usually invited her to sort clothes for the poor in the basement while they scoured the week's news at the school. Idle hands, he'd said, idle hands. Father Mulroney always offered her a Rusty Nail. Just one, now! she'd insist, but she was sure she never giggled. The idea of a giggle made her wince. Just one Rusty Nail with Father in the study where he wrote his inspiring sermons. He'd really changed the tone at St. Tom's. Made Vatican II begin to feel like something they'd all learn to live with, maybe even like.

So one cool Friday evening early last spring they'd canceled sex education. How much change could a little parish bear? And Sister Charitina had walked the path that Teedle now shoveled so slowly. She walked through the twilight with the peaceful sense of a decision well made with the blessing of all higher authority.

Lily Devlin remembered to keep her shoulders back and sit up. Slouching was sure to capture Sister Charitina's attention. She made a basket of her hands in her lap, straightened her head, and lowered her eyes, as though in casual prayer. She could feel her whole self sending the message: casual prayer. Just the way her whole self had sent the message: Ghost of Christmas Past, with her rattling chains and permanent tears. Even her mother had said she was perfect. But her father felt that acting wasn't any kind of life, so already they were ruling that out. No acting. In a way she was in casual prayer, because she didn't know what to make of the photograph she protected from Sister Charitina's expert eyes. Charred and burned. That's what happened to miscreants. Charred and burned. She felt a laugh erupt, though she didn't know exactly what was funny. Russell Crabtree still blamed her for his trouble, his long penance as a hall monitor. She'd laughed onstage when his Scrooge flubbed a line and he'd responded by throwing his cane. He blamed her so severely that not one of his friends, or any single person who wished to be his friend in some more fortunate life, would speak to her. They made a big point of it, stepping around her if she happened to be in front of them, cutting her off if she said hello to them. If they were very lucky when they were doing all this, Russell Crabtree would be in the vicinity, so the person cutting her could breathe a little easier. As long as it was Lily Devlin they all understood to be the problem, their own lives could be expected to move along on track.

It still surprised her that Margaret Foley was immune to this. She didn't care what Russell Crabtree thought or did, and that made Lily almost laugh again. She stiffened her body and waited for the urge to subside. Then Margaret nudged her elbow. Lily laughed with a loud fake sneeze and rubbed her nose, other hand flat now on her lap, hiding the curling yellowing photograph. Only Sister Mary Claire looked up at the sound and gave her a watery smile.

Sister Charitina was like a terrier at the double door, a signal that Father Mulroney was already making his perilous way. They were always worried about Father. All the nuns fretted as if he were a gigantic infant left on their doorstep. But really, as Margaret had pointed out, he was a fox. When Father Mulroney came over for drinks at Lily's house, if Margaret was sleeping over, she could be counted on to eavesdrop. Are you sure your mother isn't *dating* Father Mulroney? A hilarious idea.

He was her high school teacher!

Margaret gave Lily the long dry look she was famous for. Next witness.

Margaret was a character; that's what Lily's grandmother said. A big piece of funny business. But Margaret was in a new phase; she was losing interest in Lily and her family. As if all the drama had faded away. Your friends will like you for who you are, said her grandmother. Not for the news of the day.

Lily held the curling photo in the basket of her linked fingers. It looked ancient, all the faces oddly colored and washed away. She knew from experience that whoever took this Polaroid forgot to use the stick of bitter chemicals that fixed the instant colors. The sky was pink, Anthony Moldano's face a deep yellow, and his two little boys had fluffy gray hair. Their mother was blue from the effort of keeping them all close in the frame. Anthony Moldano's small eyes tilted down, as though with sympathy, his mouth compressed, suggesting the resolve to act on whatever was making him so compassionate. Her grandmother loved the word resolve, but she meant it tenderly Lily knew, as something that came and mostly went. Anthony in his policeman's uniform appeared not to fluctuate in that way.

Who takes a Christmas photo in June? Margaret whispered. His wife is a retard.

Actually Lily's mother had sometimes made them put on velvet outfits to pose in June when they were tiny, but she skipped Christmas pictures altogether now. Margaret sniffled and Lily gave the photograph her attention. She knew Anthony, of course, but not his wife who was just a blur. It seemed that Margaret may have scratched away some of her features.

Gross, whispered Lily, and slid it slowly across her lap toward Margaret's extended fingers and felt the relief begin then disappear as Sister Charitina's head spun around in aggrieved distraction. A noise. Eyes closed! she shouted and all one hundred and forty-eight children knew to either recall their sins or count their blessings depending on who their teacher was that year.

Sometimes Lily thought if she were captured by the enemy and tortured, she would give up her secrets right away. It was something she knew about herself, a part of her character that she was ashamed of. They heard about tortured saints all the time. Red-hot branding irons applied to open eyes leaving only scorched sockets! Just to get them to say they weren't Catholic, never even liked the Catholics, thought it was a foolish idea. And the saints said no. Then there were the World War II children who had been piled up in dead stacks because of who they were, or who their parents were. They'd been brave in ways Lily felt she couldn't be. Her grandmother disagreed. Not that they ever spoke about the martyrs and the children in piles or the possibility of torture. Lily never talked about these things, but her grandmother would sit on the blue bed in the dark and hold her hand and say that Lily was a brave kind girl, that Lily had a brave kind heart, and didn't they know it. Her grandmother would lean down and kiss her and for a brief while it was true. She was brave; she was kind.

Margaret pulled up her knee socks with meaning. Sister Mary Claire was opening the pass-through window of the milk room. Russell Crabtree's wedge of black hair was visible now beneath the half-raised metal shutter. Sister Mary Claire moved swiftly. Her intention seemed to be to give the boys, though in trouble, the full benefit of Father's presence when he arrived.

Charitina placed both hands on the glass of the double doors watching Father Mulroney's precarious walk along the icy path. Once his cordovan boots slipped beneath him tipping him for a moment; she could feel it in her own legs the tensing, the clenching of muscles and then he was fine, just fine, old Teedle ready right behind to create the human pillow in case of a tumble. He was fine and now sliding along like an ice skater, a cautious ice skater unsure how solid things were ahead. With the sunny days and the black bitter nights, you never knew what was happening right beneath your feet.

How good he was to come at all. Not that Charitina needed him. Though she did feel her own heart calm as he came closer slowly, now just under the basketball hoop and soon he would be where the children lined up in classes, according to grade, every morning, even this one, which now in hindsight seemed a mistake. So many falls and bruises. But everyone needed to toughen up around here. That's why Father was coming, to brace them all, to give them the stamina and fortitude required to ferry all these restless children out of the auditorium and into the safety of their homes, before the blizzard, only a deceptive swivel of fat flakes a moment ago, kept them stranded.

Russell Crabtree was certainly slumping on the floor. Sister Mary Claire pantomimed the emergency of his posture, chin jerking, wrists flicking, urging a straighter spine. Russell sat upright until it was possible to see the entire intriguing back of his head. The blue-white skin with the wash of freckles just between the black curls and the white collar, the clasp of his clip-on tie shiny and bright. Lily considered the brightness of his clip through her squinted closed eyes. He always smelled of blueberries as if he doused himself with jelly before school.

Probably does, he's so conceited, Margaret had offered. Slowly, slowly, Russell Crabtree turned his head and looked at Lily, looked into her face solemnly until she couldn't find her breath and Margaret whispered, Shit.

I heard that, Sister Charitina spun round from the doorway, but in that instant Father was upon them. All the children rose to their feet. The loud scrape of metal chairs against the floor and echoing coughs. Teedle pushed open both doors wide so Father could enter and the wind reached the first rows, sharp against the skin. The wind and Father's cologne.

Good morning, Father. There was a drag and a monotony to the tone that satisfied Sister Charitina. More exuberance would have reflected badly on her. She had matters well in hand. Father Mulroney gave her his private smile; more would be said about this at leisure she could tell.

Sit, children. Good morning to you. Sit now. And Sister Charitina nodded with the right solemnity. The weather may be making Father magnanimous but proper forms would be observed. Thank you, Father, they sang out slowly like a requiem, then sat in a rumble of chairs.

Father's big velvet throne was up on the dais. Teedle had delivered it from the storeroom first thing in the morning. There'd been a tug of war over that, but now Sister Charitina could see she'd been correct. Dais first, snow shoveling second. But where was Mary Claire? Father held out his coat, wet with snow and there was no one to take it. She'd do it herself. Allow me, Father, and she smiled. This was a special occasion.

You're too good, he murmured. Now, he coughed loudly and crossed himself, In the name of the Father . . .

Today the children were allowed to pray in their seats. When the whole school gathered there was simply not enough room for kneeling. Another reason to expand this old auditorium. Besides, the children needed exercise, even in the winter, she'd pleaded. Father felt the old altar and the sanctuary took precedence over the natural process of growing bodies. He scarcely needs our interference there! Father had laughed. Are we agreed then?

They were not agreed. Though it alarmed her a bit to think it and here she was holding a sopping wet coat. Of all the children in the front row only Lily Devlin still had her eyes open, watching her folded hands as if something might explode there. Poor child, well, she'd certainly done her best. Charitina lifted her chin with a quick jut, a gesture sure to catch the attention of anyone with open eyes. Lily looked up with surprise and alarm. Sister Charitina jutted her chin again and indicated the armful of sopping outerwear.

Glory be to the . . . Father Mulroney was humming along. Lily rose from her seat and tucked her hands into the pockets of her uniform. Something they'd been over countless times especially with the older girls, the implications of hands in pockets. Charitina didn't like it one bit and glanced at Father whose own eyes were, mercifully, shut. What a face that man had, too handsome really to be a priest. She'd heard he'd been the oldest son and that was that. His father had taken the pledge, like so many, on the day of the ordination, and didn't even keep faith to the end of the party. Spent the night on the Elks club lawn while his mother polished and put in proper boxes all the neighbors' borrowed silver. She wouldn't let him in the door. Not on that most blessed night. The poor soul had caught double pneumonia from sleeping on the dewy grass. Father Mulroney anointed his father in the same Cambridge hospital where his mother would be admitted a year later, urgently ready for death's door.

The guilt! Can you imagine? said Mae Manon. Charitina could not, at least not in the moment of that interesting conversation, but later walking slowly through the schoolyard, she realized why she understood him as well as she did. Of course, she thought, both orphans. Both givers.

She wouldn't hiss, but she could click her tongue. Get moving! the sound said and Lily picked up her pace.

Mae Manon stared into a coffee cup, sitting at the table. The radio played in the rectory kitchen, a big band and a female singer with a high sweet voice, singing a lullaby about a man gone overseas to war. He might be back someday; he might be alive only in her heart. Or he might give her a start, the start of a brand-new day. Lily didn't like to knock, so she coughed. Then she shook the snow off herself and the heavy bundle in her arms. Stamped her feet. Mae, she called out, and Mae lifted her head, looking angry. Who would dare intrude?

It was only Lily Devlin. She pushed back the ladder chair, solid polished mahogany, and came to the door. Later on she'd report to her sister about poor Lily Devlin. They all set things aside for that girl; it was a given. Lily's name had become a kind of shorthand for all the generosity of the St. Thomas Aquinas parish. Lily, she'd say to her sister tonight. And her sister would nod. You're a good soul, Mae.

What are you doing out in the storm, Lily? Mae asked. Get right back to school before you get in trouble. Father's not here.

I know! Here's his coat. Sister Charitina sent it. He needs another.

Mae stared at the thick bundle in Lily's arms, wrinkled now and soaked through. What have you done with Father's good coat! Her voice was as high as the lullaby. Look at the mess of it now.

He needs something else I think. Now that Lily thought of it, she wasn't entirely sure of the sense of this errand, taking Father's coat away.

There's nothing wrong with the coat you have right there! Or there wasn't before you got started with it. What are we going to do with you, Lily? You can't go on like this, you know. Mae put her rough red hand over her eyes and passed it down the length of her face, as though erasing one expression so another could appear, and just like that she smiled, and said, Well, since you're here. Since you're here, you better come right in. She'd show Charitina she could care for Father Mulroney just fine. How dare she, Mae Manon thought, but she wouldn't mention this to her sister because it felt already, even the anger, that she'd been defeated somehow. Not so fast, Charitina, she said aloud. Not so fast.

Lily looked away from Mae. Toward the orchids swallowing up the last bit of light from the big bay window. A little steamer, something used for colds, sent a filmy mist toward the cascading blossoms. Magenta, ruby, white-laced with veins of pinks. Oh, look at your flowers!

They weren't Mae's but they might as well have been. She'd been the one to put up the vaporizer and right away dead sticks began to bud. My kitchen miracle, Father said once, looking at them all and though his gaze was directed firmly toward the flowers, she got the message. She knew her own worth. Whatever Charitina felt one day to the next.

No need for you to wait, dear, said Mae. I'll bring Father's coat myself. They'll be wondering what happened to you, now. She'd be damned if she'd let Charitina pull a stunt like this one. She'd have the hole, and wasn't that the big problem here today, that tiny, tiny pinhole, the pettiness of some people. Mae would have it sewn up, the coat dry and brushed and delivered to Father's side before they finished the rosary. Sooner even.

You're a good girl, Lily, she said and now felt, watching the child openmouthed at the budding orchids, that she couldn't let her go without a little gift. Yes, it touched something to see the girl and Mae reached into her pocket and took out a scapular she'd found in the ever-growing pile in the church basement. It was true; these days she only tossed donations and closed the door. But this sweet thing had caught her eye and she brushed the lint from the image, a sacred heart, and from the blue flutes of satin surround, it was obviously the sacred heart of the Virgin. Here, Lily, Mae offered it forward. Something for your dear mother.

Then Mae walked Lily to the door, and said, Now hurry. I don't want you to get in any trouble. She closed the door against the blowing snow, pleased with herself, Charitina's knot handily untangled for once.

In the five minutes that Lily had been inside the glowing kitchen the snow had sped. Thick whorls blurred the grotto in Father's garden. High fans of powder covered the carriage barn where he kept the Cadillac. The doors there fastened tight with a black crowbar slid between the metal flaps of the lock. Even there inches of snow teetered.

Lily's coat was opening at the belly, the teal wool straining at the silver buttons. She hiked her shoulders to settle it down, but snow was already catching in the gaps and melting against her uniform. She'd forgotten her gloves. The school looked like a fat short distant mountain half hidden in the whirl.

Now a patrol car rolled silently in slow motion into the schoolyard. After a long pause the door opened and Anthony Moldano unfolded his heavy body out of the car and put on his cap. He was coming to find Margaret, which meant he'd be looking for Lily, too. Except for Margaret's normal babysitting pickups, Anthony Moldano insisted that Lily always come with them at least for the first part of any ride. See the world a little, Lido. Have a little adventure. That's what Margaret would say. This nickname, Lido, and sometimes just Doe, would fill her with a kind of sleepy joy.

In the same spirit, the see-the-world spirit, when Lily moved to London the first friend already invited to visit was Margaret. Now she was just waiting for Margaret to make up her mind.

Anthony Moldano tucked his head low into his shoulders. He looked like a gigantic black turtle. Whatever official announcement he'd come to St. Tom's to make was quickly done. At the carriage barn Lily held on to the snowy crowbar and watched Margaret duck under Anthony's big arm. Anthony liked to say they were an inspiring influence. They helped him effectively respond to all he had on his plate as a police officer. But today, Lily felt too tired to be inspiring, as if the snow and maybe the orchids and the too warm kitchen had all conspired to hypnotize her. She would cut behind the carriage barn to the courts of the Tennis Club, then to Love Lane, which connected to Hartshorn Road where her grandmother lived. Her grandmother hated snow and was sure to be home.

Just as she made it to the second tennis court, Anthony Moldano's patrol car turned slowly onto Love Lane. The echoing crunch of the snow under his fat tires, the blue flashers going. Lily crouched to the ground. She heard the squeal of brakes and the window lowered and Margaret shouted as if something were important: Lily, Lily. Doe, where are you?

It thrilled her a tiny bit, and she almost showed herself, felt the sweet urge to stand up and be embraced by her friend with relief. Lily, Lily, she heard again, but something in Margaret's voice made her stop. Margaret had played Tiny Tim when none of the boys could be counted on to behave with the crutch and something of her stage voice was there now. The shouted, Lily, oh Lido, sounded pitched in the same way, singing, a little silly.

Lily kept low and waited for them to get bored. Soon enough the blue lights were extinguished and she began to unfold herself, but instead of leaving, the cruiser made a wide swing off the road and edged down the little drive of the Tennis Club. They parked ten feet away from her, blocking the way out. Lily kept down, watching the dull swish and struggle of the wipers. The windshield filled as fast as it was cleared.

A couple of months ago, when the three of them were out cruising around in the patrol car, Margaret and Lily in the backseat as usual, Anthony Moldano had explained that vision was only one of his enhanced senses he used when tracking criminals. This had made Margaret laugh, but he was serious.

Then he told them a confusing story about his father as a police cadet. His father had failed some essential test that had to do with hand-eye coordination and left the academy in disgrace.

Before his draft number could be called up Anthony enrolled in the same police academy and trained his hands to juggle eggs while reading comic books propped on a stand. When the same test was offered to his class, Anthony got a special commendation. He brought home the certificate and presented it framed to his father with a black ink square over the "Junior." He thought his father would be proud, but instead he got a swat across the side of the head. Anthony's mother suggested a visit to a cousin in Brielle for a week or two and that's where Anthony met his wife. It was horrible.

He was quiet for a long time then said, The important thing is I have exceptional vision, certified. For example, remember Fourth of July? Boiling hot, crazy rain? Really hot and wet?

Margaret laughed and Anthony laughed, and that seemed the end of the story.

But what happened? Lily wanted to know. If she didn't hear it now, the story would vanish.

Margaret put her ponytail in her mouth.

Don't *do* that, said Anthony.

So then what? asked Lily, even though just this kind of curiosity was why they dumped her all the time.

Well, said Anthony, narrowing his eyes. You know the beach club snack shack is all painted to look like the dunes, camouflaged, right?

So there's some disturbance there, and I get the call. I go in and nothing seems to be happening, just the rain and the lousy heat. So the guy running the snack bar asks if I can help him lift some cases. I say sure. And I'm pressing about fifty pounds of frozen beef when

I see this movement in the fake painted dune, and just like that I toss the case of frozen patties and hear a scream. Knocked the fry cook right out, who like an idiot is dressed in sand-colored shorts.

Oh my god! said Margaret.

That's right, said Anthony, nodding.

He was attacking you? asked Lily.

Well no, he was probably just sneaking off to have a cigarette. So after he got out of the hospital, they fired him.

I guess! said Margaret.

Maybe he was coming to help you or something, Lily said. I mean it's possible.

Anthony looked at Margaret in the rearview mirror, then flipped on his turn signal, pulled over, and parked. He spun around in his seat to address them both. First, I'm trained to assess the situation and you're not. And if a guy is sneaking around, he's just sneaking around. This is a story about perception. Get it?

Margaret was nodding, eyes wide, a tiny respectful smile on her mouth that usually shaped toward sarcasm. She looked to Lily as if instructing her about the right decorum here.

I think I better go, said Lily. She waited for Anthony to release the lock.

Okay, be good, kid, said Anthony, but Margaret wouldn't acknowledge Lily.

As they drove away, Lily stood on the edge of someone's lawn covered with leaves they hadn't raked up. Margaret had been hanging out with Anthony for only a few weeks then. The conversations on the way home from babysitting were so intense and phenomenal Lily wouldn't believe it. He was way more reserved around Lily. Maybe so, but Lily wanted the other Margaret back. Not this on- and off-again Margaret.

Lily thought about Anthony's special senses as the snow piled up on top of the cruiser. The wipers were off now. Even if he did spot her blue coat as she streaked past them, she was too cold to wait. Her bare knees were frozen raw. She began the creep, low along the tennis court fence. At the car, she sunk down and crawled below the windows. When she got to the taillights, she stood to run, but she was so stiff she felt like a wooden doll whose legs wouldn't move.

On Love Lane, she ditched behind the Henderson's hedge for the shortcut to her grandmother's. She wished she'd just stop crying; it made her face hurt. She tried to think of something else to distract her, like Russell Crabtree and his long stare from the milk room. Maybe he was starting to see her differently? Maybe he'd finally forgiven her?

3

Nick Devlin leaned into the gilded mirror and focused, wiped his hair back with one hand, rubbed his eyes. A wince played then vanished and he tucked in his shirttails. By tomorrow evening Billy Byron and company would be in Paris and he'd be flying home to the States. Sheldon Walpole was already making his way into the suite's drawing room, a bottom-heavy glide as if to keep him upright and forward moving. Nick almost laughed. How did Sheldon ever get into the beauty business? How did anyone, really? In his case, of course, it was Lionel, like everything else. So benign, promised Lionel, all fantasy, the easiest pitch in the world. That's what he'd said about uranium, too: who doesn't want to be in on the absolute essence? You're giving them the reins to the world, the universe. But it turned out he'd given only the illusion of the reins. The rest was a suspended sentence.

Lately Lionel was saying, Now this is *supposed* to be an illusion. It's *makeup*, for chrissakes. Make-believe is the whole point.

For a very long time Nick refused to take his calls. Even now he kept low and Lionel seemed to be backing off. Life is long, Lionel said. I can wait.

This is what Nick might try to remember; the rest would fall away. His thumb pressed down lightly into her split. The hair around was cut short and very fair, unaltered as far as he could tell, even the shape of her cunt looked simple, though if he pulled his attention back, he'd see something had been done to invite a camera. But he kept close to the movement of his hand, the dark pink beneath the hay blond. Then her face. He kept his hand still, his thumb suspended almost, just the slightest press holding still, his eyes watched her belly rise and fall, rise and fall, and her breasts too small to change shape on her chest, small and round and mauve at the nipples, a lipstick color. Her throat, a soft chin, eyes ready to change in a breath kept their focus and he saw her before the ambition of the night and all she had to gain; he saw her surprise, and in that surprise a sadness, as if with him she'd lost and now the rest would be hard negotiation.

No, you're fine he wanted to tell her. You're all right. Then he lifted his hand, brushed the sides of her hips, flipped her right over and felt the weight in her body shift down, and there were shouts all around them, and laughter, and she kept quiet, but then her face turned sideways as he went into her and kept going, her eyes open and livid with a learned expression. If this was all performance he could help, and lifted her higher to him, so he was standing straight up, tilting back, and her rump something on a lever he could maneuver. Back and forth, the howling all around him, the laughter, her face gone now, she balanced on her elbows, head hanging down; he couldn't see her anymore. He slid her back down on the gold satin bed, held one foot for a moment. She laughed; this was a game and now she was winning and besides she was high. She sat up and dusted the tops of her round pretty thighs. She was very high and laughing. This would get her somewhere and he turned toward the door, ignoring the slaps on his shoulders, the laughter, the shoving. He zipped his trousers.

He'd left his drink somewhere. He'd stick with vodka; it was the only way to get through. It didn't disturb anything. Jean understood what he meant. He wasn't looking for obliteration, or even amplification, more a bridge. That's all. A very small plan. His drink was by the lamp next to Sheldon Walpole. Sheldon's suit trousers draped over the lampshade made a blocky dramatic shadow across Sheldon's downcast face. Nick plucked up his drink and took a warm sip. Formaldehyde and toasting damp wool made a foul aroma. Sheldon sat in full tie, cuff links in place and a pair of oxford blue boxer shorts that even in the gloom showed the ironed crease.

Tandy, Nick thought. Sheldon's wife had done it herself. He could see her unprotected face bent to pressing each line straight and true. Sheldon was trembling, and in the shouts all around, the thumping roar like boys at a game, Nick saw where this was going. He looked back to the pair of silky beds, the four girls, one standing now. Wobbling on her tiptoes a necktie wrapped around one thigh, she turned her back to them and made a deep bow. Oh! Fucking brilliant, was anything ever more brilliant, they shouted. Fucking arrest me.

Nick caught the trousers off the table lamp and tossed them to Sheldon. Come on, he said. Let's go meet our maker. He took another sip. Did you heat up my drink? He let it sit on his tongue and watched Sheldon shake his head.

Chop-chop, said Nick, pointing to the Gucci loafers under the ottoman. Shoes. Wait. Trousers first.

Sheldon fumbled at his belt as if he'd been struck blind.

There they are, said Nick, pointing to the shoes again. A crash behind them as the vice-president of sales went tumbling into the nightstand. Oy! He gripped the girl with the blond hair by the ankles as if she were the railing of a ship tossed at sea. Jesus, Jesus, he called. Her eyes were on the ceiling, smart look in place. Oy! The girl wobbling on her tiptoes gave the VP a single limp lash on his broad pink backside with the necktie then curtsied for the screaming executives. A dancer, had to be, if she could keep her balance on the soft and busy bed. Nick watched her do it again. Lash, curtsy. Now Sheldon was standing. We're staying?

Going, said Nick. Absolutely. Ice?

In the other room?

Genius.

Sheldon gave a gray smile. Let Nick proceed him into the small blue vestibule that led to the oversatined yellow glare of Billy's sitting room. Sheldon covered his mouth. Irving Slater shouted out from somewhere inside the glow, Party over?

Here you go. Nick held Sheldon's jacket. Too many stingers, deadly things. Come on, one arm, now one more. Sheldon placed himself into the sleeves and shrugged. Too much movement all at once made him sway. Dizzy, he gripped the marble edge of a decorative half table.

Cleaning up for Mother, boys? Irving Slater's voice rode the ripples of yellow and saffron and cerulean beyond. The Saudis love color. Reminds them of something or other Billy had explained.

41

This was the suite reserved for Saudi royalty, and not any subtier either. Only the top ultimate Saudis and Billy Byron stayed in this suite. Otherwise, the hotel scours it three times a day and lets it sit. The rightness of this arrangement almost pleased him. Still there were quiet talks under way about getting the Saudis their own suite, for fuck's sake. But for now, some priceless art smuggled out of Riyadh made for table talk.

Sheldon made a swift dive into a wing chair then pushed himself upright; he had the look of a thrift banker from Nebraska supporting a grateful farming community. Even smashed, his face revealed an open reasoned optimism, so out of step with Irving Slater who curled deeper into a love seat to better examine the fresh arrivals. Billy sat wide-legged and shiny in the only straight-backed chair.

Nick was surprised to find himself in the same room with Irving Slater. Usually they were orchestrated far apart, different suites, different countries. Nick knew from Lionel that Irving was the holdout, the burr, the one who went down to Centre Street on his own initiative and had copies made of all the court records, kept Billy back from a fancy dress ball at the Pierre to go over all the charges. Imagine, Lionel said with a laugh. Billy in full plumage—he's the rooster of course, they're honoring Frank Perdue!—listening to Irving whine out the particulars. The car waited over an hour, had to circle the block ten times. By the time Billy made his big entrance the toasts were long in the fidgeting stage. No one was happy.

Who told you this, Nick wanted to know, and Lionel made a joke about needing to smooth some large feathers. All myth, all self-flattery. That was Lionel from day one. Their mother called him the dauphin. And what about me, what am I Nick wanted to know. You're the treasure, said his mother. Pure gold, this little heart, and touched him the way she always did, the most tentative pat against his small chest.

Oh Christ. But she had been gone a long time now. Very good luck, said Nick and for once Lionel didn't correct him. And now Lionel was creating a myth about Nick: That Irving was still waiting when Billy came home from the ball. Billy scratching at the hives his feathers created up the back of his neck, in the crook of each elbow, behind his knees, in the inner thighs where the red tights already chafed. Billy, suffering, cried out: It's all a sack of lies! Irving could burn that pile of manure and get out. Just like that. Irving Slater out on the sidewalk, his soggy crap useless.

Nick thought if it did happen, it was a moment's work in the middle of a day. Irving might slip a clipping from a newspaper, no sweaty bribing of a moribund clerk downtown, just a quick column, something to implicate him, and Billy had waved it away. Forget it. Forget it. And probably Billy had, but Irving Slater stayed on it. Used the word *felon* in creative ways, suggested a lipstick: Scarlet Felon; fragrance: My Felonious Heart; blush: Melon Felony. Until Billy would look up and say, What gives? You're not making sense.

Irving Slater had nothing to do with creative; he was finance and legal and he spearheaded these in-suite entertainments wherever Billy went. Irving was the wrangler. Nick knew all about them; Lionel had told him. What's so difficult? I think you know what to do. Pretty simple.

But it wasn't simple. Here was Sheldon looking green in a room that smelled of lemons and oranges. For Billy's health. All the vitamin C kept him virile and vital, warded off the scurvy of his youth. But even the best of all tailors couldn't disguise the bandy legs and the odd foreshortening of his frame. He'd cultivated a reputation for being insatiable—anyone with a pulse—but for Billy these parties, which were identical at Claridge's or the Okura, it scarcely mattered. It all happened offstage. The shouts and grunts muffled behind heavy doors like a storm still far away. And that was the point: vicinity. Billy wanted the action where he could feel it. The rest was personal and private. He was a highly private man he told everyone. Here at Claridge's they hung a sign on the suite door that said PRIVATE. So satisfying. It was why he stayed here, those little brass screws tightened all the way in. All for him. Details. And that's what he was saying to Sheldon Walpole now. As if no one had ever said the word before, his face alight with the thought. One right detail was all it took to define a woman's self-worth. What had Sheldon learned just now Billy wanted to know. In there, he tipped his large head toward the bedroom. And Irving smiled as Sheldon sank lower into the down of the wing chair.

Well, I'd say I noticed something important about blushing.

Blushing? Irving was pleased; this would be idiotic.

Yes, we're all talking about apples all the time you know, said Sheldon. And Billy nodded.

But something else is happening under all the pink.

We're talking mottling, right, laughed Irving.

No, I'm thinking iridescence. Why not?

Done it, said Irving.

Not really, said Nick.

What would you know, said Irving.

A lot, said Billy. More than you'd think. Look at that face, he said to Irving, pointing to Nick. I don't need him to have a brain, too, but he does. So let's listen, for once.

It's Sheldon's idea.

Right, said Billy, looking at Nick. So what's he telling me.

We're thinking color when we should be thinking *glow*.

Glow.

Like the worm? said Irving.

Glow. Glow, said Billy. Glow-glow. Like Go-go. Hmm.

I was thinking a feather applicator, said Sheldon, all one piece, maybe a rotation device to reveal and retract.

You're disgusting, said Irving.

Reveal and retract. Billy was thinking, nodding. But a feather? No, won't work. You'll get the powder stuck on the first try. Forget it.

Make it synthetic. Coat it in silicone. It will trace the cheek with iridescent powder so subtle it looks like a lover's flush. It's a great idea. Nick put his cigarette down to trace the feather's movement with two fingers.

That's it, Sheldon said, nodding. That's right.

And I say it's crapola, said Billy.

Irving smiled.

Fucking moronic, said Billy. And you, you say it's good? He pointed at Nick; his hand trembled.

I do.

Then get the fuck out of my sight.

Okay, good night, said Nick, standing. Come on, Sheldon. Give me a lift.

You don't need a lift. Didn't I just cosign a lease for someplace a block away from here? Did you get this, Irving? Our new marketing manager needs Ike's old pad on Grosvenor Square. General Nick here. General Nick needs a lift to headquarters. Billy rolled an orange between his palms, setting off the scent in the overheated room. Why a lift? Tell the truth.

Then I need guidance. Come on, Sheldon.

All right, all right, said Billy. Irving, get those girls out of there, and call housekeeping. What are you running here?

We'll see you at nine, Billy. Sheldon was hoisting himself out of the yellow cushions.

You'll see me when you see me. Irving, I'm not putting a finger in that room until it's been turned over. I mean scoured. But Irving was already in the vestibule knocking on the bedroom door and the laughter inside went quiet.

Ciao, said Nick and held open the door for Sheldon. Billy brought the orange to his nose and sniffed. Some chemical here, he said. It's like they don't know what fruit is in this country.

The Europa Hotel on Grosvenor Square with its discreet satisfying side entrance was midway between Claridge's and the flat Nick had found with Lionel's help. Sheldon had picked the most protected spot at the end of the long polished bar, on the suede high-backed bar stools with a half wall between the lounge and his body. No one could wrap an unexpected arm about his hunched shoulders, or even see him without being seen first. The stools were a great concession to the Americans down the block, configured here like plush reading chairs on stilts. Sheldon's chin was lit from beneath by a votive. Steely jaw, the stuff of a fifties cartoon hero.

Tandy in good health? said Nick. Happy with the new digs?

Sure, Sheldon took a long draw on the new drink set before him. Smiled at Nick, nose flattened crooked in a way that invited the confidence of other men. That's what had caught Billy's eye, no doubt. The pugilist's face and a short smart track record at Max Factor. Otherwise Sheldon's sudden elevation to president UK-Europe was inexplicable. To you, Nick, said Sheldon, knocking a thick knuckle against the rim of his lowered glass, giving Nick the up-down assessment that was pure Billy. A crotch to crown gaze followed by a visible score, usually below what was hoped. But here, Sheldon brightened and said, You'll do just fine.

You'll teach me. That's what I'm here for, to learn from you.

If you say so.

Nick laughed, signaled the barman, pulled on the front of his hair. Sheldon was drunk. Soon they'd both be home.

Do this for me, said Sheldon.

Anything. Nick kept pulling on his hair.

Give me a high sign.

Sure.

I mean it. I want an advance warning. When you're about to tear me down, just tell me, so Tandy doesn't end up heartbroken. None of this is her fault. You get that, right? She didn't do anything to deserve what's happening.

Nothing is happening. I'm a trainee.

And a liar, and a con. You think no one reads the paper around here. Is this a joke.

Nick gave a sideways hand gesture canceling his drink. I don't know about you, but I'm done. I'm gonna grab some z's. Sticking around?

Sure. Sticking around. That's it.

Okay, Sheldon. Nick didn't pat the raised shoulders, just perused the empty dining room behind the half wall. Suede banquettes. He leaned across the bar for a light, then signed the chit from the bartender. Whatever he wants, said Nick, then left without saying good-bye. Already forgotten, he knew that, Sheldon would be sheepish and curious in the morning. Besides, Sheldon wasn't saying anything that Irving Slater didn't repeat daily.

Ignore the idiots. That was Lionel's advice. But what would Lionel know about that.

He liked this walk. Dead of the night, no one on the streets, the wild quiet of the place still surprised him. Middle of London and you could hear the treetops shiver in a breeze and breathe in the damp sour scent of those branches in the dark. At three in the morning his footsteps were the only ones on the square. He approached the fanning marble steps to his door and felt for the key, enormous thing.

He should have brought Sheldon home and let him sleep it off. Such an honorable guy, Nick thought. What the hell was he doing here?

He'd finally asked him tonight, and Sheldon just laughed. Tell me this, Sheldon said. Did he do the three-part knock?

Is this a joke? Don't know it.

You know it. Sheldon took a deep long sip of his drink, something lingering and unguarded.

We should go, said Nick.

Not done. But it was the old three. They can't help themselves. Like a fairy tale. Billy meets you by chance, or maybe it's Irving and whoever it is says he has an instinct. Right?

Nick smiled; actually it was Lionel who'd talked about instinct.

They make an offer, pro forma. You turn it down. Back it comes, not doubled but close. You're flattered, but what the fuck, you don't return the call. Is this all sounding like a song you know? Time goes by. Some messages, invitations, tickets, you feel good because you've checked them out and you've learned, because it is such common knowledge the busboys at Schraffts know, these guys are running a revolving door, that Billy spits out talent like a bad nut. So you're settled. It's just weather. But then comes the third: Clifford shows up with the car at your door and he's taking you to Billy's house. You've heard about this place and just for the story you go. Instead of the big drawing room or the library you're taken to a third-floor kitchen. Something Billy and Bunny use to heat up warm milk in the night, just the two of them. You're in a very private place. You see Bunny's headband on the counter, and some knitting she's left behind. And Billy is fucking with the coffee basket. Some cheap normal electric thing, nothing like the equipment you know is downstairs, and he's nearly having a heart attack getting the plug in the wall. You show him and he's awash with gratitude. You've never seen the guy so vulnerable and it shocks you a little. Have I got this right?

Nick looked in the mirror at the room behind them, all the banquettes long empty now. The copper shaded lamps still flickering. He had it completely right. Down to the coffee basket.

Got it, don't I. He tells you his wife usually makes the coffee. They've got three live-in help, but this is their sanctuary; this is where she poaches his egg every morning. You sit at the round table where his son, the race-car driver, learned to play Scrabble. He tells you what a shambles everything is, a total mare's nest. He gives you a few particulars, no names. And you sip the shitty coffee you've just helped make and you give him an idea. You watch the lines on his face reassemble themselves. You've transformed him. Your insight has changed if not everything, then certainly enough. He starts talking about the ground up. He wants you selling lipstick in Macy's on an executive salary. He drinks the whole cup down and pours another. So happy. He's never met anyone like you. All he can do is sit back and wonder. You're a natural—a natural wonder. He's going to name something after you; just give him a minute.

Okay, okay. Nick pulled out a handkerchief and blew his nose.

And then Billy's got a cramp in his leg, and though he'd love to talk all night, he hasn't met a brain like yours in this lifetime.

Clifford shows up in the little kitchen like the leg cramp deployed a buzzer. Yeah, yeah, Clifford, Billy says. It's nothing. But he's rubbing that skinny leg like it's broken and you say you'll talk to him later and put your cup down. Look around for the sink. No, no, smart and compassionate, what a combination.

Sheldon's lips are shiny. He stares at the back of his hand.

And I have street smarts, Nick says.

Street smarts! My fucking god. Street smarts? You are the messiah. Sheldon's cough sticks in his throat. He lights a Dunhill to calm it down.

Just so you know, he says, puffing his lips on the exhale, the good-bye has a pattern, too. That's all I'm saying. The game speeds up like you wouldn't believe. I won't see it coming, because no one does, but you will. That's how it works. So I'm just saying, give me the nod. Can you do that?

Yup.

We'll see.

Nick took a cigarette for himself. No, if you're right, I'll do it. I'll tell you.

See? His faith is justified. Billy's right about you, a decent guy. Who gives a hoot what Irving says.

Hoot? Nick laughs. You sound like my grandmother.

Irving wouldn't know a scam if his grandmother was on the inside.

4

Her father would tell her this was nothing. Just take your time, Jeanie. Take your time. She let her breathing calm down. He'd never understood her terror of driving in snow, as if it were all some nonsense she needed to get over. Maybe he was right. The snow landed in fat splotches on the glass and the wipers swept it aside easily. She labored up the last hill before the bridge just in time to see the Clury bus come to a stop at the turn ahead.

Everyone knew the Clury School bus, shorter than most and robin's-egg blue. The Clury School in Fair Haven was famous for slipping kids in trouble—academically, behaviorally—back into the mainstream. It boasted students who went on to Dartmouth and Brown, but only a handful of successes. When a friend sent a child there, everyone felt a ping of relief it wasn't a child of one's own. Nick had argued very, very briefly that Lily might benefit from a year at Clury. Two at the most. But Jean had held firm. Oh, no, she said. Absolutely not. She'll be stigmatized for life. We might as well paint something on her forehead.

Don't be ridiculous, he'd said. It will be a badge of honor. Are you kidding? When she runs out of stories about what monsters we are, she'll have something to fall back on.

What are you talking about? You make no sense. Why would she ever say anything about us at all. What a sickening idea. And Jean was right of course; Lily was very loyal. But then Doris had chimed in, Oh, yes, the Clury School. Why didn't I think of it?

Because, Jean had almost said, it's none of your business. And she was right about that, too, but she pretended to listen to Doris's argument that Lily needed a little extra attention.

Really, Doris, Jean said, when we all stop wringing our hands over her feelings, everything will be fine. She is a child. None of this really concerns her.

What can you possibly mean?

Jeanie knows what's best, her father finally said. An argument so definitive that Nick and Doris fell silent. Now they were moving to London.

Everything sounded too loud in her ears, the blinker and outside the grind and hiss of the Clury bus as it made a wide turn onto the bridge over the Navesink River. Just like a little steam engine plodding through the snow making a path for Jean to follow.

She kept her distance. She kept the requisite one hundred feet and then let herself slow some more. Felt the swath of snowy wind deepen between them. Only the two vehicles, no one behind her and it was so beautiful on the slow rise. The Navesink bridge curled into the widest views from this end, a panorama of the river channels and islands and beyond to the ocean. The cotton sky and gray lines of sea grass and punks and cattails poking out of the cracked shoreline, all the swirling tides frozen. Beautiful most of all on the quietest days, like this one, and she allowed herself a brief glance, hands tight on the wheel, just a blink of a glance toward the ocean, when she heard the screech. The school bus spun sideways in slow motion, as though drawing a wide arc in the snow with its headlights until it bumped gently into the parapet and stopped just the hundred-plus feet ahead of her. She would smash right into it and then she remembered to pump her brakes, release the accelerator and pump her brakes, like a short panting breath. Her car went into its own small spiral and she felt a wash of hatred in her throat as she came closer to the parapet, hatred for the bus driver who was endangering her.

The car slid to a stop, caught in the rugged tracks of the school bus, exactly reversed, facing the way she'd come. Her foot slipped from the brake pedal; her eyes were open but not seeing and burning with some chemical released into the air. She couldn't hear a thing. She closed her eyes to stop the sting and felt for the gearshift and pushed the car into park.

It was very quiet. The wind had died suddenly and when she opened her eyes the snow fell before her in straight thick fast lines. Like Christmas light strings unlit. The school bus, more a van really, was probably empty. The children already in school. Besides, most who were forced to go to Clury were driven by their parents. A trust issue. The bus driver cut the engine. Now the only sound was the whine of her windshield wipers. Jean was shaking so much she couldn't turn around. She watched the bus in her rearview mirror and thought she saw the hand of the driver wiping at the windows on the inside. He couldn't be hurt; the impact had been less than that of a bumpy car on the boardwalk. The bus looked completely fine, as far as she could tell, though now her back window was obscured. She was the one who could have been killed, if she hadn't been able to stop, if she'd collided right into him. Her hands were shaking; she was shivering all over now. But her car was fine she was fairly sure.

She started to press the door handle; she'd get out and talk to the driver, get his name. Though her legs felt so weak she might have trouble standing, she tried to push open her door but it felt frozen shut. She pushed harder and no difference. At least she thought she pushed harder. Her arm moved, but maybe there was no power behind it, an empty movement.

She rolled down her side window and stuck her head out for a look. She called out to the driver, Hey! But he didn't seem to see her. She tried once more to open her door, but couldn't so she cranked her window shut and tested the acceleration. It was working just fine. She could do this she found, if she thought of the car as a needle and she would stitch the road. She'd be that secure and that small, going back down the slope they'd just climbed. The car—she didn't once think about reversing—stitched forward until finally she was creeping along the curve to the yield sign. She was on land, and behind her—she only remembered this later—the lights were flashing on the bus, yellow bursts in the white cloud behind her. The driver had pushed on the flashers. The driver was fine. She would get as far as the Crabtrees' barn and raise the alarm and urgent Mimi Crabtree would fly into action.

That was the very best idea. Mimi, and Dr. Crabtree, a veteran. They would know what was needed. That was what she'd do. And she would have done it, she felt certain, if the police car, with all lights revolving and sirens blasting hadn't rushed past her onto the bridge; didn't even see her, she thought. Though she half waited all day for the phone call or even a knock on the door.

The other calls came around noon. Mimi Crabtree to say that Perry was all set, that Jean could stop worrying. Then a few minutes later Doris, in tears, saying Lily was safe, she was safe. She was dry and warm and Doris would keep her for the night if that was still all right. Let her stay with me, Doris pleaded. Let me keep her close. I was so frightened. I've aged ten years in a day!

But she *is* staying with you, Jean broke in at last. That was our plan, remember? What in the world was Doris talking about?

It seemed Lily had walked from school to her grandmother's house all alone in the blizzard. Jean sighed. Well, I'm sure you'll keep her good company.

Then, no surprise, Nick's new secretary called from London to say that his flight had been canceled. When Jean asked to speak to him, the childish singsong voice said Mr. Devlin wasn't in the office yet, but she'd be sure to give a message as soon as he arrived. Tania, that was her name. Thank you, Tania, Jean said into the fizz of the phone line, then stood staring out the bay window in the kitchen: the river and trees were invisible now.

Doris put down the black receiver and settled her necklace along the thin white line that curved at the base of her throat. All of her necklaces, good and trash, had been adjusted once she'd healed. All of her dresses taken in and then discarded altogether. She was a different woman since the surgery; everyone said so.

Even Clyde thought she was different. She crept up on him now; he couldn't hear her footsteps anymore. She gave him the creeps he said, sneaking around that way. Then he'd turn his face away and take a long sip of bourbon from a tumbler and he'd hold it in his mouth as long as he could. His mouth made a little bowl and the aroma snuck up through his sinuses and pleasantly stewed his brain with thoughts of success, all that had been his, that still was, that he'd grabbed from misfortune and worse. Everything he'd done and made and was, and a smile whispered across his black-brown eyes, a wisp of joy, until there she was standing right in front of him. He'd swallow and say, What the hell? I thought you'd gone.

Clyde was away now on one of his trips, though he planned to be back for Christmas. That just might not work out Doris thought, watching the heavy snowfall pile up through the sidelights framing the front door. She startled to hear Ruby's laugh, and then Lily's too, a deep guffaw, the two of them huddled in the kitchen. Ruby's hot milk on the stove, fragrant with cardamom and vanilla. Even from here Lily's bright red snow-burned knees looked raw where the blanket had slipped away. Doris rushed toward her, crying out, Bundle up, darling, please. Now, sweetheart, please. Then gently moved the blankets herself.

56

Summer 1970

5

What Clyde Boll missed most about work was his driver, Huey. He'd intended to take Huey with him into retirement, had selected the car—a white, deep-seated convertible. He'd ordered the caps, the uniforms, something lightweight for summer, good navy wool with silver-plated buttons for winter. Clyde was all set when Huey suffered a cardiac arrest in an underground garage in Newark. What the hell was he doing in Newark? Clyde wanted to know. Honey, he lives there, said Doris, with a look of surprise on her face. Now Huey had decided to retire, too, and Clyde could scarcely forgive him. The man has a heart problem, said Doris. But he corrected her thinking. No, Huey would not be welcome, even if he had a change of mind. Even if he came to his senses. Clyde would learn to drive himself. Briefly, he'd entertained the thought of letting Doris drive him. They could be companions of the road. An idea expressed to Jean that made them both laugh.

By the time of his retirement party on an early June Saturday, with all the plaques and testimonials, Clyde could drive anywhere he pleased. Anytime. He'd driven half the guests himself back to the train station in the evening. Pile in, he shouted and some did just for the novelty, and for the tale. The president (Not anymore, bud!) was opening the doors for them. You've got a second career here, chief, said Bart Canfield, from the backseat, clasping what was left of his hair.

Stupid son of a bitch was always the stick in the eye, could never let well enough alone. Always said the wrong thing. If it was possible to destroy, no, demolish a great idea, he was desperate, *panting* to do it. Should have fired him when I had the chance. Oh, Daddy, said Jean. And didn't she look pretty this morning. She really hadn't changed; he didn't know what Doris went on about. But what did you think of the cake! Sent via helicopter by Sterling, sorry not to deliver it in person.

I've got some, brought it home last night. For luck! Let me get you a slice. And she was up and running into the house, and he shouted something in through the porch door about hiding it from Lily, something to make Jean smile, though he couldn't see her for the moment. He watched the sparkle of the morning light shift and shiver on the water. He'd have a half cup of coffee more, then get on with it. He had Shea to deal with down at the marina, the only one with a slip worth having from here to Barnegat Bay. Then he'd stop in at Gunco's for chum and a pound of pastrami, then down to the tip of Sandy Hook to see what the boys were finding today. Plenty of chop, plenty of breeze, the air still cool enough to keep the fish coming up to the surface. He kept a rod and gear in storage at McKinney's garage; he'd stop in and pick it up on the way. He was doing just fine without Huey.

Where's my angel? he shouted through the screen door. No time for her old Poppa?

No time for any of us, Daddy, smiled Jean, coming back out onto the porch, handing him the plate. A popular girl.

Clyde took the cake and nodded. They both knew this was untrue. But Clyde agreed with the principle: just say the best version of a situation and chances were better it would turn out that way.

Getting hotter, she said.

It made him smile. That Huey, he said.

Yes, Huey didn't like the heat. Those awful suits he had to wear! Like being boiled alive.

I'd have done better for him.

I know that. But you're fine, better than fine.

Learning to drive, this had been his first destination, though he'd never admit it. A good routine, no one went to Mass anymore except Doris, and Lily because she had to. Jean put in an appearance on Saturday evenings, stood in the back vestibule, smoked on the front steps under the eaves during the sermon, then left as soon as the tabernacle closed. Clyde thought she'd taken this up for him, this practice, so they could have Sunday mornings just like this for a while. Who knew how long she'd be in London really. Since when was Nick a man to be trusted.

Any word from the big cheese?

She let her mouth look pleased, but she squinted out to the water, as if distracted.

Seems like this is working out just fine for him. I hear good things.

Do you really, Daddy?

All the time.

Now she was beaming at him, and he laughed and missed her mother. That exact expression.

59

The only real deficit Clyde had as a driver was his neck. Always stiff. As a boy he'd had scarlet fever, and that left his body vulnerable in adulthood. And the vulnerability stiffened his neck over time, made the bones brittle and the muscles weak. A load of horseshit, said Clyde. Even so, his head wouldn't turn. So at any crossroads he assured himself that his intentions were as clear to the other drivers as they'd always been in other circumstances, and sailed right through. The number of near misses involving Clyde Boll was becoming legendary in the county. He was a menace and Anthony Moldano had been dispatched for a discussion about the rules of the road. Why me? Anthony cried. Diplomacy was the answer. You could talk a monkey out of a banana. And Anthony understood this wasn't entirely a compliment, so put off the warning, the admonition, week to week.

I should go, sugarplum, Clyde said. He dropped his sunburned hands to his white duck trousers and cupped his knees. He watched her stand and move around the porch tidying up, long graceful neck, her mother's slanted dark eyes, so lovely. I was thinking about how Huey nearly dropped you when Lily was born. Boy, I should have fired him on the spot.

She laughed. *You* nearly dropped me, Daddy. Don't you remember.

Me? Not possible.

Yes, it *was* you. You lifted me out of the car and carried me all the way into the hospital. I never felt so safe in my life.

He let out a laugh. Come on.

And she laughed, too. When you put me down, that is.

He was delighted. This was his favorite story. She was offering the lead-in, and he wanted to tell it. The birth of Lily. He wasn't there when Cubbie was born, so all his pride collapsed into the first arrival. He began, Doris called me at the office, stuttering like the house was burning down.

But something shifted in Jean's face. So little displeased her about her father, but this willingness to be happy about only Lily and to erase Cubbie, even for a moment, pained her, angered her. She went into the house before he finished speaking.

She was a moody girl, always had been. He adjusted his glasses, waited a half minute to see if she'd come back, then pushed out the screen door, made his way down the painted steps. He was stiff from sitting so long. The white gravel drive was too sparkly in the sunlight; he blinked away the blinding flashes. In the car, he put on his straw hat, which created soothing squares of gray across his field of vision. He couldn't see but at least his eyes didn't feel seared, didn't hurt. Everything hurt now, a nuisance. Though of course he never complained. He waited another minute for her to come and wave, but she didn't.

All along Navesink River Road the big car coasted through a sea of new green, all the leaves barely stretched. This was his season Clyde had declared, in a rush of poetry that made Doris and Ruby laugh. His fresh good ideas had burst right into the world, as quick and on time as spring. Radio Corporation of America. National Broadcasting Company. Clyde Henry Boll.

Bart Canfield could dream all he wanted but he'd never make it into Clyde's spot. That office is closed now. No one will follow him. No one could, so Sterling said. Clyde was a one-time phenomenon. The new guys coming up the line—Yes, sir!—all cogs, not a wheel in a carload.

A screech of brakes and someone with no respect for a Sunday morning laid down on the horn and wouldn't quit. Clyde glided through the stop sign onto the bridge. And the sunshine and the breeze ruffling up all the light on the water and sending it haywire into the windshield was a shock, but a pleasant one. The air rushed through the open window deafening and refreshing. What had Jean's goat this morning? She was a prickly girl all right, but she and Lily would be over for dinner later and she'd be on to the next thing. Such a good stretch these last few months, no Nick blurring and refracting the picture. No hocus-pocus. Doris said he'd been gone too much, and Jean needed him. An irritating perspective. She has her family, he'd said, meaning himself. He thought about this, catching the tail end of the yellow light, and again with the horns. You'd think it was Midtown Manhattan. In the early autumn he'd fly to London and see what he could do to make her comfortable.

He had a headache now, and something put his stomach in a red twist. Nick, no doubt. The idea of Nick. Why hadn't he stopped the bastard in his tracks long ago. Big regret. Big, big regret. Nothing else like it. He couldn't think about pastrami right now. He just kept going down Ocean Avenue, then in through the gates to the beach road. The dune grasses waving, the river on one side, the ocean on the other, the roar of the waves filling his ears. Then a truck ahead pulls a U-turn out of nowhere and Clyde can't find the brake with his foot. The floor of the car is all air, the numbness climbs up his leg, and for a moment he closes his eyes, but opens them and the rusty pile of junk is in his rearview mirror. He takes a quick turn into the next parking lot, an empty space right there up against the dune. He lets the car coast to a stop, then pulls up the hand brake. Cuts the ignition. Rolls up the windows, and in the quiet assesses the numbness in his feet, both feet now, and the tips of his fingers. He opens the door, lifts both legs out, and tries to get the sensation of the spiny shells and jagged rocks through the soles of his shoes. There you go, a nervy pinch comes in the right side.

There you go. He grabs the side door and hefts himself upright. He can walk, certainly. No problem. But Doris is right about the weight; he'll attend to that. He can see her point. And he never picked up his rod, and his folding chair is still back at the house. But he better keep walking, moving. The circulation is good now; he can feel the sand on the beach path slipping nicely under his soles.

All the way to the top of the dune, he's panting now, and though the breeze is strong and cool and ripples his shirt, he's sweating and breathless. The waves break hard in his ears, make a dizzy thudding sound. A woman's encampment right at the end of the path. He sees the basket of knitting and magazines, two pastel recliners set on a beach blanket. The dry hot sand whirring in the wind, clotting up the yarn. He'll rest right here. He'll have a nip and a rest and be fine. No one will mind and when they come back from the water, he'll probably know them by sight.

It's a long way down to the sand. He falls over sideways before he can get into the chair. He's curled over like Jean when she was a baby, and only he could calm her in the night; at least that's the way he remembers it. Her poor mother already gone. Jean so tiny all alone. She'd wake up screaming, screaming, and Clyde would tiptoe in with a flashlight, pretend they were on their own private sailboat: Just you and me, and you have to snuggle tight into the bow of the boat, curve in tight to feel the waves rock, and she would do it, so concentrated, her tiny body curled against the ribs of the sailboat he conjured just for her, the *Jeanie B.*, and her breathing would calm down. Her cheek to his big hand, she'd fall back asleep and never remember in the morning the night sailing they did together.

6

Lily held still, caught her breath, closed her eyes, and felt the sweep of the rented disco ball come over her, lighting the inside of her eyelids with a pulse of pink, then all was black and loud again. She opened her eyes with a laugh to Margaret opening her own eyes at the exact same instant. They collapsed toward each other with swift joy then fell back as Margaret assessed their audience. A cool trickle of sweat slid down Lily's side under the gray flannel maxidress, borrowed from Margaret in a last-minute negotiation while Tommy Foley idled the car outside. Lily's mother had rationed something white that looked like a baptismal gown with puffed sleeves and pin tucks. The only outfit she was willing to pry from Lily's already packed clothes. Margaret's gray flannel Christmas dress, bought on sale two sizes too big and never worn, had leg of mutton sleeves, heart-shaped buttons as reflective as mirrors, an empire waist, and a long gathered skirt with green lace near the hem. Her mother would snort with derision at this dress, but her mother wasn't here.

Across the dance floor a jumping skirmish shook the floor, bodies lit up then unlit. Dead center in the tangle was Russell Crabtree throwing an elbow and calling it dance. Now out of the pack in one leap, caught off balance, a fantastic crumble, his khakis slipping down, yanked back up. His oxford blue shirt flapping, a tiny fringe of black hair on an exposed belly one instant, covered the next. He was beyond beauty. Lily looked away, dizzy, took a long stabilizing sip through a straw of a warm diluted Tab. From her low angle, she observed his shoulders, in a near constant shrug, wide and framing his ears. Like a vulture, said Sister Charitina. A vulture!

Lily understood him perfectly, felt her own shoulders rise up and in toward her chin, and then lowered them fast, for fear she would catch his notice. She'd just close her eyes again and clock his dance that way. It was a technique she had and she explained it once to Margaret. This way of being able to get the whole feeling of someone as if she were a radio. But human. Her brother had called her Lilio; it was his idea about her. That's retarded, said Margaret. No offense. But it is.

But Lily knew what Cubbie meant. Oh, shit, said Margaret, and Lily opened her eyes.

Margaret stared in a freeze at their tiny table littered with plastic cups and soaked pretzels, then lifted her eyes and jerked them. Lily followed the gaze. Margaret cried, Don't *look*! But it was too late. Russell Crabtree walking toward them, if walk was the way to think about all that movement. The stiff high-shouldered slouch. The shuffle that seemed to happen from the knees down. The bounce of his hair. He stopped, hovered nearby, not looking at them, but through the French doors, until Greg Kiernan, red-faced and sweating, punched his back and shouted, Case!

They tumbled left and out the doors onto the terrace overlooking the first hole. Somewhere on the dark velvet golf course boys had secured some beer. Beer, according to her mother, meant a choice. Lily was choosing between a future she could be proud of—giving nice dinner parties—or something murky and full of misery. Everyone was interested in her future. Even Momo imagined Lily keeping up her garden later on. Things had narrowed in the last two years and all the people predicting her adulthood were anxious. If she was going to plant tulip bulbs and serve crab dip, she needed to shape up.

Russell came back into view, stopped still in the doorway. There he was, a silhouette, and she felt herself go bright in her gorgeous dress. He'd noticed her. Jesus, whispered Margaret. He patted down his caved-in chest and found a crushed pack of Winstons, his trademark, put a bent cigarette to his lips, and turned sideways, so that they could get the full impact of his insurrection, then vanished under the rose pergola of the terrace.

I have to tell Mrs. Flaherty something, Lily said.

Now?

She's with Mrs. Shea on the terrace.

Probably, but now?

Only for a minute.

All right, I'm coming, said Margaret, pulling down on her minidress. Anthony Moldano made an observation about Margaret's knees the last time he gave them a ride in the patrol car. Chunky, he laughed. And she'd given him a complicated smile. Lily in the backseat watched Margaret's face try on different expressions in the rearview mirror. Proud, hopeless, indulgent. Happy.

I think I may be cramping or something. Don't come, said Lily.

You need Flaherty's permission?

No. Something else.

Don't wreck the maxi. Like it could be a costume or something.

Save my seat?

Fine. Margaret made an acute adjustment to the ribbon holding back her dark blond hair, brought it forward without creating any ripples in her smoothed-back bangs.

Nice, said Lily. It looks good now. But Margaret was studying the dance floor and nodded without looking. Lily almost sat again. She couldn't bear these moments with Margaret. Something caught her eye, a ping of a light all the way through the doors and out on the black course. Russell lighting his Winston. She could smell the first tang of smoke already. She turned to go, but Margaret tugged on her sleeve.

Be back in ten minutes, she said. Anthony's meeting us on the putting green at eleven. You know, so he can drive us home.

What about Tommy?

Tommy's a jerk. He's unreliable.

But thanks to Tommy a miraculous thing had happened to Lily back in March. Lily went over it again and again. As usual, she was spending the night at the Foleys and Tommy had boys over down in the passion pit, something his father had built in the basement. Round banquettes in red corduroy and quadraphonic stereo speakers. After their parents "retired" for the night, Tommy could invite the whole world, Margaret said, and they'd sleep right through it. Boys came and went all the time through the cellar door, but they were mostly boring, said Margaret. This night, only three boys huddled around a long purple plastic bong. Lily listened to the burbling and the coughing and didn't like it. No, said Margaret. Stay. There'll be others soon.

It was a command, which Lily found both comforting and worrisome. The stay or else. You'll get used to the smell, she said. Margaret was educating her because she had no brothers of her own. No, she wouldn't stay. Margaret could do what she liked. And soon she was upstairs; the dark kitchen felt creepy with the green stove light hissing and the dope smell still seeping up, so she went out onto the porch with its ghost furniture and the plastic sheets coating the screens. An eerie bubble with little halos glimmering from the streetlamps and the neighbor's garden lights two acres away.

Lily sat at the round covered table on a cold rounded bench and considered walking home. She'd done it before. It seemed since Anthony entered the picture, she'd become a big walker. She took a breath and felt the clingy vegetable taste at the back of her throat.

When Lily was very small she shared a bedroom with her brother, so their parents could find them both easily in the night her mother said. Cubbie's bed had safety sides because he was too young to know how to sleep neatly. When they were that little, Cubbie began to cough. Everyone thought it was an allergy. They went all together to Dr. Polk's and Cubbie had to say the letter *k* over and over, while Dr. Polk looked up into the inside of his nose. *K k k k k.* Cubbie cried a bit, just because the stick Dr. Polk put through his nostrils was stiff and pointed. But otherwise, and this was something her mother liked to stress, he was very brave and never complained. Except once, much later, during a long stay in the Philadelphia children's hospital, when the need for a second spinal tap, because the first had gone badly, made him cry. For her mother this crying was unbearable. Lily with all her heart wanted to keep her mother from knowing that Cubbie cried all the time. And that when he was very sick and his body became brittle, they would sleep close to one another as they had when tiny, and she would hold his coughs in her own chest, and cry for him, so his tears wouldn't shake him or disturb their mother who needed her rest. One thing was true. Cubbie never talked to her about all the many things that happened to him, what he felt inside his body. She had to figure this out for herself. She was still figuring it out.

Maybe tonight it would just be better to go home she was thinking, when the door creaked open and Russell Crabtree in Margaret's old pink ski parka stepped out, a flame already wobbling on the steel lighter cupped in his hand. Damn! he cried out, and the tip of blue licked his fingers. He shook out his hand, capped the lighter. Christ, I didn't see you! When did you get here?

Sorry.

He shrugged, looked toward the streetlamps as if captivated. Are you okay?

He blew on his fingers. Yeah, I'll live. And he used the wounded fingers to tap out the bottom of the soft pack, a display of three cigarettes. Here.

She smiled and plucked one from the pack. He sat across from her and held out the lighter. Cold as a witch's tit out here.

She felt a small shock at the word. She didn't choke, just took another small puff and looked toward the plastic sheeting as if there were a view.

He was flicking the ash of his cigarette on Margaret's mother's painted cement porch floor. She knew from her own mother the apple green was a ridiculous color and that the paint was porous and wouldn't last through the spring. Wait, she said. There was a beanbag ashtray in a drawer of one of the wicker side tables. She and Margaret had looked inside everything one bored afternoon. Wait, she said. And felt Russell watching her every move as she retrieved the stuffed watermelon slice with a metal dish squashed into the middle of a fabric rind. Use this.

He studied her carefully as she sat down again. This sitting back down was so important her legs were knocking into each other. He took another long drag and let the ash lengthen and hover, as if he were undecided. She waited, not hopeful. Later, in London, when she was trying to untangle all the trouble, she would think of him in the bubble and remember him as her first mirage. She was imagining Russell while he was right here in front of her. But instead of the shadowy blur and the gray backlight from the streetlamps washing over the deeper gray of his vague head, she saw his shiny black hair, and the surprise blush of his pink cheeks. Even sitting, his body seemed to rocket up from the soles of his feet. He had a small red mouth and nearly black eyes. Black Irish, her mother had said, neutrally, and, from her tone, Lily understood this was something desirable. He was hunched over his cigarette now, and his hunch and his silence told her he was a little sad, but he wasn't going to discuss it. That something had hurt him, but it was not within his power to reveal that hurt. He grinned above the glowing tip, just a few shiny teeth, his nostrils lit up then dark again. His eyes, she imagined, searched her face for some sense that for all that had happened to him, whatever it was, she got it.

You're shivering, he said.

I'm not.

I can see you. You're like vibrating, and your teeth are chattering. Take a drag. Quick. You want my coat?

Nice coat.

I grabbed it off a chair. Here.

He stood up and began a tortured twist to get the pink coat off his arms. Shit.

Don't tear it!

The rip was loud in the plastic bubble. Damn, he said. Now we're screwed.

Here, said Lily. Give it here. And she stood behind him to pull the sleeves, gently, one at a time, shimmying the pink nylon away from his navy blue ski sweater. She loved his sweater. She could smell the warmth coming out of the coat that was his, the old blueberry smell that made her want to laugh. Put it on, he said.

But she couldn't right that moment, so he took the coat from her hands and dropped it on top of her head. There you go.

Oh no, she said, holding the cigarette out in front of her. Don't let it burn, she said. Please! Margaret will kill me. Is it touching? Can you tell?

He didn't answer. She waited a minute, then pushed the jacket off her face. How did he leave so quietly. His cigarette still burned in the metal cup of the watermelon rind.

He never spoke to her again for the rest of the year and when their graduation happened he didn't even say congratulations, which was pretty much mandatory. Wasn't it funny how he'd danced right toward her then veered out the French doors like a signal. Wasn't that funny, and Margaret had seen it, too. Someone likes you, she said. But not in quite the way Lily expected her to, it was with a ripple of disapproval. But Margaret had been irritable since the flood because now Tommy was upstairs all the time. Clocking her every move, she said. He eavesdrops on my farts. He thinks he's a master detective.

By the end of June, the water had risen high in a surprise summer storm and rushed over the dock through the Foleys' backyard and straight into the porch and from there it surged into the basement, soaking the passion pit, revealing the bong and the copy of *The Sensuous Woman* hidden beneath the train set.

The brown water bubbled the green paint from the porch cement just as her mother had foretold, and in the basement the red corduroy was beyond salvage. The bong was confiscated and *The Sensuous Woman*, too, which Mrs. Foley told all her friends was conducive to screwing. Privately the friends thought the passion pit was enough inspiration for teenage boys. They need an instruction manual? And the hilarity of the bloated pages of pointers on a blow job properly administered made for a few happy nights in the wake of the Foleys' misfortune. But the neighbors took seriously the flash deluge and what it meant for property values and the seals around their own foundations. There was loose talk about French drains for a while and then July came with its perfect weather and August, searing the lawns, too dry to reawaken the resting fears.

Out on the terrace these same parents laughed under an umbrella they put up over one of the round tables. A single netted candle flickered. And one mother, Mrs. MacPherson, hugged her arms tight, one hand gripping each shoulder as she laughed beyond her natural limit, then squeezed to rein herself in. This was entirely necessary according to Lily's mother. The woman had no inner controls. She'd said some things about Cubbie that her mother couldn't forget and wouldn't repeat. Lily watched the woman who laughed, restraining herself; some snaggled teeth made her smile look tender even in the vampire light of the candle and Lily wondered what she might have said. Who would say anything bad about Cubbie? But her mother had told her people in the town were not as pleasant as they appeared and it was about time Lily grew up and understood that. The woman's smile made Lily smile too—she couldn't help it—and she thought Russell Crabtree might be able to see her already, and for a moment couldn't make herself move.

A weeping willow glowed on the edge of the terrace, its long fronds lit whitish by a thick bright moon now low in the sky. Tree shadows made monster fingers on the fairway. No one noticed Lily finally stepping off the stair onto the green; she wandered out into the hush of the night, the throb of the music a bubble of sound already behind her. The willow tree rustled as she rubbed along the lowest reach and rounded the other side. Across the first fairway, a gazebo made a black dome. She'd sat there on cold days with hot chocolate and lemonade on hot. Margaret's father was a bad golfer and brought the girls along for company when he had to fulfill his obligation as a member. They chased balls and drove the cart. Their gazebo stop by the end of the first hole was a joke for them all, the hilarious evidence that Margaret Foley's father was hopeless at something.

Such a novel idea. A father with a flaw. Lily's own father could do anything he put his mind to, and he had the kind of courage most men are only called upon to locate in wartime; he was that brave and resourceful all the time. At breakfast for instance, when he was home, which used to be weekends and now was never, he'd turn his face and look out at the water and say something about the tide, high or low, in or out, and a hush would fall over the table. Then he'd ask for more coffee and her mother was up and looking in the freezer for the kind she bought and saved just for him. She'd make a fresh pot. He didn't tell her not to bother.

Margaret's father was not only a bad golfer. When he trimmed the hedges he made flattops with bare sticks poking out, so Mrs. Foley had to call in a rescue team. He wore a hat, indoors, to cover the strange pink map of New Jersey slowly revealing itself across his scalp. How convenient, Margaret said. Every day he lost more hair. And sometimes he cooked for the family, disgusting things with clams and gelled gravies that tasted of dirty slimy socks. Whenever Lily ate Mr. Foley's cooking she understood the wisdom of her father's abstention.

A diaper smell came up from the grass and this was a secret recipe the new groundskeeper was using to keep the course vibrant in the August drought. Some poop from animals fermented in kegs. She pinched her nose and closed her eyes as if that would stop the swift stink coming to her from the ground. Lily wished now she'd worn her shoes.

Fortunately Russell Crabtree, she knew, had a summer cold. He always had a cold or a flu or a broken wrist or a twisted ankle or the worst impetigo anyone had ever grabbed out of a swimming pool. He got fleas from his dogs and lice from his baby cousin's nursery school; he had knock-knees and there was a rumor that he'd been born with a hole in his brain. In seventh grade he'd written a poem about it and then explained in a way that got him a permanent A-plus that the air pocket wasn't a metaphor. When she left, Lily would miss him.

Somewhere out here Russell was smoking. Didn't that mean, when he saw her, he might remember the night in the plastic porch? And just as she'd known, right under the black dome a tiny flash of a pin light, then it vanished as it would in a cupped hand. The poop smell stronger now and the grass sodden under her feet, she wondered if the hem of Margaret's dress was soaking up the stuff. The idea of Russell flinching from the stink when she arrived, of him having a bad reaction played in her mind, like an image caught in an air pocket, she thought, suddenly pleased with herself. If he ever wrote a poem about her what would he say?

Her grandmother told her she had eyes the color of bluebells, which was certainly poetic. All along the water's edge Doris planted bluebells when Lily was a baby. And she kept small bunches clipped in jars on the picnic table because she liked them best out in the open in the sunshine. Her mother liked to say, We name you Lily and naturally Momo plants *bluebells*. But her grandmother had gotten in bigger trouble over the bluebells, an invasive species, it turns out. All down the shoreline, along the river, the neighbors had to resort to drastic remedies to fight off the encroaching blooms. They're crackpots, said Momo. What could be the trouble with bluebells?

But it wasn't the flowers themselves Mr. Foley had explained. They took over the sod and wove tendrils through innocent soil. A plague, said Mr. Foley, then he'd finally found the solution. Some mixture of lye and ashes packed against the roots at the first sign of spring. And the new groundskeeper at the golf club agreed. Her grandmother's bluebells had popped up on a fairway or two. And Mr. Foley was given the unusual pleasure of addressing the membership with his authority. Nobody, not even the weed-killing team at the club, held this against Lily. If the blue of her eyes really matched this pest no one but her grandmother had noticed.

She saw the flicker of light again in the black dome of the gazebo, and heard a cough, quick and dry. And she realized that Russell might not be alone. She felt something stick into her toe and bent down to scrape it off when out of the darkness the cough was right beside her. Hey, she said, standing up. Russell?

But the big hand that pushed at her right in the center of her chest, clumsy like the paw of a puppy, couldn't be his. Russell's hands were slender and bony. A big Saint Bernard puppy, or even a bear, was pushing a heavy unskillful body into hers. Hey, she said, laughing. Stop. Russell?

But she knew it wasn't him. Greg? she tried. Greg Kiernan?

Yeah, what about it, he said, as if she were interrupting him in the middle of an important activity. His big body pushed harder and knocked her over. The wet grass soaked all through the gray flannel of Margaret's maxidress.

Hey! You're wrecking everything, she said. He fell down on his knees and his elbows pinned her around the hips digging the dress deeper into the grass. The strangeness of that, the burrowing of his elbows, his big face and his long thick blond hair, cut in some Dutch-boy shape, a clear concession to his mom, held between his hands. Then he dropped his hands to her skirt and clutched the fabric over her belly. His big face lit only slightly by the scant moon hovered over her chest as if waiting for instructions, and she felt herself go silent. Like the submarines her mother said had cruised nearby during World War II even into the Navesink River. Right outside Momo's house a periscope had popped up near the duck blind.

Holy Shit! she heard someone hissing. You stupid ass, Kiernan. Do you want to get yourself arrested? And then Greg was trying to elbow himself off her with a lot of exertion, but it became a slow backward crawl as if he didn't have the power to just stand up. Then she felt his weight come off her so fast she was almost rocketing up into the black sky. Come on, douchebag. This was Russell talking. Get up. And Greg Kiernan was struggling to his feet, being yanked by the arm away from her. Get out of here, said the voice that she was positive was Russell. Get out, you asswipe. It was like she wasn't there at all. She was a condition that was dangerous and as a friend Russell was dragging Greg away. For his own good. You and your pathetic johnson, she heard the Russell voice say, with compassion she thought. Yeah, man, said Greg. Anything with a cunt. Screw me. I'm disgusting. I'm just disgusting, she heard, as the voice drifted away. I'm disgusting, quieter now, sad and regretful, though with a little laughter, too. I'm disgusting, he said so far away now, and happy, and safe. He was out of danger. He was okay.

7

It was only polite to tell whoever was calling that she couldn't speak right now. Doris held the heavy receiver away from her mouth. She'd just told the last person, Kay Sheehan, that she was in a rush, and that call had lasted nearly an hour. Half the problem was body language she thought, even if the other person couldn't see it. If she sat down, and crossed her legs and nestled the receiver close, she was committed. She stood now and said, Hello whoever you are, I'm afraid I can't speak, and she laughed, too, knowing the person calling was likely a friend. Or a salesperson and in either case, inclined to be tolerant.

It was Kay Sheehan back again with another thought about Doris's health. She had fainted all of one time total, Doris laughed. In the supermarket where the entire town happened to be shopping on a Saturday morning. That's what I get for running on black coffee, she told the crowd assembled in aisle 3, waiting to see if the ambulance should be sent on its way or the hospital alerted to an

emergency coming. Jamie Ekdahl, sweet girl, made the right decision. Let's give Doris a little breathing room. And then sent her
daughter, thrilled to be assigned this task, to grab an orange juice
carton and a tube of paper cups and open them both on the spot.
Doris took a long sip, and soon was on her feet. Perfectly fine, she
said again and again.

Jamie Ekdahl insisted on driving her home. She'd arrange to
pick up Doris's car later in the day with her newly licensed son.
You're running a tight ship, said Doris, riding in the cozy clean
Volkswagen, the daughter strapped in the back still wondrous that
the juice and the cups were free! V.I.P. treatment, said Jamie to
her daughter.

V.I.P. and on the evening news you'd think with all the calls.
Now Kay Sheehan really wanted to know—what she'd forgotten
to ask the last time she phoned—was, And what did Jean have to
say about all this? Maybe she was thinking twice about getting on
any ocean liner?

Doris remained standing, held the receiver farther away from
her face and almost shouted, Why, she better get on that ocean liner!
And if I don't get my Lily out of bed ... but then she thought, That
wouldn't be the end of the world. Lily could finish out her summer
here and Doris could fly her to London in time for school. Why
hadn't she thought of this before? Kay, you're a dear. And then she
put down the phone.

Almost ten o'clock and Lily still sound asleep. Doris wrapped a
tight rubber band around the metal box with the paper label: HAIR-
PINS. Her hair sometimes smelled of the sour cherry throat drops
previously contained. Lily laughed at her for this funny smell and
nuzzled her hair. She was still a snuggle bear, that girl, and Doris felt
slightly sad thinking she'd miss the day to day of these momentous

years ahead, Lily thirteen, Lily fourteen, her Lily all grown up. Jean at fifteen was already self-possessed and turning down suitors. But Lily, Doris guessed—and hoped if she were honest—would be more like herself, a late bloomer. She hadn't met Clyde until she was nearly twenty-six and Jean was just turning three. Two lost babies of her own, but she seldom thought of them. Though now she couldn't remember why she had the hairpins in her hand or why she'd brought them downstairs to begin with.

She checked her hair and lipstick and twisted the bow on her neck scarf, adjusted her eyeglasses in the front hall mirror. She'd been married to Clyde for thirty-two years, just shy of that number, but Lily's hands felt closest, like a funny kitten, poking at her skin. She would miss that girl terribly. Missed her already. Lily? she called up the staircase, and then grabbed the banister. She loved this house; it had been her mother's and someday it would be Jean's and then Lily's. She could do that much, keep this house for them, but already she imagined a time when she didn't live here and no one alive had even seen her mother, and then one day, her brother's memory would vanish, too. Though for now Kay Sheehan was an astringent reminder. And Doris was thankful for that, could laugh at herself for still feeling, she wouldn't call it jealousy, it was a sense of propriety. Her brother Teddy, he'd be an old man now, but not really. She knew men handsome as ever. Just think of, oh, there were enough old roosters strutting around to know Teddy would have kept his handsome face, his strong, surprising body, big and tall and full of grace. Teddy full of grace and her mother said that was a blasphemy, or close enough. But it wasn't, really. Where else in this world would we find grace but in those we love? At least that's the way she'd always felt, but her mother advised against it. Called her rash, but she really meant vulnerable, suggested gardening instead where devotion is reliably rewarded.

Teddy inspired devotion, and that's why Kay Sheehan always made her smile, in a complicated way. She could see Kay still in a madras swimsuit and hair cut tight to her pretty face, legs pulled close, up on a wooden bench on the Sea Bright boardwalk, big cat's-eye sunglasses in white to emphasize a tan and the nearly white blond of her curls. She was a looker alright. But weren't they all. Weren't we all.

Doris's hand went to the scar on her throat. Jean had told her it was a terrible habit. All these years her hand had flown to her throat—oh twenty times a day! said Jean—and she hadn't realized. She'd never known. Clyde never said a word. Though, when she thought of him, that was scarcely a mystery. She'd put on a wedding bonnet in front of this very mirror; that was the only word for it, the odd construction she'd worn on her wedding day. She'd made it herself, a bonnet of cream-colored velvet and moiré silk ribbon and shaped it so it sat tilted on her head. It was gorgeous and her hair was dark and shiny. Her dress salt-and-pepper tweed, like her hair now, her mother refused to come to the wedding at all, and really it was only a priest's blessing so who could blame her. Doris never had. But Clyde never quite forgot. So much that was murky to Doris was clear to Clyde. He was always certain.

She wore the bonnet tipped over her forehead and Father Hetzler blessed them both at the railing of the dark altar, and only Teddy was there to give her away and wasn't he plenty, more than she would ever need. She understood her mother. She did. She and Clyde were blessed and then Father Hetzler let them out the side door and down the steps that Doris had swept herself that morning. She'd come by and swept away the new snow from the night before and placed a little bundle of flowers, her only bridal bouquet, a clutch of small tea roses she'd bought walking over at the florist on Avenue of Two Rivers. Scarcely a bud to be had this time of year, and she hadn't told him, old Mr. Canton, that it was her bridal bouquet. She took the wax paper bundle and cleared off the ice from the little exterior altar to the Virgin. Nothing funny in this; you saw small offerings there all the time out of nowhere as if all the most pagan rituals took place in the night and left behind these souvenirs. She put her bridal bouquet at the stone feet of the tiny Italian Virgin, then walked home to put on her good tweed dress and velvet bonnet and by the time Father Hetzler was letting them out the side door to Clyde's car, which they'd drive to the courthouse for the official ceremony and then to Atlantic City, by the time she caught Clyde's hand on the icy church side steps, her wax paper bouquet was gone. On someone's winter breakfast table she thought, bringing good cheer.

She woke up so lonely this morning. And without even thinking dismissed the idea that this loneliness had to do with Clyde. This old ache had persisted for decades, coming and going. This morning it was sharp. She unbuttoned the bottom of her cardigan; she'd take all the pictures of her and Clyde and put them away. There weren't that many, but without them the house would revert to her childhood home, except for the new light-colored drapes, the same lemony-white linen sheers in every room, cheerful ghosts, that let in the river light and the air. Her mother preferred dark velvet. Maybe Lily would, too, when her time came, when the house was hers. She could already see her beloved girl painting the walls bright blue. How she would miss Lily. She'd go look at her this very minute, but not to wake her. The whole house wrapped around her sleeping, dreaming girl, safe now. What could be better?

Yes, she'd put away the photographs, just as she had all the television sets, nearly first thing. After the whole week of family and friends, the services and receptions, Clyde's funeral in the same church where they were blessed, but not married, he was blessed again but not buried in consecrated ground because he never did become a Catholic as he'd promised her so long ago. Though Jean's mother had apparently been devout and until recently, Jean in her way was, too.

Jean had come in through the back pantry and saw the television sets stacked, wires wrapped around the tube fronts and nearly cried. The whole neighborhood had piled into their house to see the first television and then the first color television. Clyde was a marvel and a magician to bring such things home. And only dead ten minutes, his ashes, ashes! not yet scattered and his legacy was being shoved out the door, handed off to Negroes. What was Doris thinking; she had finally lost her mind completely. Jean packed as many televisions as she could fit into the Valiant—three—and drove off to put them up in her attic for safekeeping.

Oh, our Jean misses her daddy something fierce, said Ruby. She doesn't know how the world will work without him.

Doris looked at Ruby pushing the remaining small sets closer together on the pantry bench, rewrapping the cords. Yes, Ruby, she said. She doesn't know; you're right. It's a terrible thing. I'm making tea. And she let out a big sigh and so did Ruby. And then they left each other alone for a while. Something it seemed Doris and Jean would never learn to do.

Now she gripped the wide banister and made a slow aching climb up the wide front staircase. Her left hip wouldn't leave her alone, and she felt she'd adopted a wide straddle to compensate, like a sailor's roll, she would laugh, maybe with Teddy, who remembered her twirling on her toes. Amazing, amazing what happened to our bodies. But not to Teddy, and now she'd reached the top landing, and crossed down the long light corridor to the room where Lily slept and pushed open the door. Lily's hair, tangled streaky sunlit, her round cheek smashed deep into the blue embroidered pillowcase Doris always kept on this bed for her. A big book, pages crumpled under her deep hand. What was she reading? The room smelled like Lily's breath, something milky and ever so slightly sour with the warm lavender of the sheets heated by her body, and through the open window the river breeze, soft and saturated. Ruby was soaking the strange flannel dress in salt downstairs. Nothing else would work, she said.

No one thought about drowning. No one ever thought about drowning and that was a wonder. They were surrounded by water. The little spit of land made a natural point and then curved in at the last moment, and a tender hook of waving cattails and driftwood as though the house was protected from danger naturally. The tiny birds that flocked into the garden said the same; racket of chirps and trills, they said we're safe here to Doris. And she wondered about that, watching Lily turn on her back and throw a soft arm up over her head, draped across the blue pillowcase, her hand a half fist, a seashell curl of a hand so unmarked. When Lily held Doris's hand she'd play with the loose sun-marked skin and stroke down the wrinkles as if they could be wiped away like loneliness. She couldn't imagine how lonely she would be when Lily was gone; her helpless love for her eldest, now only, grandchild always made sense to her. She understood herself, though bristled at others who pretended to. Poor Doris doesn't know what to do with herself, she heard them all say in her head. She heard them now as if they were all chiming in, saying so much nonsense about her. She shook her head, and when she did felt her eyes were full of tears. Oh, she caught up a ragged breath, and tiptoed to the door. She wouldn't let Lily catch her old Momo sad.

Sunlight a rectangle shimmer on the honey-colored floor-boards of the upper hall. Ruby didn't much fuss with them, put her attention elsewhere. On her thieving boyfriend, said Jean, imploring Doris to fire Ruby once and for all, but hadn't she got Clyde's credit card back right away, left in the mailbox in a pink envelope that stank of violet candy. It could have been anyone. The dust made a soft gray frost on the high trim painted glossy white twice a decade, now overdue. She felt a stab of anger toward Jean so fierce it made her queasy. Who was Jean to be telling her Ruby must go? Who was Jean? And this she felt was the crux of all their problems and she felt dizzy with helplessness. Because what could she do. What could she do. I should have married Ruby instead of your father, she'd said to Jean recently, eating Ruby's soft-shell crabs, laughing, lifting yet another small light battered claw off the chipped blue platter. She'd ignored all the catering, all the neighbors and their casseroles but Ruby's crabs tasted like all she'd ever need. Then I'd never worry about being too thin.

The outrage! What had she done to make her stepdaughter so angry. Not enough, said Jean. Not nearly enough. But really, thought Doris, shouldn't this old fight have ended long ago? Darling heart, she'd said, putting down the crab shell, gently setting it aside, because she didn't want to hurt Ruby either, who was always in earshot; she was used to that, and thankful really. But Jean hissed at her, You're impossible. And all she could think of to calm them both down was to laugh, and tell a funny story about Teddy. Teddy nineteen, always in trouble, like our Lily, and Kay Sheehan plays a part. And she watched Jean's cheeks go pink and her jaw let go, curious just like a little girl, but she wasn't a little girl, and Doris needed to be careful; sometimes solace could do more harm.

Teddy climbing out of the low waves early September just before the war, no one knew a thing but how beautiful it was all the way out to the horizon, which was as much our own we felt as the backyard. How angry people were when the U-boats dared come, like trespassers spoiling something precious. But this was very early September, like a glass door we couldn't see through; the war was so close, but we couldn't see it, and there was Teddy stepping out of the waves.

He liked to swim, said Jean, and reached across for a piece of crab, just a small one.

He couldn't swim! That was the joke. Our father went mad, nearly beating him, did beat him once. Here Doris dropped her head.

Jean nodded and said, But Teddy ran away. He was nimble and Pop was stiff in every joint.

That's right. Pop couldn't catch him so he picked up a chair and threw it. My mother wouldn't forgive him the divot in her wall. Easily fixed, even so.

So Teddy went down to the beach. He would prove a thing or two.

That's right, you know this story better than I do.

Jean bit into the crab belly, ran a hand under her chin to catch the imagined grease, fumbled around for a paper napkin from the Dutch-girl holder. I hate this thing, she said.

It's for the picnic table.

Then why is it always right here.

Doris straightened a pleat on her blouse.

But what did Teddy do? said Jean. I can't remember.

He went right down to the ocean and dove right in, waves crashing right on top of his head, because he didn't know how to dive under them. He was always stubborn.

Not always.

He was when it came to Pop. No one would win those fights. He let the waves crash on his head, and poor Kay Sheehan must have finally realized that with all that water in his eyes she could pose as much as she wanted; he would never notice her.

Doris, Ruby's knitting. I can see her.

Sweetheart, I know.

You pay her to knit?

I don't pay her much. So Kay Sheehan leapt up off that bench. Marched down to the water, arranged her madras two-piece to her best advantage when standing, and yelled, Don't you know a real elemental beauty when you see one?

That was the Deb, Doris Elemental Beauty. I forgot that. Very funny.

Yes, it is funny . . .

Teddy called you that. I always think it was Daddy.

Well, Daddy, too, but he got it from Teddy.

It was a joke.

A kind of joke, yes.

Because you're not, really. Jean looked at her stepmother as if just clarifying the facts and Doris smiled, but not showing her teeth, just the broad slender mouth pulled wide, her aquiline nose stretched lower, her gray eyes narrowed into a nest of wrinkles. All salt and pepper in the hair now, and pulled up away from her long face in a French twist, and pearls on her ears, dangled from slim gold wires. Gold beads at her throat half concealing the white scar, her hands curled now with arthritis, she'd lost an inch of height in the last two years alone. No, her stepmother wasn't a beauty, really, so why did everyone think she was?

That would be you, my love, said Doris, reaching the curled fingers out straight toward Jean.

But why didn't Teddy marry Kay Sheehan? Jean would have just one more small piece of crab and that was it. If Kay was so eager and so sexy?

No time. And that's what the story is about really.

How so?

Oh, said Doris and she laughed, sat back in the deep chair. I'll miss your daddy. He knew all my stories. I forget them halfway through. He would know where I was going with all this.

I wish that were true. But you can't even say it with a straight face. Jean put the crab back down on the plate and grabbed a handful of napkins and rubbed at her fingers as if they were stained. Don't try that on me for one minute, but she was laughing now.

Doris could feel the relief. It was in the air, in the bright sharp sunlight like a change of season. Jean dancing around her now, soft with forgiveness. What could anything matter anymore; there was to be an ocean between them. Jean would sail all the way across and when she reached the other side, she'd call she promised, more often than Doris could imagine. It would be so easy. Jean was breathless with the ease awaiting her, as if she'd already entered that new time and could be lightened by it. She smiled at Doris fondly as though she were a distant great aunt, odd and cantankerous even, but only the snag of an afternoon. It was the new smile, pretty and bright, eye-catching and deflective. It was safe to look at Jean now; no one would be heartbroken. It was safe.

If only they'd stay right here, thought Doris. Yes, she'd let Lily sleep; she'd probably come in very late last night. A final dance at the golf club. Stupid place, she caught herself thinking, and then forgot about it. What did it matter anymore what she thought of the clubs that Jean had joined so readily. What could it matter. She had a terrible theory, and she thought about it now, finding her grip on the banister, taking the steps one at a time, butter just past melting, its scent curling up the stair. She thought how slow and tiny love was, not sky and ocean vast, but tiny like an envelope. Small and stiff and holding only a scrap or two for a very long time. So that Teddy stepping out of the waves and silly, endearing Kay Sheehan trying to get her madras straps back in place, her siren's smile turned a wide *o* of consternation and Teddy reaching her and finding the ends of the straps in the wind and tying them at the nape of her neck like bib strings, and that was the whole story. Kay knew it, and Doris knew it, and in the tiny envelope that was her theory, Doris had collected this scrap of knowledge and held it in front of her eyes for the next thirty years or more. And then sometime in the midst a second scrap of paper had arrived and that was Lily. What a sad and sorry business she was, then she called out to Ruby in the kitchen, when she knew she was audible, when she was almost on the first landing and could hear the eggy bread drop sizzling into the pan. Divine, Ruby, she said. Just divine.

8

There was a lot of nonproductive blame floating around, a lot of hassle from all sides. Billy Byron wouldn't even come inside the house; he was that angry. Lionel rubbed at the black hole behind his right eye, like a black eye really, but inside, as if someone had punched him in the brain. He rubbed that temple gently, and didn't like to think about the conversation with Billy Byron in his preposterous maroon stretch. Maroon? But that's why Lionel was here, as a favor.

Billy Byron had five houses, each uglier than the next and Lionel had agreed *as a favor* to oversee a nearly impossible renovation. What Billy wanted, and wanted on the cheap, was a re-creation of the house Lionel had kept for a short and glorious time on the Ile St. Louis in Paris. Billy Byron never got over that house, that dinner. He'd been funneled out of his suite at the Georges V into a limousine as if blindfolded; when he stepped into Lionel's entry courtyard it was as if everything gorgeous in the world was right there, every sense amplified to the last limit of pleasure. In a single beat. A miracle, Billy said, a fucking miracle.

And this before his first drink of anything. He never forgot it, and when the townhouse he bought on Sixty-Second Street refused to come to heel for the usual decorator (for the love of god, Williamsburg Blue?), Billy begged Lionel to come and work his magic. Begged. Remember?

Billy didn't remember. Lionel sat in the cigar-infused maroon leather bench seat in the back, one big cup of an imprint where Billy usually sat, but he moved over, made Lionel sit there instead, and there was something mildly revolting about that. He was made intimate with Billy Byron's peculiar frame and its contours, as if his essence was being suffocated through his pores by the leather's clammy embrace. Hallucinating, he reminded himself, and made a mental note about a plausible chemical remedy he could prepare once Billy had completed this little ceremony. You—Billy was pointing at him—*you* are going to speak to the adjuster.

Of course, said Lionel, and his mood lightened because that really was the best way.

Billy felt it, too, and let Clifford the driver unlock the doors.

Now the insurance adjuster was pressing the electric buzzer, one of the few wires still intact after the fire. Let it go, yelled Lionel to no one who could hear him.

Kitty snuggled down into the blankets, her blond baby hair tangled into a little rat's nest near the crown; he put his hand there, then kissed her angled shoulder. A pretty thing, her skin nearly green it was so transparent. Kitty, he hummed, and sniffed the Pears soap and opiated hash scent in the tidy curve of her neck. She was a tiny string, a delicate instrument. His fingers quickened, and the black hole behind his eye receded; he touched with the softest part of his hand, the warm mound at the base of his thumb. She'd told him she could feel it from stem to stern when he did that—a first, she insisted—and it had made him laugh, scoff, but he kept it in the repertoire. He brushed the warm base of his hand against the tips of her shoulder blades, her back, and felt the downshift, the move into her coming on fast, her back arched in her sleep, then the buzzer shrieked again. Fuck off! he shouted. But Kitty murmured and turned deeper into the duvet. And Lionel grabbed his black kimono and located his black velvet slippers and closed the door gently behind him.

Climbing down the inner stair, and it did have quite a stench, all the smoke had gathered there like a flue and caused the skylight, the best thing in the whole place, to go gray with grunge. Lionel wouldn't look up, because his neck was precarious at the moment, some gymnastic feat with Kitty had given his spine a twist, and the thought of that made him laugh and doubly furious at the factotum with his thumb on the buzzer below. Lionel wasn't getting paid for this he would remind Billy Byron; no money was passing hands. But if he played his cards right, the insurance would give him the kind of cash this place really required. So he folded the kimono higher on his chest. He'd play this straight. No fucking with the guy's head by appearing nude at the door. Though, in other contexts, that worked quite well.

He was expecting something dumpier. So when he opened the door on a svelte young man with a bow tie and a pink checkered shirt, a tight blazer with white piping, someone express from a Twiggy shoot, he let go of his flap, and said, Coffee?

Roger McKintrick gave back a helpless grin, and Lionel amended the offer. No, no, he purred. Something sweeter.

Lionel wouldn't mention the jacket right away, though he was curious. Roger, Roger McKintrick, followed Lionel obligingly into the kitchen, the *downstairs* kitchen Lionel stipulated walking in; the upper one had already been dismantled. Who needs two *full* kitchens? Lionel threw up his arms to show he was with Roger when it came to stemming excess. His arms went up, the robe fell open, there was a short kabuki of the closure, something that friends re-enacted with mixed accuracy at Lionel's memorial. All those years later, it was this gesture that won the most tearful laughter. Now it didn't fail to win the notice of Roger McKintrick, who sat back in the leather desk chair rolled to a red lacquer pedestal table and felt a kindred spirit reigned here. They would be able to talk sense. They would come to an equitable agreement, something in the open and close of the kimono assured this. He'd had temperamental house-wives in New Jersey up to the eyebrows, weeping over shattered Lenox bowls and their mother's cultured wedding pearls melted in flames. Though he'd never seen a kimono except in photographs and then on women entertaining American soldiers, cheering them up, Lionel's folded silk was grounding, clarifying. Something he wouldn't say later when forced to defend the exorbitant sum allo-cated and disbursed in a single payment to a case of minor smoke damage in an uptown double duplex.

Lionel was pouring grappa and promising a tour, but then clasped his head and cried, Fuck!

What is it? said Roger.

Standing back outside on the sidewalk when this tableau re-played in his mind, he knows that he'd offered his hand, but all he really remembers is the grasp, and the feel of Lionel's warm mitt through the fabric on his forearm. Then Lionel lifted the other hand, the one covering his right eye, and said, Where did you get this jacket? It's got to be Derek Voose?

Roger knew about Derek Voose, but the knowledge was so brand-new that to be accused of owning such a jacket shocked him.

Migraine, whispered Lionel. Just fuck me.

Roger knew about migraines, too. You poor thing, he said.

It's hell. And no doubt I deserve it. He gave a wan smile, one of his best.

Bed, dark room and bed, this instant.

Do you mind?

Mind? Of course not.

You'll come back?

Of course.

Angel, groaned Lionel.

Not a bit, said Roger, and found his company-issued briefcase lodged against the red lacquer pedestal. He started to say something about the table and something he'd seen, just out of the blue, in a little shop upstate when he remembered that they'd have time for this later. Lionel shuffled to the door, all gratitude, but when he held it open to allow Roger to leave, the morning light rushed in. Both arms flew up to shield his eyes, and then the last glimpse Roger had of Lionel was the famous tug of the flap and the humming, rueful, laughing, Mercy. That they never met at the townhouse again didn't much matter. He'd seen enough, and no doubt someday they would find each other in the same room, somewhere. Roger wouldn't be an insurance adjuster forever.

Lionel let the front door close with a whisper then bounded up the central stair. Kitty! he shouted. Kitty, my love, we're late! We're late! They were to be aboard the *QE II* by three or they wouldn't get on at all. Not even Lionel could change that.

9

Lionel would be the very last to leave. He'd already sent Kitty down to find the driver with the suggestion she circle the entire island and find them a place to have a quiet drink. That they'd end up at Eddie Condon's was a given, but it was a nice activity and Kitty could stretch out in back and let the sunset play through the tinted windows. Polaroid technology! Lionel had told her and how the thick cameras that spit out photos on the spot were relevant to the windows on a rented limousine was beside the point. Take me to Potter's Field, she said to the driver, Potter's Field was everyone's favorite joke. They intended to end up there. Life is for the loving, said Lionel. He was against ceremony and breath devoted to the already gone. The exception was his nephew and namesake, but they didn't discuss him often, at least not in daylight. Only at night, and only once really when she first met him, had Kitty found Lionel sitting at the end of the bed, smoking, dropping ashes on the carpet, saying, Poor darling, poor darling. And she curled herself around his hips, just like that, a warm pillow, and he reached over her to find a glass or something on the bedside table to drop the cigarette into, before he leaned back into her belly first and then pulled her arms, her hands into his lap. Thank you, precious girl. That he didn't seem to entirely recognize her in that dark room didn't much matter.

When Cubbie was born, he arrived a month early and at New York Hospital, not at the sleepy riverside maternity clinic like Lily who was late and round and had a flame of red hair. Cubbie was born tiny with the creased face of an old lion and Lionel had what he'd always wanted, and with a sweetness he could never repay Jean and Nick gave it over to him, Cubbie. Lionel the second. Eighteen months younger than his sister Lily—Lillian—named for their mother. Jean half-asleep in the green glow of the fluorescent claimed the next baby was hers; they were not to reach back to any more Devlins. She'd done her job and they could both be satisfied. Satisfied? They were jubilant and Eddie Condon played a new song that night just for Cubbie. "Cubbie's Lullaby." Eight years later he promised to bring everyone in his ensemble on his own private bus down to the Jersey Shore, the whole enchilada, to play Cubbie's own song. The kid had a song. We want to play it, he said, over and over, but no one was taking the message. Instead a high school sophomore with a wavering alto soprano sang "Ave Maria" all by herself. Like everything else in the small private funeral Mass she stuck to the Latin version, the less comprehended the better.

But it was a big party the day the Devlins set sail and Eddie Condon had access to the right ear at Cunard to get them the room with the best acoustics. The whole rig is padded, every note sinks, except in the discotheque and so they had the farewell there, all daylight and harbor views irrelevant. And if there'd ever been a "Cubbie's Lullaby," by now, three years later, it was forgotten. Rosemary Clooney stopped by and sang a little "Stormy Weather" as a joke, then "Someone to Watch Over Me." And Jean took a turn on the dance floor under the disco ball—everyone stepped back to make room when Rosemary waved her forward, come on darlin'—for a slow refrain in her husband's embrace. Moe Dailitz had the good sense to bring a showgirl on each arm. It was, all agreed, an excellent party. With press to cover what they printed the next day as the happy end to a very long story.

Tommy Foley knew how to get back from the West Side pier to the Sea Bright Bridge in under an hour he said, so their mother gave them her car to come to the send-off. Last thing, Lily showed Margaret and Tommy her L-shaped room, the only window tucked in an alcove on the short end with a tiny padded seat. For your poetry writing, laughed Margaret. For sensual pleasures with your miniature lover, said Tommy. Then, All right, Meg, we gotta go. Good trip, Devlin. Happy sailing and all that jazz. He gave her a quick heavy squeeze that she could still feel when he backed away. Margaret draped her warm arms over Lily's shoulders. Don't stink up the place, all right?

Yes, all right, said Lily. Don't you.

Right, said Margaret, with a wince that Lily couldn't come up with anything better to say and Lily felt the sink of a missed chance. All right, she said again. She had to go back to the disco immediately her mother had said, and they could find their own way to the gangplank. Hey, wait, Lily said. I can call you from our house! She was nodding fast. There's a special phone for long distance right in the house.

Good, said Margaret. And that was it.

Now Lily felt her father's hand on her head, just at the top like a cap, light and kind. She was leaning out as far as she could get on the very last rail, watching the harbor peel away, a busy blur; everything was a loud pressure on her ears and smelled of smoke and tar. Don't cry now, bub, said her father and Lily tried not to.

Margaret will visit us, he said.

She won't, said Lily. She won't be allowed to, Lily amended because she didn't like to contradict her father, though her mother claimed contradiction was Lily's vocation these days. It was Anthony Moldano who wouldn't let Margaret come to London, even if she pleaded and said, Just for the culture! Lily already knew he couldn't spare her.

What are you doing in there? Jean called out.

This one, Nick said, holding out the black cocktail dress with the satin hem. He'd brought it home from London that spring.

All right, she said. How's your head?

Blasted. Decimated.

No, she said and joined him in the walk-in closet. Everything about this suite was larger than need be. Palatial, presidential, royal, but the most sleek and modern of ocean liners had set aside corny titles. The suite had a number and a letter that signified an almost fantastic preferential status. They're laying it on a bit thick, said Jean, after the two stewards had finally left them alone to rearrange their skillfully unpacked luggage. They each had a walk-in closet, and Nick had walked into hers. Come out, she pressed her mouth into his upper arm, leaned her forehead into his shoulder, the reliably salty smell of his skin as if he'd eaten the Cape Cod beach of his childhood. Her heart slowed down; she could feel it. The party and then the overpowering garbage smell of the pier had made her sick, but he soothed her, just the scent of his skin. Come out now, she said. Don't have a bad head tonight. Let me give you something.

The champagne, he laughed, croaking. Christ, I think I was slipped a mickey.

No doubt. Billy Byron sent it, along with the coffin-sized basket of fruit.

Give the guy a chance.

Sure, she said, and let go of him.

Don't start. He was quiet and turned to her. She put both hands against his forehead. There, she said. Her hands were always cool.

He sighed. Closed his eyes. She watched his face, a small tremor under the left eye, and she smoothed it away. Kept her hands light, so as not to hurt him.

That's a help.

Good, she said and brought her hands down against his chest. You're clammy. You have a fever.

Yeah.

Let me check. She moved away to go find a thermometer; there must be one somewhere. She knew she'd packed it, but hadn't seen it yet. There was a mirrored dressing area between the walk-ins with a low tufted stool, as if Jean were expecting a dressmaker.

Where did you go? he called out.

Here! she said. Take an aspirin. She opened a long shallow drawer beneath the white marble veneer counter in the bathroom. They'll regret all this, she said to no one.

Aspirin makes it worse. Where's my kit? Where'd you put everything?

Nothing can make you worse.

She had on a wrap, something velvet and new. Isn't this hot? he said, coming into the bathroom. Loo phase one, he'd called it, just a long bank of sinks and mirrors and drawers. The tub and shower and toilet each in a separate chamber. He hiked up the back of her robe and pressed into her. She looked up and saw her face green in the fluorescent lighting over the wall of mirror. Snap that off, she said. The switch, right there.

Nick loved this bass. Listen to that, he said to the girl writhing in and out of his open hands, and he laughed to think this sound would have been impossible even a year ago. Brand-new! he shouted and pointed out some contraption floating near the low ceiling, metal tubes tucked into black quilting meant to keep the sound crisp and dry, hard on the bones, meant to move him to action his body had never known. Look at you, he yelled and now she smiled. Her white strap a flicker of glowing lavender in the strobe. He'd gone in the wrong direction, had a couple of stingers, and now the vibrations tickled his feet straight through the shoe leather. He wanted to laugh, wanted to hail something; he also felt a tug of some inner gravity, felt himself melt into an off rhythm way behind the beat, and to his surprise, and shifting interest, more interest, she met him there. Slowed her undulations in and out of his hands to something his body could mimic. Her backbone suspended on a silver string. Look at you, he whispered. So pretty!

She wasn't actually and he'd seen her earlier and dismissed the whole notion of her look. A silver-white dress too big on top and tight around the bottom, a bottom that looked square and unhitched when she walked, too much motion below, too much smiling above, that was his first pass. But now, now that she'd located this beat and her whole body had synchronized itself with the sound he understood her for who she was, a forerunner, a herald. I'm new, she shouted. Just like you! New something, she was saying. Oh yes, she was utterly new.

You are! Newer than new, he shouted back, nodding, smiling. New! And there she was, her hip bouncing, slipping off the palm of his hand.

Jersey! she shouted.

Oh for chrissakes, he said. Please, he shook his head. Slowing further. Feeling the crash come fast now. Please, he tried laughing. Have a drink.

Can't! she yelled, swiping a hand across her breasts. She'd done this before, part of a whole selection of gestures meant to keep him reaching and retreating. Come on, he said, irritated, panting. It's hot.

Nope. He saw her lips move, couldn't really hear her now; his ears had clicked off at Jersey. She spiraled around, hands moving down her body, checking for breakage, funny this, and now the hands made that pass across the breasts again, checking, protecting. Stay here, he yelled. I'll get you something. He did a cha-cha-cha to make her laugh, up-tuned to catch the spiking rhythm. She spun away across the floor. Stingers, he cried to the bartender when he reached the bar. No, make that vodka rocks, splash of OJ. Two por favor.

Jean had fallen asleep so quickly. She and Nick in the white expanse of soft bed that rocked, she could feel it, though how could a vessel this large swing like a hammock. But it felt like that to her, Nick warm and open to her, her body nestled into him and for the first time, she felt the beginning of possibility. They slept, but she tucked her body in close to him, sure they would make love again sometime in the night, and this resting sleep just a start, just a margin between all they were leaving and then. The rocking. The softness of her body. He was right; she only needed to pry herself out of that house, out of their whole world for a while. Then she'd come back new. The last morning she'd awakened at home there'd been grackles at the feeder, the largest with a tucked wing and a puffed chest frightened off the small and female. But two little ones kept circling back to steal the pumpkin seeds. One to tease the large injured grackle, the other to feed and flee. So odd to see them there every year. Only in late summer and then they vanished. When Cubbie was tiny she told him to come indoors; she said she worried the big grackles would carry him away. But then she'd become a bird herself of course and find him; any mother would she'd said. She was dreaming when Lily asked to hear more about this. Jean admitted that usually the blue jays were the most aggressive and had little interest in stealing children. But if they did steal Cubbie, how far out over the ocean would the birds fly? The knock caught volume. A thudding in the dense wood, and a muffled voice in the corridor. She hoped they wouldn't wake Lily whatever it was. Nick was gone.

Here, she said quietly, inward, as if answering an unkind teacher. You're just disoriented Nick had told her once. It's normal he'd said, but wasn't that long ago? She'd put a robe somewhere handy, and there it was, near the fruit display, the black velvet wraparound she could barely make out, rolled in a lump like a sleeping cat. Lily must have played some game with it. Nothing was her own anymore. She pulled herself up out of the heavy stiff sheets and felt them drop away from her body like a loss. What is it? she said, but softly. She arranged the robe, belted it tightly, ran her hands through her hair, bent low to snap on a lamp, a false nautical sheathing glowed orange. Here, she said, and opened the door to a young man who looked bewildered to see her as if he were expecting something forceful, someone who might help.

Mrs. Devlin?

Yes? she said.

I'm very sorry.

But of course he'd come about Nick. Shall I follow you? Is he all right?

Yes, thank you, Mrs. Devlin. I'll wait right here.

She almost remembered where everything was, but packing for a cruise, everything was accessorized and matched, nothing to throw on in the middle of the night. She put on a sundress and a blue cardigan and sandals, and felt a fool. Here I am, she said, snapping closed a white straw purse, and stepped into the cool dim corridor. Which way are we going?

She followed the young man through a maze of galleries and long public lounges with oversized chairs bolted into sociable clusters. Finally they came to a kind of antechamber and she laughed to see the earnest neon flash above a double padded door. DISCO! in a rakish scrawl. Back where she'd started. The bass thudded against her chest as she stepped through. So dark, much darker now. Pink cove lighting etched the ceiling, but little below could be made out immediately except the bar bottles and the piercing sparkle of the mirrored twirling ball. It must be very late because there was ammonia in the air as if the drudgery of antiseptic reversal was already under way. She half expected to see him collapsed on the dance floor, and already her body felt charged with electricity, becalmed and charged just as before. But then of course, of course! The overhead lights would be on. Just there, Mrs. Devlin, said the young man, and pointed to a booth, a high horseshoe of leather, and her husband head down on the small round table.

Thank you, she said, and she heard her own voice disembodied and polite as if she were being shown to a table at lunch. She smiled and nodded and went to the booth, put her straw purse down on the banquette and stood and looked for a moment. He was only asleep, only resting. She touched his cheek, cool enough, no fever now, put her hand on his back and felt the rise and fall of his breath. What was the big emergency? She almost felt angry to be brought here this way in the middle of the night, but then she spotted the young girl shivering and hunched over a couple of booths away and understood the problem.

The girl's face was invisible, like all faces of all young girls now, this one masked by a swatch of long straight hair. Jean almost wanted to brush it behind her ears so that they could speak to one another, but instead she knelt down and looked up through the veil and said, You must be very tired; it's incredibly late. The girl opened her eyes and focused. There you are, said Jean and thought didn't she know how to do just this?

Here, she said. Let me get you some water. Jean brought the water, and knelt down again, the pulse of the dance floor jarring her knees, the bass line still playing thick, but like a blanket, something to hide under. Here you go. Tell me your name. I'm Jean.

The girl shook her head, which was a good sign. That's fine, said Jean. I've come to take you back to your cabin. The girl seemed to accept this, and no wonder. It was a voice Jean used with Lily all the time: this is the plan. Here we go. She stood and offered the girl her hand, which was not taken, but the girl stood now too, in her tiny dress, a silver sliver of nothing. Red panties and a white brassiere and a very flat chest, all visible, Jean wanted to throw her sweater over her. She did. She wrapped the sky-blue cable-knit cotton around the girl's pointy shoulders. She smoothed back the girl's hair and smiled. You must be a very good dancer, she said. And the girl looked relieved, as if this were a conversation she could finally understand. She was a good dancer. She always had been.

A whole series of ideas had got Jean this far, to this walk with a slumping sleepy girl across an indoor recreation room on this ocean liner early, early in the dark blue morning. Wait, said the girl, Stephanie, who'd caught something on the heel. Just a minute please. She sounded like a girl Lily might go to school with.

Stephanie's parents had the suite on the level just below the Devlins. On the AA level, the Devlins resided on A. The best of the best, just as Nick would always have it, or nothing at all. And hadn't nothing been visible for a long time now. Stephanie's mother had not taught her to cover her mouth when she yawned. The girl had an enormous tongue, white with sugary soda and some residual braces on her bottom back molars. Her shoes looked like Mary Janes with a modest heel. Something for a preteen, but Jean was guessing fifteen and just. She hadn't been much older when she met Nick so didn't she know the way it felt. And he couldn't help it, if he didn't know how to turn that off. He was like a flower: he bloomed and then the bees came around.

A flower! her father had bellowed at her. She'd made the mistake of telling him this theory. Such a mistake. But when he finished calling Nick a list of names—she couldn't remember a single one— she understood her motive. She'd been lonely, and now she'd be lonelier. As long as she understood that, she could contain herself.

She always knew her father had loved her. One thing he'd said she took to heart. That Lily should be told what had happened, all of it. So she'd never be caught unawares by some prying nobody. All right, Jean said. He'd asked for a promise, and she'd given him one she meant to keep. But not yet. Because wasn't that the best thing about this move; it would buy them all a little time.

She looked down at the crouching girl and felt the tiniest rocking under her feet. This Stephanie had extremely fine hair at the top of her head; even in the half light her scalp was nearly visible. Your mother must worry about you, said Jean. Let's try not to wake her.

Part II

10

Delays at Heathrow, then an interminable search in U.S. customs at Kennedy last night, every pouch, every zipper, well after two when he'd finally sunk into this elaborate bed at the Sherry-Netherland and now a noonish green light severs the blackout drapes he failed to draw closed completely. He didn't quite get undressed, apparently, and still wears his shirt, open; one cufflink bites into his side. The phone blinks red fast and then calms down to a pulse. He'd had the wherewithal to turn off the ringer. The woman beside him looks familiar. As he rises to sit, he sees that she, at least, has folded a tiny dress with some care on the pink chaise longue. She has black hair that rises in a confection over her face and a trace of raspberry-colored lipstick still pretty against her skin. She's a pretty girl. Very pretty girl. A pretty girl who seems to have bled all over the bedding. A sodden tampon lays neatly next to her charm bracelet on the bedside table. The whole room smells like beef and freesia, her misguided perfume. He thinks he might be sick and finally juts himself upright onto his feet and veers into the loo.

The glare of the white marble tile is piercing even with the shade drawn. He tosses the joint on the sink into the unflushed toilet, dashes water on his face. His eyes burn. He can still catch her butcher's scent on his hands, wipes them on a towel and ignores the fast blinking red on the wall-mounted phone. He's got a belly now from all the cortisone, and his face is swollen, too, under the eyes, puffed along the jaw. Moonface he calls Lily, but he has one himself this morning; he looks like her, he thinks, then forgets about her. A suit hangs pressed in the dressing area, a blue striped shirt with a white pointed collar, ironed and starched; his shoes are polished. Someone's been in here, when did that happen? He slides up the shade and watches the tiny yellow taxis push and grind to cut each other off on Fifth Avenue. From this height, with a squint, they look just like the Matchbox cars Cubbie crashed together. He stares for a while. The park treetops mesh in the sun already so high the light washes away the green. A point he made a while back to Billy Byron— the light and color thing. Listen to Picasso here, Billy said. But Billy got it. They should be thinking day and night, right? Night and day. And that was the launch of a whole new line of foundations in development. We'll name it after you, sweetheart, Irving Slater said.

He was useful and he was insightful and that was a surprise to everyone. That this was actually working was news he'd like to keep from Lionel. He hears a low groaning laugh from the bedroom. His watch is in there somewhere; maybe she'll just take it and go. He screws on the shower taps to blistering. Then picks up the receiver on a telephone and dials 0.

Mr. Devlin, good afternoon, sir, says a young Irish voice. Messages? he asks. Several, sir. She reads off a list, including Lionel.

He grimaces into the mirror, studies his back teeth, feels his heavy beard, rubs his tender scalp. There's a saddle-shaped bloodstain, a big brownish butterfly, across his upper thighs, his dick. He says thank you, hangs up, then retches. Okay in there, lamb? The girl calls out. He remembers her name—Vivienne—then kicks closed the door and retches some more.

Been to Versailles lately? asked Irving Slater when Nick came into the meeting. He's referring to the hair pomade tester Nick dutifully wears that stinks of thyme and gardenias. So wrong, really a downer, and only experience will convince Billy that flowers and herbs have no place in the modern men's line. Nick was on the minute, yet the meeting was already under way and Billy Byron was in a rage. Not only were the new Scheherazade lipsticks corrosive in the test markets, but his wife, Bunny, had come home from the Colony Club yesterday evening with devastating news about the whole backstory. I thought this was about seduction! Right? Of course he was right the eight executives parked at the table frowned and nodded. So right. Scheherazade: Don't Say a Word. Whose idea was that? No one could remember at the moment.

Now I'm getting a whole thing about the dead wives. Bunny beside herself. It turns out the girl is a big talker. Is this really what we're after? This lipstick keeps your date from chopping off your head? He laughed. It's ludicrous. Such violence. Believe me Bunny couldn't sleep. And all the stories are about cuckolds. The wives are screwing everything—garden boys, genies, demons, each other. It's mayhem for the husbands. They have to kill the wives just to keep things under control. Scheherazade understands that. So, she *anticipates* her husband's completely natural reaction to their wedding night—he'll need to keep her in line once she's had a taste of the unquenchable experience, so she tells him a story of unfaithful wives offed and satisfies the urge. So the story replaces the act. Get it? Interesting. Something in that we can use, but what? asks Billy.

Well, said Nick. I thought the stories were more about heroes, actually, which is a plus. Anyway, the lipstick names could alter the stories in our favor, like . . .

I'm speaking metaphorically. When I want your opinion, I'll ask. Plus there's another problem. A key test group in suburban New Jersey had lips that required the emergency attention of a doctor. Not just cracked, cratering! said Billy. One actually contracted herpes, but legal has already asserted that can only happen to those with the predilection. But for fuck's sake. Kiss Me? Kiss Me Sheer? Kiss Me Frosted?

Now they'd have to go out to the labs themselves; that was the only solution.

Irving, Irving, get the mechanics, said Billy, meaning the drivers. Then he collapsed back into the pale blue swivel chair at the head of the conference table and spun to the windows overlooking Central Park. He hid the side of his face with his hand. The eight men around Nick visibly gauged whether they would need to travel to Perth Amboy today. He rubbed along his swollen jaw. Billy hadn't even glanced his way. What the hell was he doing here. Why had he flown to New York on an hour's notice? Five housewives in Brielle with chapped lips needed the attention of UK marketing?

Mrs. Blatt? said Irving to Billy's secretary, throwing up his hands. What's the delay? And she looked alarmed and placed the call from the nearest extension. The cars will be waiting on the Madison side in fifteen minutes, sir.

Fifteen minutes? said Billy, still facing away. It's an emergency. Call back, Mrs. Blatt. Five minutes.

Nick's training period—the sitting around at Saks and Bamberger's watching women peer down into countertops, clocking their interest, seeing what whetted the appetite for more and what they could pass on—hadn't included the laboratories in Perth Amboy, New Jersey. Some fluke of timing, so Nick was curious. For the others, from the looks of the downcast resignation, dropping in to shock the geniuses screwing up at research and development was a tedious routine.

The cars pulled around to a service ramp in the back of a long gray warehouse not far away enough from the Amboys to quell the stink. Foul odor seeped into the waiting cars from the oil refineries while one of the drivers jimmied the lock on the cargo entry. Billy in the car, examining his palms, was quiet. He still hadn't acknowledged Nick, though Irving had shoved him toward this car with the two of them and Mrs. Blatt. Nick thought he was being tested, but like a child is tested, given the cold treatment until he came around to some right way of thinking.

The driver finally broke the lock and waved them in. Billy looked up then addressed his palm. Why are we coming in this way?

A surprise? said Irving.

Good, right, but Clifford always takes us to the awning.

True, said Irving. But this is unexpected? This will answer the right questions; we won't get the usual obfuscation techniques.

I see. You know, Clifford is hitchhiking to Georgia. His mother is ailing. Were you aware?

No, I wasn't, said Irving.

I'm concerned.

Well.

I mean the situation just being a person down there, Jewish, Negro, it doesn't matter. It could be me. You know what they do, right?

Well, at least he'll be traveling alone. No mixed signals. Irving smiled at his own wit.

Yes, good point. What do you think? Billy nodded his chin toward Nick, but kept his eyes on his hands, now the nails, began buffing each one with his pointer finger.

I think, said Nick, trying not to watch the wiping finger, something mildly repellent in this, the waxy liquid shine on the nails, the circular caress. I think that Clifford is a good man.

Maybe a stupid one? asked Billy.

Maybe he knows how to handle himself.

I wouldn't lend him a vehicle. He asked, you know, but what would that look like, right? I don't have anything appropriate for him in the pool to drive out of uniform; the car would be a signal. Hitchhiking he's normal. It's a protection, you see. But still, I worry. He's the only one who seems to know anything around here. Did the moron get the door unbolted.

He did.

Well, what are we sitting for. You're a time waster, Devlin. You're pretty and you're smart, but tell your brother I'd like what he promised sometime soon. We clear? Now, let's get the fuck out of the car. And Irving, try not to look like you ate the goldfinch. Because believe me, you did not.

Once they'd walked past all the cages of stunted rats and then the pens of frightened, injured rabbits and then vials of sludge that looked and smelled of shit, not even the intriguing new wall systems, just installed, designed in Denmark for this very conference room could shift the mood. It's a slaughterhouse out there, said Billy. Plain and simple. Why didn't anyone tell me? Why has this been kept a secret? When Clifford drives we go straight to the laboratories, sniff the tubes, test the colors. No rabbits with chopped off paws.

Billy put his face in both hands, covered his eyes, and appeared to be stifling a sob. Sir? tried Irving. Billy, sir?

Billy Byron shoved back his modified captain's chair and bolted from the room. They all waited, speechless, around the teak table. It was common knowledge that conference rooms were visible and audible from outside. So many executives had been sacked for whispered quips when Billy left the room that silence was almost mandatory. They sat there. The lights were dimmed by some remote switch and the heat cycled on and off, then around five, a janitor opened the door dragging a garbage trolley and surprised them. Oh, Mr. Byron went a long time ago, talked to all the rabbits like he knew them personally. Such a good, kind man. He raised bunnies on the farm as a little boy, you know.

That's nonsense, said Irving. He grew up on Flatbush Avenue behind the Esso station. Where of course it's possible his mother kept a pen or two. Christ. Let's get out of here.

Nick pushed the lower buzzer on the angled townhouse on East Sixty-Second Street and felt a slight shock, like there was some kind of short in the wires. He hadn't been here in months and from the pile of collapsed construction debris just inside the iron fence under a moldy tarp, progress on the renovation appeared stalled.

He half expected a party, then Lionel opened the door in his kimono and looked nearly asleep, which didn't rule out a dozen intimates in the kitchen. But it was only Kitty and the baby. Kitty's gauzy Indian blouse opened to the waist, one enormous breast revealed, her nipple dark as rust with the baby's sleeping cheek flattened to it. Baby Lionel. Lionel Katherine Ivy Devlin. They were calling her Junior.

The baby winced at her dreams, her legs a series of chafed red folds, her diaper, from the doorway, smelled saturated. Beautiful, Nick murmured coming in and he kissed the top of Kitty's head. Nicky, she whispered. At last.

Here, take mine, said Lionel and pulled the big padded desk chair back from the red lacquer table. Lionel sucked in and squeezed between the end of the countertop and the wall to the back corner and into an elaborate bamboo patterned dining chair. He swept his big hands across to gather up the playing cards spread out on the table. Honeymoon bridge, he said. Mrs. Ivy is staking me.

Looks like a rummage sale in here, Nick laughed. The two of you, a pair of hippies, now?

Yes, we *are*, said Kitty. We really are now, fully, and I want to be, really, all the freedom and love. That's what we want for our girl.

Yes, and Kitty's mother is upstairs resting so she can provide the auxiliary freedom and love. This is Junior's first snooze in several days. But Lionel looked surprisingly happy.

You both look good on no sleep.

Well, that's Mrs. Ivy's job, right darling? She wouldn't let us stay up if we wanted to, said Lionel.

That's right, Nick. Mummy wants us to rest. So I can recover.

Yes, I was sorry to hear you had a hard time. Jean was concerned. We both were.

Aces now, said Lionel, reaching his hand toward the baby. Yes, it was big melodrama around here.

It was! smiled Kitty. And Lionel knew exactly what to do. He was a miracle worker.

Oh? said Nick, trying not to sound surprised. Lionel usually evaporated in any kind of medical emergency. Allergic to hospitals he liked to say. His scarcity when Cubbie was in so much trouble still galled. Lionel was just a coward, and suddenly Nick couldn't remember why he'd come here.

Well, Lily, of course, Lionel was saying. So I had some experience. What an ordeal! Kitty was shaking her head. I can't even imagine, she said. I mean we had our moments—she paused to beam at Lionel—but nothing like that. Poor Jean, poor Lily!

Nick wasn't sure what they were talking about. He tried to make sense of it, but then spotted the small wooden penis-shaped hash pipe tipped in the crystal ashtray among a carton's worth of cigarettes. Just the usual nonsense. But something half jabbed at his memory that he couldn't really bring to mind. It was as if Cubbie had erased much that came before, or even since.

She's turning fourteen, you know, Nick said. Right after Christmas. She's very young for her class. They didn't reply, and he began to wonder if he'd spoken aloud when Kitty rearranged her hold on the baby and reached out to touch his hand. Of course, we know, Nicky.

Lionel was frowning. He sighed and said, Let me show you something. You'll like this. He began to wrestle himself up out of the corner. The kimono opened and Nick caught a glimpse of the sagging belly, the drooping cock, an old man's apparatus and it shocked him slightly, as if Lionel could never be anything but invincible. He looked up as if the thought were a betrayal, even if

117

Lionel was a bastard. Lionel was studying Nick and Nick now saw the display was a calculation, a ruse. He wouldn't fall for it; he'd find out what Lionel had promised Billy Byron, because he remembered that's really all he'd come for, though he was touched to see Kitty, and the baby, despite her name. Standing, he bent down to kiss her again, No! Don't go! she said. Not yet!

He'll be back, said Lionel. Come look, you've got to see this.

Oh, Lionel, called Kitty, but they were already trudging up the inner staircase. Just wait, said Lionel. An eerie lavender light seeped down the stairs. Nearly there! shouted Lionel, and below the baby began a tentative howl. Oh shit, well never mind, Mrs. Ivy's a bulldog; she'll take care of it. Look, look! My masterpiece!

Nick craned his neck to see the huge skylight Lionel had concocted and commissioned. Some stained glass—it's all antique Tiffany, said Lionel—had been deformed into an image of a gnome gripping a red wand. It was lit up by an ad-hoc series of black lights clamped at random onto the banister. That's obscene, said Nick, half laughing.

Don't be ridiculous; it's priceless. It's Billy Byron discovering his first lipstick formula. Get it?

What?

Yes, and there's more. We're doing a whole series of painted murals, like the stations of the cross, up the entire staircase. More modest, of course, nothing to steal from the grand finale. I have this young Italian kid. He's already penciled in the pivotal moment when Billy fires his older brother, Melvin Bolkonsky. I'll show you. Then we've got the nail formula they could finally sell. Anyway, twelve separate images. Billy won't believe his eyes. Though I'll have to reignite the place to pay for it, Lionel laughed.

You set the fire? Didn't Kitty nearly die?

I'm joking. What's wrong with you?

This is Billy's place?

Of course it is. You knew that.

I don't understand. I thought you bought this after the Wellco deal.

No, that went south. And Billy needed his investment reimbursed more swiftly than the courts would allow.

What are you talking about, south.

We're just doing Billy a favor. Giving him the house he deserves. None of the other indentures could deliver.

We?

Me. Obviously. Kitty is my muse. Lionel smiled and adjusted one of the dangling black lights. And Mrs. Ivy is like an engineering department. She keeps all the paperwork straight. Hey—Lionel sniffed the air—do you smell something burning?

The house smelled like all of Lionel's houses, like every place they'd been together since their mother died and Lionel took over. The bleach, the BayRhum a strange salute to their long-lost father, the carpet dust like the house of an old woman who'd held on too long to her belongings, where did it come from? But here it was.

Where's Mrs. Ivy? Junior's in a snit down there. The baby's muted wails began to sound desperate. It made Nick angry. You're a prick, you know, he said. Jean is completely heartbroken.

What are you talking about? Come on, you're jet-lagged. You're out of it. Stay here. Don't go back to some stupid hotel.

Fuck you. Why would you name her that.

Name my own baby? I think I'm on solid ground here, guy.

What about Cubbie, your namesake, never to be replaced.

Jean is fine, Nick. She told me so. All right? She blessed this, I mean literally, you guys are the godparents. We're doing it at Thanksgiving. It's all set.

I don't fucking believe you. You lie for breathing. Nick angry at himself now, he'd never been able to say anything but generic curses to Lionel, protecting him. You were a scum to Cubbie, he tried. And now you're a sanctimonious ass to poor deluded Kitty. Cubbie hardly saw the back of you when he was so sick. When he was dying you never came, not once, not even once, you stupid con.

Nick.

Fuck that, and what hole have you gotten me into with Billy Byron? What's the big plan, what's he waiting for? What did you sell me for this time?

Sell you? I told him you're talented. Hardly a stretch. Lionel quenched a yawn. Come on, all the old people need to sleep. You too. Mrs. Ivy will be up soon and on duty, then we'll find you a bed.

Just tell me what Byron wants.

Lionel tucked his kimono around his belly. Smoothed the top of his head. Nick waited. Lionel sighed.

He wants you to take over UK-Europe. UK first for a few months, then the whole shit pile.

No, said Nick.

You're welcome, laughed Lionel. But Nick was already stumbling down the half-lit stairs. He stopped. What does it get you? That's what I want to know. Then I'll have a half chance of not being destroyed in the payout.

Destroyed?

Just tell me, Lionel.

Peace of mind?

Nick didn't say good-bye to Kitty, but made himself close the front door gently. One of the babies had been colicky and now he couldn't remember which. Maybe Lily, because Jean always made the joke about lifting infant Cubbie as if he was made of glass for fear he'd be the monster Lily had been, yes, that was it. But Cubbie was a good baby and Jean always kept him close. He looked just like her and she loved him. It was so easy.

11

Five in the morning, the phone bleated beside him and it was Jack the driver. Sorry to disturb, sir, but I'm asked to deliver you to the office.

Now? Nick watched Jean turn again and sigh. She'd been restless all night and they'd had a long whispered argument about Lionel and his plans. But only the latest of many. They agreed it had been a rough, lonely beginning for Jean and Lily in London and Jean was already aching to go home for Thanksgiving. Thanksgiving? They just got here. Besides it was the first he'd heard of a baptism. When did she say yes to that charade? Her face was away from him now, her hair streaky and long on the pillow. Every time he looked at her she got blonder. He touched a strand. Still soft.

Sir? Jack said. I'll be waiting outside in five minutes.

It's the middle of the night, Jack.

Beg pardon, early morning. There's someone to see you.

All right. Okay. He rubbed his face. Do I have time for a shave? I've been asked to bring you straightaway, sir.

He'd heard about Billy's unannounced visits. Half the office had probably gotten sneak warning calls late last night. The place would be humming like midday no doubt. But when he got to the lobby at Duke Street, Nick needed to find the lights. No small thing. The switches were tucked behind a panel disguised to mesh with the wallpaper, a hand-painted, repeating pattern of a silver perfume bottle on a pink ground said to match Bunny Byron's complexion as a new bride. A fable.

Nick took the elevator to 5. The lights were already bright in marketing. His secretary, Tania, sat typing at the desk perpendicular to his door, back straight, an anxious crease between her eyebrows.

What in the world? he said and smiled. But she started and stood up.

Mr. Slater's waiting to see you, sir. She nodded toward the half-open door, taking a quick breath.

Nick frowned as if she wasn't making sense. I'll bring you some coffee, sir, right away.

He pushed the door wider to find Irving Slater standing at the window looking down at the rooftop of the neighboring building. Lousy view, Irving said.

Not so bad.

We can do better.

Nick went over and stood next to him, looked down at the slate-topped dormers. A triple chimney next door needed work, bricks lay in shards, the pointing collapsed. In the bare beginning light, it looked moody, paintable. He liked it.

I'm fine right here.

Sends the wrong message, said Irving. This is the servants' quarters, don't you think? I mean it's got to be. I can touch the damn ceiling. But he didn't bother to demonstrate.

Nick sighed and took a seat on the narrow navy sofa. He pushed aside a stack of British *Vogues*, all tagged and sorted by marketing resources spent.

Irving Slater sat on the windowsill and let his eyes close. This wasn't my idea.

Of course not.

Remember that.

I believe you. What are you talking about?

Billy wants you to take over. He likes your ingenuity.

Nick laughed and then coughed when Tania came in with the tray of coffee. She poured two cups then left, closing the door very quietly. Nick offered Irving a cup and he took it.

Effective immediately.

It makes no sense, said Nick, sitting back.

You're telling me.

Is this about Lionel in some way?

No. I don't think so. It's instinct; that's all Billy said and that he wanted me in London at the office before you got here. A surprise party. He loves that kind of stuff. So, surprise. Happy?

No.

Well, neither am I. It's a mistake. You have no experience. And frankly you're not that smart. The rest. Why bother going into it now, we've been over it.

Nick didn't respond. He felt a wave of exhaustion. He hadn't slept well since coming back from New York. Seeing Lionel had put him in a foul temper and now here was Irving Slater looking like death's messenger standing in his office before sunrise.

THE LOVED ONES

I'll talk to Sheldon when he gets in, said Irving. And then fly back to New York this afternoon. To give Billy the good news. Give Sheldon the bad, Billy the good. Irving smiled.

Nick shook his head.

Don't thank me.

No.

But Nick stood and put down his cup and Irving extended his hand.

A half hour later Nick was at Twenty-one Cheyne Walk looking for the buzzer marked Mr. and Mrs. S. Walpole. He'd been here only once before when Sheldon and Tandy insisted on inviting all their favorite London friends to meet newcomers Jean and Nick. Now Tandy Walpole opened the door in a blue wool bathrobe, patting a set of curlers under a scarf. Sorry! I'm a sight! she laughed, then welcomed him inside.

12

Lily came home from school and once again found her mother's new friend Emma Hocking collapsed in a graceful twist on the drawing room sofa. Her slender neck craned back in happy disbelief at some bit of gossip Lily's mother was retelling. Usually about Lionel, who Emma knew from his many trips through London before they'd arrived. He hadn't come even once since the move, a story in itself—Nick was being impossible; he'd canceled Thanksgiving this week!—but her mother usually stuck to the old stories.

Now Lionel's on his very best behavior, or so he says. Her mother tossed up her hands in surrender, and Emma laughed, lifting her own hands. They looked like they were doing some kind of sofa ballet.

Studied at the Joffrey, all right? she'd told Lily first thing, the day she arrived, as if Lily had confronted her. Sleek and streamlined, no sequins or shirts cut to the navel for Emma. Her mother trimmed back the new gear accordingly. Fewer tassels, more gunmetal velvet trousers and beige suede hot pants cut to show off her slim hips and mask a very slight belly. Miniature! Emma cried out. Practically invisible! Her father had used the word pudgy, but that was an extremely bad day. A day, as her mother pointed out, when the doctor Cecil Bathrick ended up in their bedroom at midnight administering the epinephrine again. Her father's asthma was aggravated by the London air, and more than once in these early months, he'd needed an intervention.

Not as scary as it looks, love, Emma told Lily. She had a bit of asthma herself. As if to prove it, she removed a tiny silver peanut-shaped pill holder on a chain in her purse. If you ever spot me panting on the floor, she said, solemnly, just one of these. I'll be right as rain. And Lily agreed to intervene.

You don't want the epinephrine bit if you can help it. Not that it's bad, not at all, and it doesn't hurt, for all that the bastard is sticking a prong into the middle of your chest. They numb the skin first. No. The problem is the moodiness. Just appalling. A real nuisance for your dear old dad.

Emma knew from the inside everything her father was up against in London and she was here to offer her help. Don't know why I bother, frankly. She laughed. In fact she laughed in the same style she liked to use when her father was right there. Hand to her breastbone, shoulders forward as if to protect the delicate nipples beneath ivory silk that were suddenly all Lily could look at. Emma had a genius for directing attention all around her body. Lily wanted the opposite, to send the attention away, to fling it out onto the street to be run over by taxis. Especially when she was caught and held in the unhappy gaze of her mother. But the best thing about Emma was how distracting she was. Her mother relaxed and laughed in ways that felt very old to Lily, as if her mother had been saving in a special storage this set of gestures and smiles.

For Jean, Emma had a different laugh than the one she offered to Nick. Chin up, eyes blinking bright with appreciation. You're darling, she'd say catching her breath. Then to Lily, whispering, though Jean was right there: It's your mother, love. She's the one who's interesting. But don't tell his nibs.

Emma was all stretch, no strength, muscles like taffy. Huge problem, she said, hovering above the great silver ashtray with a brown cigarette as if she might fail to make the reach otherwise. Everything Emma did was riveting and that's why Derek Voose found her invaluable. He was lending her out—a loan, mind you, don't get any grand ideas—to organize a party to announce Nick's new promotion. King of the Bloody World! said Emma. But to Lily it seemed that all Emma and her mother did was talk about New Jersey.

Today the story about Lionel was a sad one, the fire story, and Emma, listening, forgot to make a gimmick of her hands or her enormous eyes. She listened as if dumbstruck, startled out of her role and mission. This, Lily thought, might be why her mother held Emma's attention. Since London, she'd begun telling all the Cubbie stories, but in a hidden way; today Cubbie hid behind Lionel. Lionel at the water's edge in their backyard with a brush fire early in the morning. Lionel crying, poking at shards of toys with a rake handle, making a foul plastic stink that filled the house for days after. That he'd barely made a dent in Cubbie's things was beside the point. It's only a ritual, Lionel had said. And her father, in a kind of stupor—her mother said later: why had they ever let Lionel spend the night anyway?—punched him hard, but in a strange spot, the throat. Lionel suddenly couldn't breathe and turned purple. But her father couldn't see that; he was so angry, or the putrid smoke was blinding him and making the tears run down his cheek, so her mother had to save Lionel herself. Mistake! she rolled her eyes, cue for a laugh, but Emma didn't smile.

So I made him stand up her mother said. I walked him out of the smoke, and talked to him like a baby who can't stop crying. It was like that, his refusal to breathe. I stroked his chest and soothed him; all while Nick is dousing Lionel's infernal pile of Cubbie's train sets and car models. All the things he'd made himself. Even in the hospital, he loved to assemble the models. Nick had lost his mind; they both had. Lionel purple and looking like a heart attack. Me, holding him, calming him back to breathing. Nick taking water from the river in his hands and dousing the fire with sprinkles, weeping. Of course, I chose the wrong brother to comfort. I worry still. Her hand went to her mouth and her eyes wide with a blasted look, as if all expression was already done, like her eyes had expired. That's why her mother wore the fake lashes now and all the other stuff, Lily thought, because her eyes didn't really say anything anymore. All of Cubbie's models were lost except one. Her mother pointed to the gray battleship that's found a place on the piano between two new candelabra, her latest find from the Silver Vaults.

Nick took a very long time to forgive me. As for Lionel, we didn't see him or hear a word until the indictment, and then it was like nothing had ever happened.

Right, Emma nodded, frowning as if her mother had raised a questionable color choice.

It was nothing in the end. Some screeching in the papers. It all finally came down to a suspended sentence for something very small. Thanks to my father, because he—

And Lionel?

No, he was out of it. The magician.

I'd heard something about this.

Lily! Her mother finally noticed her again, stretched out on the rug beside the backgammon table. Why are you eavesdropping? I'm not!

Emma's smile was meant to be understood as false but winning. Lily imitated it as she peeled herself off the carpet. Back in her room she pretend grinned into a wicker oval mirror. Emma Hocking said she was strategically placed to offer aid and guidance to both Lily and her mother because her age was nearly the halfway point between them. But closer to my mother, Lily said. By a year, mate, don't be so effing literal. So, Emma was twenty-five. Her hair short and auburn, eyes gray—sometimes sapphire, she insisted—tiny bones, long limbs, conical breasts easily observed, to Lily's fascination, through the Italian silk menswear shirts she wore, tailored to fit just her. No makeup except spiked black lashes and a plain beige lip gloss. A man's jewel band wristwatch slid up and down along the tendons of her forearm. My father's, she said, with something like reverence. Lily stared. Her own father had a new watch, a gift just last week delivered by courier with a note—ceremony to follow!—from Billy Byron when her father was named managing director UK. Maybe it would be hers one day. Preposterous and ostentatious her mother declared, a diamond wind-stem on a man?

Uncle Lionel wears one!

That's precisely the point, said her mother and then looked confused.

But Emma Hocking would change all that; she'd soon make Lily's mother see things differently. Wears you out, darling, all the boy tricks, she said. All their little games. But wasn't it Emma who supplied the information her mother was missing. Filling her in on the people who crowded the cocktail parties and the Sunday brunches on the King's Road. Who were the film people, who were the oil people, who were the untouchables and hangers-on. And she was the first to point out Vivienne Vimcreste, though at the time she seemed like another flashy girl among many. Her mother looked a little happier already. Lily began to sleep through the night. Some important task had been lifted.

For the last two weeks of October, she went to class and did her homework as if nothing else had ever required her attention. Her teachers stopped thanking her for deigning to join them. She began to know the faces of her classmates in repose, just listening or bored. Lily watched their sleepy faces, mouths ajar, eyes cloudy, listening to the drone of their teacher go on and on about Prince Myshkin, and she felt a powerful affection. Especially for Lawrence Weatherfield who once winked at her before dropping his head on his fist for a nap. For a moment she felt as normal as she had at St. Tom's, where every curve of every eyebrow was known to her. Lawrence had eyebrows bleached nearly white by the Saudi Arabian sun, brown hair like the center of the black-eyed Susans still blooming right now in Momo's backyard.

Now listen to me, my love, Emma Hocking said one afternoon, laughing. Listen very carefully. But she studied Lily without speaking. Brought herself upright on the sofa. Emma shook her head, mouth etched in a line of mild disgust, and rummaged in her vast handbag for a tube. A color corrective. Give it a whirl.

Lily opened the tube and sniffed. A swift chemical scent like peroxide, no masking sweetness. That's right, the real thing. Not for amateurs, mind you. She carried these things around because, really, love, you never know what you're going to run up against. Derek Voose routinely gave Emma his most difficult clients, because she had the touch. How fascinating that men's faces could be improved.

Her father put on a bronzer now every day, right after he blew dry his hair with the round brush. This blustery rain-choked afternoon, when Lily came in from school, Emma cried, The sight of you, good lord. And this is when Lily first began hearing about Peggy Moffitt. Emma had determined, and apparently her father agreed in principle, that Lily, with a little discipline, could be her double. So Lily, to her mother's nodding approval, became one of Emma's projects, too.

Lily called Margaret that night, the unscented professional cream concealer sticky and itchy under her eyes. I'm being remade, she said. Into what? Godzilla? Hey, Anthony Moldano's wife mentioned divorce this week. Oh, no! said Lily. Oh *yes*, said Margaret. Yes, indeedy do! said Margaret imitating Momo, but imperfectly. Still it was her phrase and Lily was happy to hear it. Between Lily and her parents were two dressing rooms, a marble bath, and three plaster walls; even so when she laughed she turned her face into the rust-colored carpet.

So, obviously Christmas is out, said Margaret.

But why? said Lily. Why? You've got to come; it's all set. Shit, whispered Margaret. The asshole just woke up. And the line went dead. Which meant her brother Tommy was around and would eavesdrop. The line buzzed and echoed. More and more, when Lily called, Margaret was unable to talk. Lily replaced the heavy phone now and stared at the bottom of her father's desk. Lying this close to the legs, she caught the funny stink of the gleaming wood, not the usual canned furniture polish from the States. Lily knew their new charwoman, Mrs. Veal, made her own concoctions.

Bacon fat, right?

Nothing like it, little miss.

Her father said that Mrs. Veal had a face like the blunt end of a hatchet. Her mother told him to stop, but Lily thought Mrs. Veal just looked like a nun. She could really see her sharp little eyes and shiny nose, her big cleft chin, her whole face wrapped on all sides with a stiff white cloth. Mrs. Veal's face would fit right in at St. Tom's. No one would talk about it. But not in London, where her mother was increasing her beauty by the day, and her father was becoming a true expert. People whose faces would seem normal— all different faces and bodies—were now filtered through the new understanding. Tonight in the library where she now lay, Lily's face had been discussed by her parents, as if Emma Hocking had opened up an intriguing new topic. Her father had an idea. I'm going to show you just what I mean he said to Lily's mother. He framed Lily's face with his hands, like an artist, carefully erasing the parts he wouldn't keep.

On Saturday, as a special favor arranged by Emma Hocking, Jack, the chauffeur, drove Lily to a photography studio just past all the antique stalls on the Portobello Road. She was backlit and photo-graphed wearing her mother's long lavender water silk caftan. Just wait, her father declared. This would be definitive somehow. They were all going to learn something important. The photographer had done sensational work for British *Vogue*. When her father got the proofs, there was one in which Lily had forgotten to smile. She studied it and knew she'd been thinking first about Russell Crabtree and then about Peter Healy. It seemed she was trapped in a bad situation no matter where she lived. Backlit, draped in purple silk, hair carefully teased she'd been thinking any kind of dance, maybe just any kind of boy, would be a problem.

133

Peter Healy was on the older end of her class, already fifteen and training for the Olympics as a cyclist. Every day he carried crucial parts of his custom bike into the morning assembly at school. But for the freshman mixer he'd been required to leave the bike at home and put on a jacket over his racing shirt like all the other boys. Lily was doing the free dance with a big group of girls she barely knew with her eyes closed, just flapping around waiting for it to be over, when Peter Healy grabbed her by the arms. The slow dance started and everyone stopped spinning and draped their bodies over each other. They were in the same algebra class and now Peter Healy's chin dug into her head and his fingers gripped her shoulders in a rubbery way, but with rough tips and scratchy nails. The lights were lowered until only a sparkling spiral bounced off the walls, and he leaned himself completely into her, torso stiff and heavy. She felt breathless under the weight. Hey, hey! she said and he opened his eyes.

Hey to you, he said, and that was so sweet, as if no one had ever said such a witty thing. She smiled. And then serious, like a chore, his slow big face came toward her, watching her eyes until he had to twist and bend to find her lips. She laughed—she couldn't help it—and tried to get out from under him. He pulled back just enough to say, Relax, babe. His mouth pushing hers felt like a moving jelly sandwich, slimy in the middle with a crusty edge. She started to recoil, but he had her head in a wrestling lock; he made a point of his tongue and methodically dotted along her upper lip then poked at her teeth, and something in this was a little beautiful. But then he stopped, leaned back and gave her a narrow-eyed look, as if he now had some ideas about her face, too. Suggestions. Then he eased back to an arm's-length distance, fingering her elbows, still slow dancing technically, and let her in on the important preliminary trials in New Mexico last summer that he'd won.

I'm usually either first or second in my age level for the Americas, he shouted toward her ear. North and South, both. Not just North America.

When the music merged to a fast song he released her elbows and bounced away. The next day Peter Healy rode his famous bike from Kensington, where he lived, to Grosvenor Square and said he'd chained the frame to the iron spike fence. When Lily opened the door, there he was with his seat and his front wheel under his arm. She remembered that second of beauty she'd felt. She tried to conjure that, looking into his sweaty face while he looked back at her, eyes blank. He might be a little scared; she was. Come in? she said. She couldn't believe he was here. But he stood, rocking back and forth on his feet, stretching his calves, on the landing outside the apartment door. He wouldn't come in. He was really sorry he said, watching the rising toes of his cycling sneakers.

No, she said. Don't worry. She thought he must be apologizing for kissing her too soon. Come in? But he looked up at her sharply now. Listen, all right, I just said no.

Why did she repeat herself? She flushed. She could feel her whole body kind of fade and wobble. She said, I only meant no about the apologizing? Lily laughed but it sounded like a nose blow. He looked disgusted, maybe even angry. Yes, he was angry, but why?

Look, I need to keep an eye on the future. A little poor judgment now could have lasting consequences. His father, he told her, thought Lily was bad news. That if he got involved even superficially she'd stick to him like glue and he'd never be rid of her. Now you know.

Then he flipped the bike seat up over his head without losing the grip on his wheel. He smiled his first- or second-place smile as he caught it in the other hand, nodding at her, because didn't they both know he was kind of great. She smiled because he was smiling; also the sweetness reappeared in his dimples before he trotted back down the stairs, waving his bike seat without turning. She wanted to follow him. Hey, she called, wanting to understand the crucial mistake she'd made with his father, but then Mrs. Veal was behind her on the landing. In or out, love, said Mrs. Veal. I'm doing the floor whether you like it or not.

Out, Lily said and ran barefoot down the marble stairs, but Peter Healy's bike was already gone. He'd vanished from Grosvenor Square. How could he do that in seconds? In the lobby, Cyril in his booth only nodded. They would both ignore the crisis of her feet by not speaking. When she came upstairs again Mrs. Veal wouldn't let her in. We all have to live with our choices, now don't we. What would your mother say, you chasing after boys in the street. She'd have your hide she would. I've half a mind to tell her.

But Lily knew that anything Mrs. Veal had to say wouldn't get much of an ear from her mother. What a strange woman, her mother had said early on, staring down at a little arrangement Mrs. Veal had made on her dressing table. Two white greasy candles from who knows where and a half-budded half-dead pink peony in front of a snapshot of infant Cubbie and happy Jean. She thinks I'm a saint, said her mother, shaking her head, looking deeply into the picture. Lily had laughed, but her mother didn't.

Maybe she'd call Margaret for advice, but all she could do now was sit across from their door on the stairs and wait. Peter Healy and his silver medals. His flat pointy sneakers and ugly bike tights, his scratchy fingers. His heavy head digging into her scalp.

Lily flipped over onto her hands in a maneuver she'd forgotten she could do, kicking her feet up into an astonishing balance, defying gravity, amazing the upper reaches of the stadium with her stamina and grace. My, my, little girl, she heard above her. That's a florid display.

Beryl Sutton grasped the banister carved in relief into the curved plaster wall and let her descending foot dangle in the air. Lily had been warned the Suttons had blackballed an American child in the building. Unprecedented and undesirable, they'd said in a written note to the estate agents. Lily had danced it out like a tune. Call me undesirable, yes, I'm— But her mother had been worried about the peace of her new home. It's very hard to relax when the neighbors are irritable, said her mother. Remember the Beesons on Momo's street? He was arrested for assaulting the mailman!

I won't attack anyone.

All right, said her mother.

Now Lily stood up so that Beryl Sutton could make her way down to the landing. My dear, you are shoeless, she said. Lily thought it best not to respond; she looked down at her feet as though mildly surprised. And silent, Mrs. Sutton said. Well, perhaps we'll speak to one another at a later date. Thank you, she said when Lily stepped aside. She changed her grip on the railing and made a slow painful-looking descent past Lily, who curtsied. The half squat she'd learned in toddler ballet. Oh, I see, said Mrs. Sutton. Very good. Very good. She made an abrupt spitting sound and Lily could see she was stifling a laugh. Lily looked away. Yes, good-bye now, Mrs. Sutton choked out and continued down the marble flight to the lobby.

There's a large American infant on the landing, Cyril. Call the exterminator.

Lily couldn't hear the response. She sat and leaned her head against the banister and closed her eyes. She could feel the calloused palms of Peter Healy slide around her neck, dry and sweaty at the same time, the pine tree–scented lotion in his hair kept any distracting wisps from flying in a race. She inched her chin up for the kiss.

A sudden *tap-tapping* step coming up the stairs startled her. Her father paused at their door to adjust something about his suit, happy, she could tell by the tilt of his head. 'Ello, guv! she said, close enough to Tania his secretary's accent to surprise him. He spun around smiling, hands in soft fists, knees twisting, dancing. Can't go in yet, Daddy, she said.

What? he said, squinting almost as if trying to recognize her, as if she were sitting in some deep shadow. She giggled. Don't be funny. It's me.

No shoes? Then he found the right expression, wry, a tiny wrinkle of disappointment, always there now. What's going on out here, Lily.

He ran a hand along his chin, as though her answer and a decision about a quick shave were competing now for his attention. Whatever this is, cut it out. Come inside. He rummaged in his trousers for a key, but then Mrs. Veal held open the door. Wasn't expecting you, sir.

The sweep of marble behind her gleaming wet and fragrant with dish detergent. Keeps the shine, sir, she said, when he glanced at the bottle in her hand. Nothing urgent, Mrs. Veal, he said. I won't disturb you. And you, he said to Lily, winking, because now it was all a performance. You watch your p's and q's. And then he was already tapping back down the stairs.

Daddy? Do you want me to bring something over to your office? she called out, but got no answer.

You see? Everyone's got a job to do today, said Mrs. Veal. Saturday morning's not just for lounging around. But she relented and let Lily tiptoe inside along the dry edges of the long foyer. Be quick now, she said. Speed it up. And don't you finger my walls while you're at it.

13

Derek Voose kept an austere workaday duplex on Mount Street and a famous cottage in Goring. Just a hop, he said when he called Jean the morning after Nick's celebration party at Annabel's. We all need a postmortem, dear girl. Come for a quiet supper; bring the princeling. You'll barely know you've left London. Emma will be there, he added, as if that needed saying. And Anna Percy-Flint, who adores you.

Jean said yes, curious to see the fabled place. The scene of the social crimes Emma Hocking loved to report on the following Monday evenings over spaghetti carbonara. Soused, stoned, and randy was the usual roundup. But other details, Burt Bacharach dropping in and noodling on the piano, Peter Lawford running to the off-license for a forbidden brand of gin in the charwoman's Rover. Giving her a wet kiss in exchange for the dented bumper. The poor woman nearly had a heart attack on the spot, said Emma. All this made it sound intensely glamorous, even as Emma was waving it all off as business, business. Derek said on the phone and Emma agreed later, this would be a quiet gathering, just the family. Jean knew she was stupid to be flattered but she was.

The smaller drawing room opened onto a garden they'd glimpsed driving in as the sun went down. Dahlias and more dahlias in the summer Emma told Jean. He's a fiend for the beasts; can't talk him into another bloody blossom. Now it was just urns and hedgerows and dry leaves. The snug room with saffron walls—a paint like patent leather—had seating in a wide navy blue satin U before a fire. Birch logs piled in an artful display, enough to last the night.

True to his word, it was a quiet gathering. Derek fed them motherly food. A gluey-tasting shepherd's pie and a trifle for dessert. Potatoes and cream and more cream. Cognac handed round had takers dozing off in fat armchairs. But those still awake nodded in agreement that the night before, the big celebration, had been a hit. Derek mentioned the marvel of Jean's dress. A red silk Jean Muir found by Emma. He ticked off a list of women who'd looked hideous. And that was it. A strange letdown, as if all that preparation had produced nothing at all. I'm sure I got everything wrong, she tried, smiling.

What's that? Derek looked around at her blinking, waiting to understand, then roared, Not a bit of it, darling! And then he was on to the next event. Some boring obligatory pushy mess inflicted by Robin someone at Les Ambassadeurs. Can no one think of anything new?

Emma and Anna Percy-Flint had just settled down into private whispers when Nick wandered in from the next room and stood before them, waiting for a verdict, confident of the results. And so he should be, thought Jean, unscathed, that was Nick here. He laughed at these scrutinizing women and why not, what could they find wanting. She relied on this. She'd begun to believe in his resilience and thought she might even catch it in some way. That was all she needed to do. Stand and be judged on something silly, like the mesh-metal vest she wore tonight or her long fake blond braid, and be found fabulous. Nick loved all the costumes.

Anna Percy-Flint threw out an arm and grabbed the end of Jean's leather skirt. Come here, you sweet poppet, she tugged.

Jean looked at her, uncertain where she could possibly mean; they were sitting only a foot apart on the U-sofa.

Here, dearest, come right here, said Anna and she yanked Jean closer into an awkward cuddle.

Christ, I'm completely zonked, said Emma and lifted herself from the low sofa and stretched.

Not you. You stay right here with me, Anna said as Emma drifted off toward the kitchen. *You* don't move until I tell you something important. She had a slim silver pipe in her hand and she used a table lighter shaped like a gun to ignite the black ball and puff. She kept a loose arm around Jean's shoulders until the ember reddened and glowed. She held her breath and croaked, Go, go, pushing the pipe to Jean. Who touched it to her lips.

Don't kiss it, shouted Anna, laughing, choking out smoke. Oh good lord. Try again.

Jean wasn't interested in trying again, and she waved to catch Nick's eye. She was ready; they could leave now. Anna, pipe dropped into a bronze bowl, turned to Jean for a full embrace. Precious girl, she said, and Jean sat back and stared as if to bring Anna to sense, though kindly. She liked this Anna in some ways, but Anna was moving now in a kind of spiral, her head circling, eyes closed. She pressed her bobbing head against Jean's shoulder, and then when the mesh scratched her cheek, she decided to embrace Jean to her chest instead. There, love, she crooned. Just a sore boots, that's the all of it. And Jean was wrapped into the cool silk of Anna's caftan, a black Greek cross wedged between her breasts. Here with the breasts and the cross and the tester fragrance—celery, cardamom?—and the silk.

He was your little angel, said Anna. Am I right? And god plucked him right back, and now you're wondering why. Anna sat up again to give Jean a long look.

To say that Jean was wondering why was like saying that she was breathing; nothing separated her from that question. This Anna was only the latest to try to break to her the news of her lifetime. If nothing else, she thought she'd finally left this problem behind in New Jersey. She couldn't stand Doris's cow-eyed kindness, and now a phony baroness with breasts exposed and crucified was going to explain it all. But to her surprise, Jean found she was listening.

My Digby, said Anna. There was wine somewhere and Anna pushed past Jean's knees to grab a bottle by the neck. Here love. She poured into both their glasses. Digby took his brother for a drive, poor little fuckers. Something funny happened; that's what he says. They saw something leap on the side of the road and they looked and the wheel turned on its own, said Digby, like another hand had taken it and given it a twist, into the ditch they went. We heard the sirens, you know, but the night is full of sirens. Always something, right?

Jean listened like she could finally hear what someone was saying to her.

Yes—Anna nodded, took a sip—yes, Digby.

Jean stared, knowing whatever she could ask might be cruel. When Nick appeared, standing in front of her, bouncing a knee lightly against her, she looked up almost wanting to protect him from this. There was something, not the information, but some other thing that had her spreading herself out like a sheet between him and this Anna who had lipstick on the tips of her teeth, who was grabbing now for the lighter in Nick's hand. And then before Jean knew it, she was wrapped in her long cape and huddling through a foggy moonlit courtyard to their car.

They pulled out onto the highway, and Nick said not to worry, he'd tied a string on his wrist to remind him which side to drive on. He waved a bracelet of twine.

She lost her son, said Jean. Did you know?

Who?

Anna Percy-Flint, she had a son who died in a car accident. I think his name was Digby, but it might be the other one who died. I couldn't be sure. And I couldn't ask.

Oh good lord, Nick said. God, I don't know if I can drive. He started to laugh. I'm going to stop.

Why?

I'm too stoned.

I'll drive. Pull over.

You need the bracelet. He started plucking at the twine.

Pull over, then you can give it to me.

Nick stopped the car; it was a quiet village road, and late. He got out of the car and stretched his arms up over his head. It's nicer here; there are some stars. Can't see the stars in London. Maybe we should get a little place out here. Don't you miss that?

Jean slid into the driver's seat; the warm leather felt good, reassuring. Get in! She was suddenly afraid someone could come out of nowhere and hurt him. Get in! she cried.

He opened the back door of the Bentley. You can be Jack for a night. You can't be any worse a driver than he is. Nick slammed the door shut and lay down. Jean locked the doors. I'm not sure I know the whole trip.

You'll be great. It's easy. Don't worry.

Jean sat looking out at the darkened houses along the road, all very sweet and safe-looking.

Did you know about her son. Had she told you about him?

Whose son?

Anna Percy-Flint, her son was killed.

Oh, bullshit.

Jean turned around and looked at him over the top of the front seat. Nick.

Nothing—that's the rule of thumb—nothing that Anna Percy-Flint ever says is true. It's just fun. Improvisation. Believe me if Anna has a son at all he's tucked into Cambridge with a nice boy-friend, just like his papa.

But she told me.

Sweetheart, she told you something she thought would interest you.

Jean turned forward, her hand to her mouth; she could feel her hard breath on her fingertips.

Are we going? asked Nick. It's all a game, that's all. Jean read the gilt letters on the pub sign across the way, the George and Dragon: a green beast curled a heavy tail under a dim light. As soon as her hands stopped shaking she'd start the car; in the meantime Nick's breath slowed to a quiet snore. She looked at the deep curl of the dragon's tail and wished she could lick it. Maybe she was just stoned, too.

14

The short wide curved stair made every arrival an entrance. Lily felt her legs go heavy. She forced her feet to shamble down each step until she could squish into a cluster of older kids who ignored her. From there she searched out Peter Healy's location. He was yawning by the one open window to oxygenate his muscles; slowly he stretched one calf then the other, his long green eyes dull with boredom. By the end of the month, right after Thanksgiving, he'd be at Concord Academy in Massachusetts where he could really train properly. He told Lily he was making a disciplined departure from the American School. He'd just skip but that might put his academic record in jeopardy. Lily watched him with so much sadness and he did not watch back. She'd told Margaret later over the phone that his ambivalence was that intense. Maybe.

Yeah, maybe, said Margaret.

There were too many American high schoolers to fit comfortably into the tearoom of the Working Men's College. It was half belowground and smelled vaguely of coal fumes. The pebbled glass windows, close to the ceiling, were sealed. Only one, Peter's, actually opened onto the sidewalk. All the others held animated leg shadows rushing by at head level. A feature wall depicted a faded bare-chested swimmer clutching a trident standing on a wave of pistachio ice cream. He'd been defaced and repaired many times in the short months the American School had camped out here, renters until the new school building was completed in St. John's Wood.

Now, rolling blackboards with chalked lists were wheeled into position and the headmaster, Norman Phipps, announced the location of their classes for that day. This daily morning assembly was a crucial organizing strategy for the school. He cleared his throat and a *shush* went through the room. Ladies, he began, and this caused a rupture of dissent. Gentlemen, buffoons, and laggards, your kind attention, please. It was widely known, the only attendance taken all day, was done right then by his secretary. The speech reminding them of the merits of a progressive education ended when she gave the nod: All accounted for, sir. Then the students siphoned out, some to the newly assigned classrooms, some right back out the front doors.

The problem was a disagreement about the use of coal. The workingmen liked to burn a tiny bit of coal now and then, completely illegal, and it left a hollow stink on everything. So the Americans were stiffing them for part of the rent, and every night the workingmen locked different classrooms. The American teachers complained about the soot settling into the weave of their new cashmere sweaters, but the workingmen didn't care and as far as Lily could tell the students didn't either.

Lily was the youngest in her class, the youngest in the school. At St. Tom's there'd been a handful of Christmas babies in her class, but at the American School Lily seemed shockingly immature next to her classmates. At least her mother thought so. She'd said this once or twice, but then she contradicted herself, saying that Lily had changed dramatically between twelve and thirteen. She wished she'd just please, please, pause for a moment, just stop. Lily was difficult now. Lily wouldn't listen. But she did listen to her mother. All the time, she thought. Especially in the middle of night, when she'd find her mother up and thinking again.

If anything, Lily felt more mature than ever. Soon she would catapult beyond these older freshmen. She'd enrolled in an open Russian literature class with mostly upper classmen and then fell behind almost immediately, too sleepy to make sense of Prince Myshkin's misconceptions. He liked everyone, and that was a mistake; that much Lily understood. When she began to sense the depth of her failure—how lost she was, and so fast!—she too wandered back out the front door once Mr. Phipps's secretary waved the all clear.

Anyone could do whatever they pleased in this school. That was the responsibility part of the system, said Mr. Phipps, with shining eyes. He was passionate about the open assertive vibrant minds being created even in the less than optimum conditions of the Working Men's College.

Lily hadn't slept very well the night before, and by late morning she was already hungry for lunch. Long after the house had gone quiet, she'd awakened in the blue-green light of the army's security lights next door. The long end of the apartment and all the bedrooms looked out on the courtyard shared and guarded by the neighboring United States Army headquarters. She'd listened to the buzz of an emergency generator, always kept on low alert. Beneath the buzz,

Lily heard a tiny cry like a cat or a baby. It was hard to know at first and she listened hard, moving out of the covers to the bars on her windows as if to push them open wider. A tiny sound, but when she listened too closely it went away. She lay back down on her flat pillow and waited. This kind of waiting would have reminded her of her brother if any reminding were necessary. It was like an idea of what someone else might be thinking about Lily in this moment. Maybe Peter Healy. If he came into her bedroom and found her listening for a kitten in the blue-green light. He'd think: She's lost her brother. It hasn't been so long, really. He'd sit down, maybe not beside her that would be too strange, but on the other bed, maybe he'd sit cross-legged and tell her jokes to distract her. It was a nice idea, but she knew it didn't have much to do with her brother.

For the first weeks at school, Lily had tried the tearoom for lunch, but now not even the teachers could be forced to stick around for the boiled sausages with bits of hard fat like rubber knobs and thin grainy mash potato mix. Everyone except the Christians went to the pubs.

The only bad thing about the pubs was the deep embarrassment of going into them at all. The little pockets of friends seemed more conspicuously together than they did at the scarred tables of the tearoom. The Blue Pumpkin wasn't the closest pub. It was up on the High Street, near the tube stop. But Camden Town was mainly working class, the skinheads in heavy boots and workingmen in thick jackets looked unhappy to see the temporary tenants arrive at lunchtime. Only the Blue Pumpkin welcomed the Americans, so they crowded in for thick cheese and chutney sandwiches and sausage rolls.

By eleven the Blue Pumpkin was already crammed. In a far corner a clutch of ninth graders toward the back looked like sophisticates with legs crossed and heads tilted back, smoking. The girls in Lily's class were beautiful in a way her father would approve of. They had long hair cut in wings around cheekbones that even in the masked light of the pub looked gleaming. There was something about their fringed boots, velvet chokers, and sequined bodices, something potent and meaningful. They were much more than what they had to say about who they liked or hated that day. And they understood, these beautiful girls, that it was better if they didn't talk so much. That talking wasn't so important.

Lily, balancing her sausage roll and a slopping half pint of shandy, edged through the crowd and asked to join them and they were very polite. Very polite. She found a spare low stool without spilling. Twice before she'd done this and they were always courteous, which should have been good. Smiling such smiles they could all be models, easily, why bother with school? But her father was saying lately that being beautiful wasn't necessarily enough. The really interesting women, he said, had brains, too. He thought her mother should try to do something with her life. He'd mentioned this now several times to her mother's incredulity. Her mother had made him a home, had, well, the list went on and on and to articulate it was infuriating. Then her mother would say that perhaps Lily's father was in the middle of an adjustment phase.

Lily's mother in her velvet chair and her silky velvet robe smoking long slender cigarettes her eyes dark and forlorn, her hair long and blond, was certainly as beautiful as the dramatic girls in Lily's class. And her mother's drama—her adjusting husband, her lost son, and now Poppa, too—was more important to Lily than anything she heard at school, or just louder.

Today Lawrence Weatherfield was eating lunch with the girls, too. His strange sun-bleached eyebrows looked even whiter and his dark curly hair was pulled back in a ponytail, showing off brown eyes, heavy lids half closed as if ready for another nap, but he was laughing about something, about his family. They'd come from Riyadh and Lawrence was staying at a hotel with his mother. His father, tying up loose ends in the Middle East, was expected by Christmas.

To Lily, Lawrence looked nothing like a boy who'd lived all over the world. He wore a navy blue L.L.Bean sweater and baggy light brown corduroys like every boy she knew in New Jersey. But to the listening girls, his head bowed over a double portion of sausage and mash, he listed the countries: Indonesia, China (only for a few months), Thailand, Tunisia, Rhodesia, Japan, and finally Saudi Arabia. London was a big compromise made for his mother, Lawrence said. The mental health posting. When he looked up at them his eyes were long and ungiving and full of laughter. He asked to bum a cigarette, wiping his mouth with his hand, and three of the girls threw their packs at his chest.

All this was very funny. Lily ate her pastry roll and watched the changing brown eyes of Lawrence Weatherfield. Every once in a while they swept her face and she felt a quick alert to freeze. She'd hold tight and wait and then the sweep settled on the girls cuddled on the banquette, passing cigarettes, sharing drags. Lily thought about Russell in New Jersey. Something about Lawrence, even in such a different place reminded her of him, how they were like two fat plants with big foamy leaves drawing all the moisture. There was something very tiring about how charming and deep Lawrence was. He had Sartre tucked into his back pocket; he talked about *Naked Lunch*, which sent a jolt through the table, while his eyes narrowed and smiled and slid.

Okay, Lily said, standing up from the low stool, nearly knocking it over. She picked up her plate and mug, saying, See you all later, with a dopey little finger wave. Stop waving, she thought, but it didn't matter. Lawrence had begun to whisper something to Mirabel Kendrick and everyone else leaned forward hoping to hear what made her usually tranquil face turn red, eyes blinking, laughing tears.

Lily brought her things to the bar. Even though she'd only walked a few feet, looking back at the laughing girls, it felt like she'd rocketed miles away. She left ten shillings in a teacup for tips and pushed out into the cold overcast day. The winter air was penetrating here—because of the damp, that's what her father said—and Lily could feel that. She stood for a while not knowing what to do. It was too miserable out to go back to the Working Men's College. She picked up three chocolate flakes and a pack of Rothmans at the red news kiosk and considered, then went down into the underground train station, where it was still cold, but at least she was out of the skin-coating drizzle.

It was exactly this cold in December when Cubbie died; that was true. And New Jersey could be damp like London, though her father said London was worse. But her grandmother had driven her up the Garden State Parkway to the turnpike in a terrible rain, past the oil refineries with their blistering smell to the high double bridge with all the water down below, over the state line, which her feet passed first, then straight up the avenues to the cross street and into the half-moon entry drive.

Lily's father waited for her under the awning at the hospital, his blue coat flying in the wind. He opened her door and waved to Doris behind the wheel. Then her grandmother was pulling away, which surprised her, and her father hugged her close then sent her through the revolving glass door. The hallways are long at the children's hospital as if walking through them you might find yourself in a different city if you went outside. The colors changed and when they arrived at the green corridors, Lily and her father took the elevator. Cubbie was in his regular room and lights were bright and the television was on. Her mother was talking to a doctor, but it must not have been important because she stopped and kissed Lily, and the doctor stepped out.

Cubbie looked very tired. Like he was sleeping with his eyes partway open. Which was something he could actually do. Lily said hi, but Cubbie was too tired to say much. He smiled a tiny bit and his eyes were swollen like he'd been crying, and bloodshot. Lily asked him, Are you crying? And he moved his head on his pillow such a tiny bit no. Cubbie's blood vessels were very close to the skin, and his skin was a pale yellow like a tan had faded and not been replaced with new tan. He hadn't been outside for a long time. Lily put her hand on the bump of his feet and both her parents followed the doctor out of the room. Lily listened, but Cubbie wasn't going to talk. She put her face down on the bed and her shoulders, too, next to his legs, just the way they did at home, sleeping in the bed under the blue shelf with all his models, even when his bones were very brittle and she had to be so careful, but now she kept all her weight off the bed, so nothing at all could hurt him. She put her face against the weave of the blanket, lightly, and the rest of her she suspended just above the bed but close to his tired self like always. And she held still this way and watched the television like in the den at home. Cubbie was very quiet. His body didn't move, just a small tremble close to her face like a butterfly might make. So when her parents took her to dinner later at a big table all to themselves and told her that Cubbie wouldn't be living much longer Lily did know that. Then Momo arrived in Poppa's new Eldorado to drive her back to New Jersey. Two days later, Lily woke up at her grandmother's house and she didn't have to go to school.

15

Thanksgiving was a downer for everyone. All the pressing, unanswered phone messages from Lionel. The baby would have to wait to be baptized it seemed, until Nick could come to his senses. And Jean had pleaded for the long holiday weekend in New York. We don't need to even touch New Jersey! Lily wept as if the world hinged on the slight chance—if she *can*—that Margaret Foley would get on a train and meet her in Grand Central Station. No, everyone had been unhappy. Even Vivienne Vimcreste told Nick she really fancied a holiday. I'll bunk at the Sherry, too. Different floor, of course. Jean refused to cook and they ended up, last minute, at the Europa, just the three of them staring at the overdone steaks and potted shrimp. Nick decided to cheer things up, at least at the office.

As executive director Sheldon Walpole had kept a modest suite on the second floor with gray-flocked wallpaper and an oak desk he'd brought with him from the States. Now a big rectangular dent in the beige carpet marked his departure. The desk installed for

Nick floated in the imprint. Not enough light, Nick said. And Tania agreed and had a funny idea. Have you seen the library?

On the third floor, tall leaded windows and handsome bookcases filled with old volumes. A gorgeous hush to the room. They left everything, said Tania. It's a crime really. Can't imagine why the children wouldn't at least take an atlas or two. But the mansion that housed Billy Byron's London interests was purchased with fixtures and fittings intact. Nick's new office would be suitable for a lord said Tania. I mean truly, sir.

Nick settled in. The old velvet piles had just been carried out and the new Italian leather sofas brought in, arranged and rearranged to his satisfaction, when Tania came in one morning to say that a Mr. Freeball Krill was shifting and squirming in the general waiting room. He's a starer. I'll say that much for him. Good concentration. Asked me my age!

What did you tell him?

Don't make me laugh, sir. Think the gentleman slept in the pub by the smell of him, said Tania, giving Nick a postcard. Handwritten in black ballpoint was a name he knew. Should I send him on to the embassy, or try one of the help services?

Nick shook his head, flipping the postcard to read the fine print on an advertisement for a car wash in East Orange, New Jersey.

Makes you wonder. They see a nice American coming and going and right away take liberties.

Show Mr. Krill in, please. Bring a tray of coffee, super strong.

Mr. Krill looks well past the coffee point if you ask me.

I'm sure you're right, but coffee would be fantastic. That nice stuff from Selfridges.

Right away. Ah, here he is, sir. Mr. Krill. She held open the door and pressed back against it, dodging the drifting hands of the man.

Freeball Krill?

Just a joke, Nick. Funny, yes?

Super. How did you get to London, Harry? Nick didn't bother to stand.

Same as you, Nicky, the big swim. He climbed over the arm of one sofa on his way to Nick and then glanced around to see if this move was noted by Tania.

Nick waved Tania out the door then reached and opened a lower drawer, pulled out two packs of cigarettes from a carton, tossed one across the desk.

Much obliged.

Nick watched him fumble with the pack, then clicked open a gold lighter and held the flame, while Harry leaned in to take the light. He'd let his fingernails grow long and snagged.

Looking well, Harry.

Um. Harry Lewis tipped his head high up, opening his throat to take in more smoke. That's the answer, the full punch, all you really need sometimes.

Glad to help.

You do help, Nicky-boy. You know you do.

Nick sat forward and studied the ripped open cigarette pack. Nice day out, he said.

It's a mess out there, raining dogs.

Come on. Take a stroll. See the sights.

A stroll?

Good idea, right?

You mean you're not coming along, too much to do? Right here at your nice big desk.

I think so, yes. We could have a drink later. Where are you staying?

With you.

Very funny.

Things I could tell that little pouch in the front there, oh, the things I could say, Harry laughed, his mouth crumpled tight, chin puckered and pink. Oh, he said, taking a long drag off the cigarette. You know what I mean, Nicky. I mean, my god, she'd be running for her life, and I can't really blame her when I think about it, when I put myself in her shoes. I'd be doing more of a favor really, a service, when I think about it.

Who's stopping you, Harry.

All in the right order, that's my motto.

Nick laughed, Yes, that's you, Harry. Mr. Symmetry.

You're laughing in my face? Is that it?

There's nothing here. This is all it is, a blank slate, Harry. You've come too far. You really have. Anything I could do for you is back in New York, not here, and not much there anymore either. Keeping a tight bead on lipsticks and powder. I could ask Tania to make up a nice parcel for the missus.

Tie my boots, Nick, with your fucking goody bags.

Look around.

I'm looking.

Then look harder.

The door opened after a muffled tap and Tania pushed in a wheeled cart. Coffee, sir, hot and strong.

That's the ticket, Harry smiled. You always wear skirts like that to work, girlie?

Thanks, that's all, Miss Cordell.

Cordell? Must be in the book. I'd like to see how the locals get on. Should I give a call?

Thanks, you can go. Close the door, please.

What, too rich for old Freeball. That's what you're saying, Nick? Your secretary? Come on.

Any mustard out there, doll? Harry leaned back, craned his head around to shout through the closed door.

Tania knocked and was back with a tray of pastries. For the coffee, she said.

Yes, sir, said Harry. Mighty thoughtful, that's all I can say.

And you've said plenty. Close the door, thank you.

A Miss Cordell, is it? Just as it should be. What other treats and surprises, Nick? So many changes and not even a postcard to send the good word. And everyone wanting to know how you are. Lionel most of all.

Lionel knows how I am.

I wish it were so; I really do, said Harry, and gave a thoughtful sigh. This is all very nice though, he said. Almost like a consolation prize. Maybe you'll think of it that way later on.

Nick watched Harry toy with the cigarette a bit more, licking the filter end with a white swollen tongue, then flicking ash into the pastry. Dangling it from his fingernails nearly scorching the surface of the desk then glancing up.

You're a three-year-old, said Nick, sighing. Lionel, too. You're like the fixer from *Romper Room*. Nick picked up the heavy white phone. Tania, put a call to my brother in New York on the calendar, please. No, this afternoon at five. We don't want to wake him. Thanks. Happy now, Freeball?

I'm always happy. It's a mental set, really. You can do it, too, he said, and brushed off some ash from the sugar topping then ate the pastry whole.

The minute Harry left the building, Nick told Tania to cancel the call.

*   *   *

Somehow Jean had plugged in the wrong electrical adapter. She didn't know there was more than one kind, and now the whole apartment was teeming with electricians recommended by the Grosvenor Estates, summoned by the porter at the insistence of Mrs. Beryl Sutton on 5. She'd had her fill once and for all time of American ingenuity after the last war and she was livid.

It's a catastrophe, she complained to Jean, all bumblers and thugs with fat wallets and wives like call girls. They were standing in the lobby, waiting for the lights to return to normal. The chandelier gave off a low ominous hiss Jean tried to ignore.

How is the little girl faring? Mrs. Sutton wanted to know.

Perfect, really, a lovely change, such an adventure, said Jean.

Oh good lord, what nonsense, never saw such a gang of miscreants and scoundrels as the board of that school, all Saudi money, you know.

No, I didn't.

Oh yes, and the Jews? Mrs. Sutton lifted her chin with meaning.

The Jews? asked Jean.

Absolute powder keg. I don't exaggerate.

No, of course not. But? Jean frowned.

But, my dear young lady, your daughter better know the way to the exit doors, that's all I'm saying. No peacekeeping forces in St. John's Wood, I daresay. No Dr. Kissingers pulling stunts outside the chemistry laboratory, Mrs. Sutton chuckled.

But they're in Camden Town.

Just you wait. Cyril! What's the prognosis?

It's a fright, madam, sad to say, an unlucky plug, that's all.

Unlucky? Unlucky? Hopeless morons. Please fetch me a taxi,
Cyril, and let Felicia know I've given up on this day once and for all.

Of course. Right away.

No need to say right away, Cyril. I'm aware of your timetable.
Mrs. Sutton withdrew a handkerchief from her skirt pocket, a large
checkered square, faded from many launderings. Jean watched as
she tapped the underside of her chin, tenderly as though wiping
away the fallen tears of a child. It's very disconcerting, she said.

It is, said Jean. And I'm very sorry.

You're a good girl, said Mrs. Sutton. I can see that now.

No, I'm not, said Jean.

All a charade then?

Jean shook her head and smiled.

Just as I thought, she said and she was off.

Jean took a seat in one of the large claw-footed leather chairs
at the far end of the lobby. There was a fireplace that bore a subtle
scroll of ivy. Tiny red berries and a half dozen red velvet ribbons.
This muted decoration struck Jean as just right. She felt a sudden
wash of relief not to be going to Fifth Avenue this year after all,
not to be tugging Lily through the crowds to Rockefeller Center.
Maybe Nick had been right to keep them here. No angels with glit-
ter falling off their trumpets, no Santas. This discreet holly could
be turned into a houseplant with a deft removal of a couple of
bows. She considered the rightness of this and wondered how it
happened. It's the Jews! she thought and laughed, how ridiculous.
She reached over and untied one small bow. And then after a while,
she plucked apart another.

Haven't you done enough harm for one day?

Where had Nick come from? What are you doing here,
sweetheart?

The estate agent called the office. Highest, *highest* alert. Let's finish the job, he laughed.

She looked at him, handsome in a blue suit she suddenly couldn't recall. Did he change at the office? Come on, he said, gently, as if she'd been napping. Let me take you to lunch.

16

Lily's mother told her it took time in a new place to make friends.
But for her mother the friends came with the fixtures and fittings of the flat. Emma and Anna arrived at the first party and, as
her mother said, never went home. They were always available—for
lunch at the wine bar, trips to the Silver Vaults, or backgammon and
pasta by the fire. Her mother scarcely had room to think she said.
She confided she'd really given up on friendship. She'd discovered
its profound limitations.

It's very sad. But not for you of course, your life hasn't even
started yet!

I think it's started, Lily said. It's started for me. Her mother
laughed but really she listened to the percussion of the sidewalk,
waiting for her father now. She'd fallen in love with him all over
again she said. Not that she'd ever stopped! Even in her pajamas
she kept on her eyelashes.

But I don't get it. What about Anna? And Emma? asked Lily.

Heartless, her mother laughed. One worse than the other. Emma Hocking had been saying something untrue about her father, some nonsense about a tart named Vivienne Vimcreste. Couldn't tie her own shoelaces if she had to, mental health of a flea, but then she has other talents, said Emma. And her mother decided she'd heard enough. As for Anna, Jean was sick of people's overweening sympathy.

But as far as Lily could tell no one was offering much of that anymore. Early in the autumn the phone calls from the States had converted to cards, quick notes to say a benefit committee was lost without Jean or that Sister Charitina was finally getting her new gymnasium, a miracle. Only Doris still called on Sunday afternoons, and those calls were short, and often over by the time Lily wandered down the hall to say hello. Lionel called occasionally. She'd come upon her mother hunched over the library desk once in the middle of the night. Get out, her mother whispered, covering the receiver. Then later she came to Lily's bed and kissed her forehead and said that Lionel just needed some advice.

About what? Lily asked.

The usual, her mother said. She sat looking out through the bars to the green lit courtyard, waiting. Lily watched her mother's face, her eyes, so bare and small-looking now. Her father was overnight in Paris again on business. I miss Poppa? Lily tried.

Oh! her mother said. Oh, honey, and she held her hand and rubbed along the top of her back like Lily was a little girl. And as she rubbed Lily felt her mother become calm and finally tire out.

Sweetie, Poppa always wanted me to tell you something.

Lily smiled at her mother. Poppa was full of ideas about everything but especially sports. He thought Lily should be a great and noble sportswoman. Didn't matter what she took up as long as she was triumphant and if possible famous.

Is it about sports? Too late for the Olympics. Look at Peter Healey! He started training at four or something.

It's not about sports; it's about Daddy.

Well, maybe he was five.

Daddy helped Uncle Lionel with something a long time ago and things didn't go well.

Lily watched her mother in the light from the well. Down below, the usual scurry among the trash bins always made her shiver, but her mother was the one trembling now. Lily touched her mother's hand and she recoiled and said, This is bad timing. You don't need to know this yet.

Daddy always helps Uncle Lionel.

This was a different kind of help and Daddy got in a lot of trouble with the government.

Because he hates Nixon?

No, no, her mother laughed. No. Something else. It started before you were born or just after. It lasted awhile.

The help?

Yes. For quite a while.

But not anymore?

No. It's all over now. And Poppa just wanted you to know in case anyone ever brought it up. In case one of your friends' parents ever mentioned something. So, now you know.

Lily felt her mother's hip against her leg, felt the muscles stiffen and now she held both elbows as if making a neat container of herself. She blinked away from the window toward the dark hallway.

Okay, said Lily. Thanks.

Yes, okay. Don't say anything to your father. He can be so touchy!

Not Daddy! Never!

Her mother laughed and her hip went soft and she leaned down to kiss Lily on the forehead. Good girl, she said and she smelled like Scotch and honey. All right, she whispered as if Lily had fallen asleep. All right, angel. And Lily felt in that moment her mother loved her; she just needed to keep it very quiet.

Just off Curzon Street, on the second floor above the nearest green-grocer—asparagus like dirty straw, ten bob for four wilted stalks? cried Mrs. Veal—a satanic coffee shop had opened, which for a brief while, to the dismay of proprietors, the American students made into a way station between Camden Town and Belgravia. Lawrence Weatherfield had discovered it, and until he was suspended from school and sent to Switzerland his social authority was nearly absolute.

One day, as she got off the tube at Oxford Street, Mirabel Kendrick turned around when they were up on the street, squinting in the sunlight and said to Lily, Oh, it's you? Come along with us, right? And Lily, astonished, wandered down South Audley behind them. They were all dressed in black; even Lawrence Weatherfield had on faded black cords and a blackish crewneck sweater. Finally they climbed a crooked stair into a black-draped room with flickering hex sign candles and an espresso machine. Sour herbal incense burned in tiny alcoves where the images of demons leered.

There was the ordeal of stepping to the espresso counter to order cinnamon toast and then finding the only empty spot beside Mirabel in her hooded cape. Mirabel kept a thin nearly translucent hand tucked into the black leather trouser pocket of her boyfriend Elkin Barr. Her hand stroked in an undulating motion and she smiled at Lily, benevolently, like a saint on a Mass card. Her cape hood framed her sorrowful, tortured beauty. They'd been coming every day for weeks Lily discovered, and now Lawrence told what sounded like an ongoing story about his Indonesian nanny, Puni. This time Puni fed him Popsicles made of tainted water and his mother's crushed-up Valium—just to keep him serene, ma'am, so baby can be peace—and his mother accepted this! Though she did hide the Valium, which was difficult because the jars came from Hong Kong and were *massive* like beer kegs. We had a pharmaceutical *pantry*, said Lawrence. Bigger than this room! Though he scarcely remembered that time. Now his mother was religious, or spiritual, and his father Lawrence said, raising his eyes to Mirabel's exquisitely unresponsive face, was *scarce*. He watched her until something shifted and her eyes, rarely anything but benign and detached, skittered to Elkin, who opened his and said, Well, if Mummy's ever stuck you know where to send her, mate. And Mirabel snuggled her hand deeper and slowly removed her gaze from Lawrence's.

Lily said, What kind of religion? Lawrence turned and grinned. Take your pick, love.

Love, mate, it all came from the Working Men's College, but Lily heard only the endearment, the possible interpretation of *you are this to me.*

Elkin made a joke about Lawrence and his mother camping out at the Dorchester. So bloody convenient. Lily was stunned and wanted to ask if it was really true, but then Mirabel said something about a pinch in her calf and Elkin and Lawrence studied her as she bent to rub from knee to ankle along the torn black fishnets and went silent beneath the static of the ambient guitar. This meant Lawrence and Lily were neighbors now and she hadn't even realized.

Then the very next day the satanic café was closed for good for unknown reasons and she was the only person getting off at Oxford Circus again. So she began walking up Park Lane every once in a while. She'd walk slowly past the Dorchester, set back in its own triangle of sidewalk and driveway, an attribute so special it seemed to reflect on Lawrence. Lily would slow way down and feel her whole body alerted to the possibility that Lawrence might suddenly appear through the revolving door and see her. Lily, Lily! he'd shout and she would spin around. Lawrence? Then he would come up to her. Wait! he'd be saying as he walked to her with his slow slouch, but a tiny bit rushed. Hey, can you wait? His religious mother might be left standing near the doorman, calling out, impatient, but Lawrence would keep coming to Lily, his face open with delight. I was hoping I'd bump into you. Love.

Then Lily would be all the way past the Dorchester and the Park Lane traffic sound would rise pounding, deafening, and she'd be exhausted, so exhausted she felt she could almost lie down on the sidewalk and sleep right there, but the men on the street stared, stared at her body in a frightening way until she'd reach the Hilton and the underground walkway and go down into the echoing tiles, past the buskers, who she felt sorry for and would give all the notes in her pocket, every time, then up into Hyde Park to find Achilles. By end of November Lily was walking along Park Lane every darkening afternoon.

As the weather got damper, the statue of Achilles became slick with icy drizzle most days. The pedestal wasn't hard to climb, even in her maxicoat. Others sprawled there to enjoy the vista of the park, the sliver of Serpentine spread visible beneath the fading trees, the dirt scent of grass mixed with the high sweet tinge of hashish. The joints were passed to everyone and she learned to hold in the smoke without snorting.

Lily would lean back and find a strange comfort here among the traveling international students with their guitar cases and backpacks. She could almost see her room with the bars and the shag carpeting from here, see her mother come in through the glass and iron front door with new shopping bags, see her drop everything in a lump on the front étagère and rush into the library because the phone was ringing and the police who'd found Lily were just calling to say she mustn't be frightened because Lily might still be okay, they were holding out hope, but she must come immediately. And her mother would faint and the policeman—the bobby—would be saying, Madam? Madam? Can you hear me? Mrs. Veal would rush in, pluck up the receiver and shout, And why would you disturb the poor woman with nonsense, shame on you, then slam down the phone. Missus? she'd say very gently. Now Missus? I'll get you something soothing. And Mrs. Veal would help her mother very slowly make her way to the rust-colored sofa, and tuck a quilt, maybe something satin from the guest room around her shivering legs. Oh, I'll give that girl a piece of my mind when she dares to show her face. You just wait. Lily's mother would protest, but softly, She's only a child, Mrs. Veal.

A child! Why I was taking care of the whole family when I was her age. A child? Well, that's you Missus, too kind by half. I'll get that tea, now.

You're the kind one, Mrs. Veal. A smile would break across Mrs. Veal's face, and a blush (a little bronzer would do miracles her father had said).

Lily imagined her mother worried sick about her, wrapped tight in celery-colored satin. Then she thought of Lawrence ordering extra cinnamon for his toast in the satanic café and rubbing it on his pinky finger, then onto his lower lip and licking it with a small point of his shocking pink tongue and she'd been mesmerized. Though he hadn't looked at her, it was still possible he thought of her when he made this gesture. Lily's grandmother said that Lily should always let love slide and flow like water, and once her face was wet with drizzle and her hair fragrant with foreign dope, she'd slip down Achilles's pedestal and walk home quickly in the dark on the park side, too damp and sad now to be caught in front of the Dorchester.

The first week in December, Lily was doing her slow-motion walk when she spotted her father's blue Bentley crawling down her side of Park Lane. She was at the point where a sharp fast left turn could squeeze her past the doorman and into the hotel. Nearly four o'clock and traffic was snarled. If he leapt right out of the car, impatient, he would see her. She dipped into the nearest door, into the lobby and down the stairs where nervous waiters were preparing for tea. The waiters ignored her; they were accustomed to American children lost in the lobby. Hold on there, mate. She heard his voice from somewhere nearby. High and low, smooth and crackled at the same time. Holy shit, laughed Lawrence. Look what the cat dragged in.

Oh, said Lily.

Mater, I'd like you to meet my school friend, oh shit. Is it Natalie? Nancy?

Lily.

Well, how nice. Are you staying here, too, dear? asked Lawrence's mother. Everything about her shimmered. From her winged plum-colored hair to her patent leather boots. Lily stared and Lawrence's mother laughed. Well, she said. Aren't you adorable. Will you join us for tea, Lily?

She actually spoke. No, no thank you. Lily couldn't fathom how to leave now, and felt her breath go very shallow. What if her father suddenly came through the door? It was possible. Her father was unpredictable now said her mother. Keeping us on our toes she'd sigh and take a long close-eyed drag on her Dunhill. What I'd give for an American cigarette, but she had plenty of those stacked in a kitchen cupboard. They were both unpredictable. Now Lawrence was studying her face like she'd seen him study the satanic artifacts at the café, carefully, thoughtfully. Everything here is meant to do something very specific, you know, he'd told them. Yes, I learned about this in Indonesia where they're pretty keen on devils. Very keen, he told Mirabel, who smiled her mystical smile. But now he watched Lily with the same interest.

Mums, may I show Lily the Bernford?

His mother laughed. Poor Lily. You and that Bernford! Then she sighed. Ten minutes, or I start tea without you. Lily, you are about to see the dullest painting in the entire world, bar none. But Lawrence and his father are besotted. Go. I hope you'll tell me what you think. She grasped Lily's forearm and smiled without wrinkling her face, more a beam of delighted approval. You'll settle this once and for all, Lily!

Come on, said Lawrence, and walked toward the waiting elevator.

I'll figure it out for you, Mrs. Weatherfield, said Lily.

Lawrence's mother raised her eyebrows. Good girl, she said and blinked as if distracted then turned to survey her impact on the room.

Hey! Hurry up, said Lawrence, pushing her into the elevator. Penthouse, Jeeves, express, no stops for the proletariat, si'l vous plaît.

Sir. The elevator attendant nodded and pulled the lever.

Listen, I hope you brought your naughty lace? No grubby cotton knickers like the last time, Lawrence said, stepping out at his floor. Lily glanced at the man who seemed to be counting something beyond her head. We're going to look at a painting, she said. She smiled at him, but he closed the gate.

What kind of religion is your mother?

Self-veneration, it's very portable. She can practice anywhere.

I don't understand.

Neither does she. Lawrence edged an enormous key out of his tight pocket. Welcome to the shrine. He opened the thick white door onto a very prim-looking room with flounced skirts on two high narrow beds, lace curtains yanked back within heavy satin drapes held with hooks and through the panes Hyde Park shimmered green and wet. Lily wondered if she'd been visible all along, if he could even see Achilles from here.

You share this with your mother? she asked.

Lawrence choked. No way. Come on, I'll show you the beast.

I thought you loved the painting?

You're very literal.

Lawrence opened the adjoining door and they went on to the drawing room of the suite, smaller than she would have guessed, and Lawrence as if mind reading, said they were economizing. It's nice! she said, but it wasn't. Two long narrow windows let in the grim afternoon. Two heavy sofas were covered in shiny brown brocade and faced one another, two rickety gold tables piled with ashtrays and magazines. Everything was unhappily paired. Sit, Lawrence pointed to the window-side sofa. And sit up straight, he laughed. She smiled though she didn't see the joke exactly yet. She sank into the too soft cushion and a puff of old soured perfume rose up as if his mother had spilled some long ago. Something in the smell made her worry.

Lawrence rummaged in a trunk-like suitcase open on the floor. A fight to the death, he said, between the chambermaids and the trunk. We open it—he tossed a stack of embroidered squares on the armchair—and they come and tidy up and we can't find a thing. Lawrence piled some ceramics wrapped in plastic on the rug. Blue-and-white Japanese cups and bowls wobbled then tipped. Here we go, said Lawrence. He stood and adjusted the wide black belt that hovered just at his hips. Don't move, he shouted as she stood up to see. I said stay where you are.

Lily sat. She held very still and felt alert, like something needed her protection here, but she wasn't sure what. Lawrence was grinning at her. Almost a frozen smile, as if she was supposed to understand something beneath it, something private and important. He kept his hands behind his back. Is that it? she asked. Is that the painting?

Shut the fuck up! said Lawrence, but in a whisper, which made Lily look to the other door, closed on the adjoining bedroom. Would they wake someone sleeping? Maybe his father.

Are you watching? And now he was shouting. Can't you keep your fucking eye on the ball?

Lily knew her mouth was open and closed it, blinking. She thought of her father, possibly in the lobby, and what he would say if he found her here, in Lawrence's suite. He would come right in and say, Sweetheart? Everything okay? Yes, she was sure of it. Lawrence dropped the object he held in his hands, hid it from her, covered it now in the embroidered squares. Sorry, he said. You failed.

I did?

Yup. He was walking toward her, watching her carefully. But these, he said and he bent over and reached out toward her hands, crossed at the wrists, fingers clutching her knees. Lawrence picked up one hand in both of his and murmured, Perfect, as if speaking to himself. Perfect, he said again, and looked deep into her eyes as if she'd been keeping something from him. He took the hand he held and spread open the fingers, his touch ticklish and odd, then he lay the hand down in her lap, and tapped it up, farther, tighter toward her belly, and she let her hand be moved, and watched it almost like a puppy being prompted into place. He arranged her fingers splayed at the top of her thigh and then quickly, much more quickly, brought the other into place, so that her hands made a basket shape over her crotch like rice Chex or that plaid bikini bottom she'd wanted so much; neither of them could breathe well, and Lawrence's eyes were tearing. A loud crash right outside the door frightened them both. Jesus fuck, cried Lawrence. Better go, he said in a rough voice. Better go right now. Right now. Get out.

Lily stood up and felt her legs were trembling as if she had ruined some essential thing and that chance was over now forever. Lawrence was looking out the window, his face pulled down with disgust; when he glanced back his eyes were slitted and angry. I thought you were gone.

Lily found the vestibule and the door. She had trouble with the knob and finally got it open and she was out in the corridor, ready to weep; then she was weeping with her failure and her loneliness.

Poor young miss. The chambermaid had a black hairnet that came down over her wrinkled forehead and made the skin bunch the top of her nose. Poor young miss, she sang again, and opened a brand-new box of tissues for Lily. That little boy is very nasty, do you hear? Find your mother, now, and think no more of it. Just a terrible dream. Not touching right? Please say not touching.

Lily thanked her for the tissue and shook her head. Not really. The chambermaid waved her away. Go find Mama, now, she said and wheeled her cart toward the suite.

17

Harry Lewis made an odd spectacle in his gold suede dinner jacket, sitting, or more squatting, at the blackjack table, as if he might be required to spring off his chair at short notice. Stitched up in Hong Kong, he told Nick, fingering the cuff, identical to something he saw on Sinatra in Vegas a couple months ago. Saw it; had it shipped right here. Feel.

Very nice, said Nick, but you smell like dead game. Harry grunted and nodded, called the dealer a cocksucker, but quietly, caressingly, and in turn, it seemed, he was allowed to occupy the side chair next to Nick without playing a single hand.

Cold feet? You? said Nick.

Studying, kiddo, watching the experts in their lairs. Look at this clown and his upright chest. The baby-blond hair combed sideways? All a front. The Sicilians would run at the sight of him.

This got an acknowledgment from the dealer. A faint smile.

He's the master. The sensei. Right, Kimpton?

No response.

All right, said Harry. I've seen enough. Deal me in. Nicky? Stake me.

Nick reached into a pocket and dropped a thousand-pound plaque on the table.

Two more. Come on. A little faith, please. And Nick obliged. On his other side the woman's arm pressed into his gave off a shiver as she lifted and peeked at her dealt cards. She'd lost and lost again. No visible backing. He began to notice a jasmine scent about her, an old-fashioned perfume. He tucked a hundred-pound chip into her evening purse, a tiny gold seashell left unclasped on the green baize edge. Grazie, Signor, mille grazie, she said, with a tragic glance before dropping the chip on her scant remaining pile.

Harry overdrew his hand right away. Kimpton, you lying bastard. Then he scowled over at the woman who was still in the game. What, you're backing the table? he said to Nick. He knocked back out of his chair. Come on. Let's split. Presto.

I want to see if she wins.

Oh, she'll win.

Nick smiled, Signorina.

Yeah right, Tarzan, said Harry. Come on. And he pulled Nick up and out through the throng toward the next room. Look at this place, said Harry. It's amateur night. But I'm telling you, that Kimpton is an artist.

How do you know? said Nick. You played one hand.

You think I can't tell the difference?

Okay, you know.

I do know.

That's what I just said.

Nick turned to watch the woman through the crowd; her dress had a lavender sparkle in the straps, so subtle, just that touch on a black dress, simple. He looked back at Harry. Ciao, Harry.

Now, don't be cross.

Cross? He laughed.

Grab a nightcap with me.

Not tonight.

One. Just one. I'm a dick. Right? We know that.

Nick nodded, slightly, still watching the woman, who now gazed up at him. Her eyes were slow to focus, and then opened with a recognition that was more than gratitude for a tossed chip. She'd won, maybe for the first time tonight; he could see it.

But not here, Harry was saying. It's stupid night. Let's go to Annabel's. What do you say?

Actually she didn't rise, but it seemed to Nick she was almost levitating, the tiny sparkles on her shoulders, her eyes moved into his. He reached into his pocket for what he had left.

Yeah, cash in. We'll get a drink.

One minute.

Nick zigzagged back across the room and he could feel the place now, out of Harry's muting range. He relaxed and shifted in and out of the bodies, smiling, nodding, saying hello, until he was back at Kimpton's table. He pulled the rest of the chips from his jacket and the last thousand plaque from his trouser pocket.

He leaned down to say something while Kimpton swept in the cards. She turned. She had very warm-looking skin, deep apricot color to her cheeks, a clever dot of white lipstick centered on a full pretty mouth, black hair in a precarious pile with tiny jeweled fasteners, long narrow amber eyes. Cara mia, she said. She seemed to speak in his ear. He bent closer as if to listen, bent into the jostling around the table. He pulled her hand gently from the fold of silk in her lap and placed the chips in her open palm and felt the give in her body, just like that. She bowed over his hand and startled at what he'd offered her. He touched her shoulder, smiled, and turned away.

Obliging, isn't she, said Harry when Nick caught up with him.

Nick shrugged. But he was happy now. Harry couldn't touch him.

You didn't even have to send a script. She got every cue, like a tango or something; she's good.

Whatever you say, Harry, always so valuable.

Harry tilted his head sideways, gave Nick a look like he was taking aim at something.

But Nick was much too light and he would hold on to that all the way out the door to the sidewalk no matter what Harry had to say. Then it was gone.

Chill damp slick-feeling air, the stinking exhaust of a taxi just passed. Two in the morning, and Harry was still on his toes, looking for action. Nick felt in his pocket for the plastic whiffer and gave himself a quick blast.

Yeah, offer *that* thing to Miss Hot Pants.

Nick stood and caught his breath for a minute. He could hear the wheeze start up in his chest, feel the pull. What she really wanted—he paused, took a breath—was *your* number, Harry. So what could I do?

What's the matter with you?

What? Nick felt his own cheek as if testing for a fever. Nothing's the matter. I just don't feel like a drink.

I mean, what? I'm supposed to be impressed because you can make a hooker smile by giving her money?

Nick laughed. It's not that.

Really?

No.

Because I think you're sending me a message, baby.

Nothing you don't already know.

What do I know? Harry stepped a little closer, put a hand on the cuff of Nick's coat. This is what my grandfather would say was fine goods. A garment guy, you knew that. Did you know that? Harry smoothed down the collar, plucked at the stitched notch. Very nice. Is Derek taking care of you these days? His breath juniper strong, Give me a kiss, doll, he whispered.

Let it go, Harry.

What's that? The coat? Sure. He put his hand inside, pushing gently into Nick's chest. Where's that fat wallet, he said, feeling down his side. Give me some of those big chips. You know you'll get better than a smile, right?

Nick lifted up his arms for the frisk, Harry humming a tune. Nick leaned in closer, put his hand over Harry's, pulled it up slowly, turned over the palm and kissed it. Harry grinned. That's right, baby. That's it.

Night, said Nick and started walking. So long.

Fuck off, you faggot.

Yeah, yeah.

Hey! I ran into this Vivienne kid who said she knew you. Now there's a kick.

But Nick was already tripping his way across the cobbles of Curzon Street. Back of the hand waving over his shoulder, Ciao, Harry-bird. He bent over coughing, then straightened back up. Good night.

You can run, baby, sang out Harry. Oh yeah, you can run.

Nick was out of sight, around the corner, and Harry and his stupid menace were extinguished in his head so thoroughly he wanted to laugh. Bumbling prick. Lionel's bird dog. Harry used to guard the files on West Fifty-Fourth Street, collected all the chits, the order slips at the end of the day and looked them over like someone who could read a number. Then he'd flex his jaw in a way that conveyed threat more effectively than a cocked gun lying on the table. But who needed to be threatened? They were crating cash, at least in theory, on paper. Even the runners, even the kids going to the deli for coffee were just putting off buying Cadillacs for their mothers until they had the time.

We're doing a friendly service. We're like farmers, spreading the bounty, Lionel would say over a late dinner in a back booth at Mike Manello's. He'd lay his hands on the thick white cloth, wrists together making his fingers flutter like the branches: It's like we've got a ladder and we've got a tree, but that tree's upside down, deep in the ground and full of rare fruit. We're just divvying it up as we find it, giving everyone a bushel or two. It's kind of beautiful, really.

And Harry, who listened when Lionel spoke like he'd smack anyone who sneezed, said, Yeah, it is. And when the tree is bare, we'll seal up that crap hole for good.

Lionel smiled, rubbed his hands over his eyes, and yawned. Harry pulled out a lighter with the Knights of Columbus crest and flicked it open like a torch and Lionel wheezed with laughter. Choked and wheezed until Harry's thick flat-nosed face went red with pleasure. Harry, you're the reason I sleep at night.

But Lionel, it turned out in the end, was doing nothing that could be proved against him. Even the eventual fire that took out two floors of file cabinets and a rigged steam bath was deemed an electrical failure, while Nick had signed most of the phony order forms for stocks tied to minerals that had never been mined or even found. A tree underground? Fucking Lionel. Only Clyde, by some back-channel miracle, had kept him out of federal prison. Now every time Harry started to lay out the next project, Nick cut him off. Don't want to know.

Oh, you'll know all right, Harry would say. Can't be helped. That kind of knowledge can't be stopped. You'll like this, Nicky. It has international flair. Just like you these days.

Nick would laugh and Harry would laugh.

It's all about movement, like a river. You'd be the river. Think flowing, and Harry made his hands move like a current.

Forget it.

But every once in a while Nick was curious. He was coming up toward the American embassy, past the wooden cart where most mornings, a woman in a green cardigan sold just-budded peonies out of season by the fistful. He'd bought some earlier in the week for Jean, came in with his arms full, smelling like new plucked parsley. He'd bought the whole lot, everything she had left. But Mrs. Veal stopped him at the door, No you don't, Guv. She's given strict orders. Anything pink, no matter who the sender, right back again.

Pink?

That's right. I know my duty. Clear as day.

Mrs. Veal.

You want me to take them off your hands now, sir?

That's all right. It's fine, thank you, Mrs. Veal. So he continued on to the office, dumped them wet on Tania's desk instead. I don't care, he said. Whatever you want, Tania, just get them out of sight. And she'd blushed, Right away, sir.

He stopped still and listened. He could swear he heard Harry sneaking up behind him and spun around to catch him. But it was quiet now. Scanning the shadows, peering into the square, he couldn't see him hidden anywhere. Nick grabbed hold of the iron railing, and felt his body sway a little. Finally he let go, and stepped back to look up at the front windows of the flat, all dark for once. He missed that, coming up to the house, and seeing the porch light yellow as a moon, and the blue night-lights for Cubbie and Lily, and Jean always reading late, always waiting up, so the light from their room shimmered through the French doors and then out in wavy lines until it disappeared over the black invisible water.

He thought about Clyde, what a tight knot he'd tied around Nick for all those years. But a knot that had clarified, narrowed his choices. When Lionel's tree proved rotten, it was Clyde who forced Nick back into life for Jean's sake. Saturday mornings, Clyde and Huey would pick him up and drag him along on all of Clyde's usual rounds—the track, the golf club, the marina. And any jerk who wouldn't give Nick a straight handshake had Clyde to deal with. But Clyde was dead, and Cubbie was dead, and Lionel was a soulless prick who'd used him and now wanted to line him up for a second round.

He pawed through his pockets. Maybe he'd dropped his key along with everything else into the lap of the girl with the sparkling shoulders. The front door had long been locked for the night. Christ, he was tired. He sat on the wide step for a moment and caught his breath, tried to draw air deep into his chest, but it caught in his throat, as if Clyde and Lionel and Harry all had their thick claws right around him. He closed his eyes and the black water filled his head. Then he opened them, saw the sharp lights of the American embassy like something in a prison yard. What were they thinking when they built that place?

18

Lily sat on the floor in the narrow hallway outside her bedroom. Her mother had given her the servants' quarters and put in purple shag carpeting throughout, but all three rooms had bars on the windows left over, apparently, from the general during wartime. In this back area was also the loud spare American refrigerator and its ticking black transformer box. Her clothes were in crazy piles all around and this was the problem. Her clothes. There was no good place to keep them. Her room didn't have a closet and she couldn't be counted on to put them in the wall of cupboards her mother had designated in the adjoining room. All the special tags and markers, like a professional laundry, it just wasn't appealing. But it made things easier for Mrs. Veal who took all their dirty things some mysterious place on Monday evenings and returned Tuesday mornings by taxi with a canvas-sided cart on wheels. All this was taken to be sorted out in the room next to Lily's. Mrs. Veal refused to tidy up any mess. You're a very big girl, aren't you, love. Of course Lily didn't want her tidying up. But she didn't remember to do it herself either. So the piles grew and fermented.

Just for a change, some nights, she'd begun sleeping in the cool tidy unoccupied guestroom. There was a lot of space, no bars on the windows, and the gray silk drapes were calming. The bed she slept in had a welcoming cavity.

For two weeks, Mrs. Veal had been on holiday visiting her truant son in a reform school up near the Welsh border. You better watch yourself, said Mrs. Veal. We know he's not the only one who knows how to vanish. Mrs. Veal winked with her entire face. It catches up. You'll see.

How did Mrs. Veal know what her parents did not? Keep your eyes open, dearie, that's how you get on in this life. Mrs. Veal was giving Lily tips lately, and mostly Lily appreciated it. But Mrs. Veal was gone and now piles of clothes and books and makeup and records and her guitar that she didn't play but liked to look at had ended up in the guestroom. Clothes all over the floor, her makeup open and smeared on the ivory dresser top. A sticky bronzer with sparkles embedded in the antique finish. Her mother would kill her. But her mother never came into this room unless there were guests and so far, that had happened exactly once, when Kay Sheehan's grandson spent the night on his way to North Africa. Then her mother had a conference in the guest room with Mrs. Veal about body odor and young men. Boys, really. Not a blessed thing to be done about it. Mrs. Veal was the authority. They had a good laugh about the sheets, and shooed Lily away. Not for your ears, love. Not yet at least. Not for a good long while, said her mother. And she looked at Lily fondly, as if she were pantomiming the wry happiness of motherhood. No one could see through this act and that astonished Lily. She was waiting for her real mother to return. For the most part, she was patient.

Lily was mortified by the idea of Lawrence and for a week she'd stayed far from school, wandering into Hyde Park instead, or sometimes Oxford Street, keeping an eye out for her mother especially around Selfridges where Jean liked to waste time as well. But she grew lonely and finally went back to Camden Town, and even to the Blue Pumpkin and there he was. Sitting by himself, his curly brown hair looking longer and wilder than at the Dorchester, his skin pale. She studied him through the lunch crowd with a sinking sadness while she ordered her sausage roll and shandy. He had such intelligent eyes. Now he was staring toward the door and spotted her. He waved and shouted hello.

It was difficult to move. Lawrence was flagging her over, delighted and surprised. She found a way to inch toward him. Where have you been hiding, love? I'd just about given up; he patted the bench seat beside him. As if they had become very close while she was gone. He was grinning at her as she pulled out a chair instead. No, no, over here, you'll miss the show. Come on.

Outside on the sidewalk Mirabel and Elkin were having an argument. Lawrence pointed through the window to the top of Mirabel's cape. Look, it's actually *vibrating*. That's rich.

What happened? They're so perfect.

Allegedly, he's an animal. He's been getting a bit insistent, Lawrence laughed. Then he whispered, If only. Because he was glancing around she wasn't sure he was speaking to her. Elkin has so much shit lodged in his bloodstream, not a chance he's an animal in any capacity. Get my drift? It wrecks the machinery. You know.

Sure. Lily bit down on a sausage roll, but didn't take her eyes from his face. She swatted at the pastry crumbs from the crushed velvet bib of her overalls. Well, she said. Good thing you're okay? Is it now?

You said last summer in Umbria you gave that stuff up. Right?

Did I, said Lawrence looking out the door. Mirabel's face visible through the etched glass looked unhappy, just the slant of her cheek and it was obvious. Elkin's all right, said Lawrence, distracted now. He shot the cuff of his denim blazer and regarded for a long time the oversized watch on his pale freckled wrist. Lily studied the way his hair belled out at his chin. His mother made him cut his bangs above his eyebrows in a way he thought looked stupid, but she liked it, the semicircle of wavy hair framing his changeable eyes. He was just her height, but his narrow long torso made him look taller sitting straight-backed against the red banquette cushion studying his father's watch. Two days, he said glancing up, two days and a knockoff wristwatch. My father flew in from Riyadh over the weekend to visit the block of cheese.

You don't say that to her face.

I say a lot of things.

Like what?

Like how about we get an apartment and quit farting around the mini suite. I'm sick of all the cleaning ladies in and out. It's distracting.

From what?

From what? Everything, he sighed, exasperated, and studied the new angle of Mirabel's head. She appeared to be clutching her hair, but in a picturesque way, as if her anguish at Elkin was a game.

My mother's like that, said Lily.

Like what?

She displays her problems like it's all under glass, all in a museum.

Lawrence moved his head in slow motion, dramatizing his attention. You've got a shitload of food on your clothing there, mate. But his eyes were clearer now, and he nodded as if suggesting she should continue.

She's always up in the night smoking and staring at nothing. And then when I try to ask her why, she gets pissed off.

Pissed off?

Well, yes, she does. I'll just be saying, Hey, are you okay?

At least she's got feelings.

I don't know.

Better off than the block of cheese. My father's never moving to London. Bethany can fantasize all she wants, but we're stranded until she figures out that we should pack up the trunk and go back to Riyadh. Hey, come here? Lawrence knocked the back of his hand against the banquette.

Lily nodded but didn't move.

Come closer. You're wrecking the view, he said.

Oh, sorry, she hoisted up her book bag.

No, leave that shit. Just come here. I think Elkin's making some progress, see?

Lily sat closer to Lawrence. She could feel the hum of his body now. Her breath got ragged and loud. She tried to follow his gaze out the etched-glass door to where Elkin's head now appeared a dark and inscrutable hank of hair.

You can just tell he's begging, can't you? I'm embarrassed for the guy.

How do you *know*?

Elkin was nodding fast and Lawrence turned to look at her. It seemed his eyes took a minute to focus on her, almost as if he was perplexed to see her there and he was evaluating whether it was a good or a bad development. Lily, he said, finally. Little Lily.

She wasn't little at all. Lily blinked too quickly, and her body nearly started shaking under his scrutiny. Lily, he said, his voice full of happy recognition. He leaned back as if to take her in, the delight of her. This was shocking, the happy tenderness opening up in his face. She remembered a whole list of advice from her mother, from Emma. She put her legs in the position her mother recommended as most attractive, ankles crossed, which was difficult in her boots. Then tried to get her knees angled sideways and banged into the tabletop, spilling her shandy. Beer poured off the table into their laps and then soaked the red banquette.

Christ, said Lawrence, jumping up, swatting at his thighs.

Lily wanted to weep as the warm beer saturated her overalls.

Lawrence was casing the crowded pub, but no one seemed to notice they were sopping. All right, don't cry. We'll just cruise out the back way. Right by the loo there's another door. He offered his hand. I've got some old jeans in my locker at school, maybe some for you, too.

Lily knew getting into a pair of Lawrence's spare jeans was impossible, but it humiliated her to have to say it. Her lap was a big dark wet blotch; she couldn't stand up like this.

Lawrence picked up her book bag and her coat. Cover it up. Let's go. And she followed him out the service entry of the Blue Pumpkin and back to school.

Inside the main entrance to the Working Men's College was a staircase leading down to a pair of mahogany doors that most of the

American students ignored. There on the basement level was the library. In theory the Americans had access, but in practice the place was never used. Political tracts in leather sleeves furred with dust and unpopular nineteenth-century novels never checked out by the workingmen. All magazine subscriptions had long lapsed, except a small stack that seemed fresh and urgent brought in by the librarians themselves. Two crenulated men wore white visors to shield them from the buzzing overhead sun-bright fluorescents. Lawrence waved. Good afternoon, Minks, he whispered.

One man looked up and acknowledged approval of his tone of voice. Lawrence led Lily across the gray glass walkways past the spiraling ironwork stairs leading farther down. History, religion dispatched in four rows each. At the end of the walkway there was a table surrounded by half-broken chairs. He paused to point out some new light brown scratches among the many scars. LOW III. She reached out to touch it. You? What's the *o* stand for?

Don't! he said. You'll wreck it. She yanked back her hand. I'm *kidding* you. Sheesh, rent a sense of humor. Come on, come on. Follow me.

They veered down another half corridor. A low porcelain water fountain gurgled bubbles around a rusty drain. Thirsty?

This isn't our part of the college.

None of it's ours. Lawrence opened a half-glassed door on to a small storage room. Wooden lockers lined the walls with typed yellow index cards indicating various supplies, paper patterns, wrenches and screws. Some doors were ajar and inside Lily could see a helter-skelter jumble of junk. In the corner, a daybed with a quilt that looked like the one on his bed at the Dorchester, a pin-tucked seafoam-green satin bunched on top of an inch-thin mattress wrapped in beige wool. You sleep in here? Lily was shocked.

Sometimes. It's not hard to get in at night. Not at all. It's embarrassing really. I'm embarrassed for the workingmen. I just come when I'm bored.

Lawrence jimmied the latch on a wooden locker marked DEAD BOLTS. Inside there were tiny drawers for machine parts. Here Lawrence had stuffed his belongings: some jeans, T-shirts, socks, a plastic stunted toothbrush.

I don't believe you!

He tossed her a pair of blue corduroys. Lily held them up and felt a wash of misery; her *hand* would barely fit in these.

They'll stretch. Don't worry. They'll be nice on you. He was smiling at her. And then he was stripping. Taking off his pants and underpants, which were wet with shandy beer, and he was standing before her with his stick pointing out like they were playing in the woods behind the old house. She laughed and shook at the same time.

Get out of that wet thing, he said in a granny voice. Come on now, dear heart. Hurry up. You'll catch your death.

Lily shrugged off her coat, then unhooked the clasps of her velvet overalls. She shimmied them down then tried to hide her legs. Her mother was shocked, shocked she'd said, by the state of Lily's thighs these days, and Lily could only guess that this was a universal revulsion.

Give me that. Lawrence reached forward.

I don't think so.

Come here. He stepped toward her, acting normal as if he were still dressed. What are you hiding back there? And he pulled the overalls just slightly away.

Don't! she cried, but he already was peeking down at her. He pushed the overalls back against her.

I see the problem, he said.

God, she said, and thought she would throw up, immediately, which was exactly what had happened the night her mother had been so persuasive about the state of her thighs. She'd thrown up. Said, Good night, Mom, and then puked about a minute later in her bathroom. Had a ring of red burst blood vessels, tiny ones, for about a week. What's wrong with your eyes? her mother had said, then forgot. Mrs. Veal didn't drop it though. Don't start with that nonsense, she said. You know what I'm talking about. None of that in this house.

You've got on Marks and Sparks panties, and the nasty nylon ones, too. Lawrence looked somber now, shook his head. I never would have suspected it. No wonder. We'll fix that in a hot minute. He was rummaging in his stolen locker again. Here you go. He tossed her a pair of black y-flaps. Catch!

Lily stooped to pick them up off the floor.

Okay, I'm turning around. Not watching. Counting to fifty and you'll get the dry undies on you. And she laughed to see his small flat fanny, hips tilting nonchalantly. One, twenty, forty-two, twelve.

It was during the counting, Lily successfully out of her panties and struggling to get the tight black briefs on, that there came a tap on the glass. Minks the librarian's long index fingernail, *rat-a-tat-tat*. What's this? he said, eyes averted and staring at the same time. Think you can do what you like in the tunnel, any time day or night. Think again, laddie. The big feck is already on his way. I called him, not taking this one on. Minks tapped the glass again, as a signature.

Lawrence was at the door, saying, Come on, Minks. We had a deal.

Not this deal, boy-o. Not on your life. I'd get that wee pecker squared away if I were you because his nibs sounded in a twist.

They both were dressed in their wet clothes again before Mr. Phipps and his astonished secretary arrived. She was meant to take Lily aside and get the story from a woman's perspective. Now, you do know what I mean by the word "molestation"? Lily nodded. And how about the word "rape"? Lily nodded again. I know those words, she said. We're all clear here, Mr. Phipps, his secretary shouted. Going off to the nurse, now, sir.

A week later, Lily began classes at the Little Flower, a tiny international school for girls in South Kensington run by the Ursuline nuns. And she slept in the guest room every night, because she could no longer tolerate the sickly green lights off the army's courtyard. Only with the curtains drawn and the comforting dip in the mattress holding her body could she fall asleep, signaling to Lawrence through the shortcut back streets to his high bed at the Dorchester that she didn't blame him at all; she only missed him.

19

He'd just settled at the baccarat table at the Curzon House Club with drunken Oliver Cordier, the director of sales Paris when Kimpton came over and leaned in like a waiter, Sir.

Nick pulled back his chair, waving to Oliver to continue without him. Kimpton said, Mr. Lewis has asked me to convey a message. But?

Kimpton handed Nick a folded piece of paper and bowed very slightly.

Nick opened the embossed ivory sheet and read: Kiddo, going back tomorrow. Nothing more for me here. Come say good-bye.

Nick looked to Kimpton as if he could explain, but he wore the same mask as when he was dealing blackjack. Okay, thanks, said Nick and shoved the note in his pocket.

They played until about midnight, Nick on a very short but elegant streak, then Nick poured Oliver into a taxi and walked over to the apartment where Harry was crashing. Some Hong Kong–based friend of Lionel's with a pied-a-terre tucked away in Shepherd Market. Nick had been once before when the lift was out of service and Harry was too drunk to climb the stairs alone. Mostly he remembered the lit vitrines, recessed glass-fronted shelves with tiny pre-Columbian figures that in the eerie bluish lighting seemed to haunt the place. Other than that, several white sofas and in the only bedroom a vast bed raised on a mirrored plinth with a black fur spread.

He rang the buzzer and waited for Harry, but it was Vivienne who answered. She opened the door wide and stepped back in a pose. He could see she was very high by the way she held her head, an exaggerated backward tilt, eyes twinkling and fixed.

Hello, hello.

Surprised? she said and pushed her slim hips against his as she kissed one cheek then the other. He put his hand to her face. Don't you look—

Marvelous?

Yes, he said. But she didn't. She looked rickety and gray-faced. She'd cut some jagged new bangs close to the hairline. Tight black curls now fell just to her chin. He'd been putting her off and lately she'd stopped calling.

Maybe you just miss me. She twirled around as if to show him a new outfit. He'd seen it before. A pale-blue knit dress, with black lace stockings and a black velvet choker. Her boots made them nearly the same height. She leaned in to put her nose against his, which took more coordination than she had available. Lover, she whispered and he kissed her with some tenderness. She was a good kid. He'd been stupid here.

She tried to draw him inside the foyer and closer to her. Wait, he said. How did you get here?

Not exactly off the map.

It's kind of you to give Harry a send-off.

She shrugged, eyes closed. He's not so bad.

Ah, well, Nick smiled. Let's head up.

All in good time, she said. Then did what she always did and pressed a hand to his dick and let the satisfaction of the result come into her face. Hello, hello to you, and she pulled him to an alcove on the other side of the lift. A place where people stowed tied bags of trash until morning. He could smell potato as she lifted the hem of her dress and yanked down the lace tights. Wait a minute, he said.

Don't think so, and she pressed her back into the wall and spread her legs wide. A black lace hammock stretched out at her knees.

He put his hand between her legs and held still, as if covering her up, slowing her down, shielding her from something.

What are you doing?

Nothing.

She looked confused. Her eyes, so dilated the blue was erased, filled with a sudden sorrow.

Harry shouted down from the fourth floor. What the hell's happening down there? Vivienne, did you swallow him?

When they reached the top landing Harry stood in the doorway to the flat. About time, Nicky. Thought we would die here waiting for you. He nodded toward Vivienne. The party that is.

But there wasn't much of a party. A slender man with a puff of pink hair and kohl under his eyes bent over a low Moroccan table where a backgammon board was midgame. He sorted out a variety of pills in a blue dish then carefully placed two on his tongue, eyes closed, chased by what looked like a gin and tonic. Yeah, we got very antsy here waiting for you, so we're playing games to pass the time. This is Chandler Bader. Chandler, Chandler man, open your eyes.

The man stood, carefully, as if assessing each separate limb for stability. This was almost comic and Nick smiled.

Vivienne's killing us here with her moves, said Harry.

That's right. I'm crushed. Chandler patted his sleeve as if to indicate where all his resources had once been kept. Yeah, only Harry here's keeping me alive.

Least I can do, said Harry, before the Vivienne cat takes you down completely. He looked at her thighs, the twist of black lace now askew. He let his eyes trail up her body, land on her small visible nipples floating in and out of the deep loose neckline. He took a slow inhale as though standing in a field of flowers and smiled. But Nick knew this was all a show. Vivienne was far from Harry's interests. He wasn't sure why she was here at all, except to irritate him. He should have told Harry he'd moved on, but Harry probably knew that.

Apparently Vivienne was winning. I've got them both on their hind legs. So to speak. Yeah, we're on to objects now, she said.

Objects?

Right, but not talking any bodies, said Chandler, not that kind of object. There's been a little bit of a drought here on that level. Except darling Vivienne, of course, but she was waiting for you, mate. Yeah. So we're betting stuff. Cash is boring. Chandler closed his eyes again and tilted down into the sofa as if knocked sideways by boredom and Nick laughed. He was that far gone.

I'd like to crack the glass on that shit, said Harry, pointing to the lit vitrines. There's some cute bits of gemstone, did you know that, Nick? Take a look. But then, I'd have no place to stay when I come back.

Nick nodded. This was a mild threat. Don't think you're done with me.

I don't like little rocks, said Chandler. Forget it. Vivienne here bet a dog. Some kind of corgi named Eli. Can you see it?

You bet your dog?

Not mine. My mother's.

She won, she won. Don't get all perturbed, mate, said Chandler. Anyway, I'm not sure I really wanted a dog. Yeah, she won my guitar, a really good handmade satin jacket, and also a little diversion with my drummer, which will be a snap to arrange.

What happened to the no-bodies rule?

Not really, Nick, said Vivienne. The diversion's just a laugh.

She sat knock-kneed across from Chandler on the edge of another white sofa and bent close to the doubling cube as if to reorient herself to the game in progress. There was a banked fire going. Nick realized that Harry had filled the grate with American charcoal briquettes. What, are you crazy?

A little atmosphere, Harry said. So Vivienne here. Hidden talents, kiddo.

Nick had never seen her play before. She smiled up and said, I'm really, really excellent, Nicky. Watch me.

He sat next to her and the sink of the sofa, the scent of charcoal, the muffled knock of the rolling dice on felt, all relaxed something as if he'd been walking for miles. He took a long swallow of the vodka Harry handed him, eyes closed. It tasted like toothpaste. What is this shit?

Peppermint, right? My house specialty.

Give me something human.

Name it.

But Nick didn't know what he wanted, maybe just sleep. Chandler was shaking the cup hard. You've put a hex on these things—he rolled—hell! I knew it.

Vivienne nodded, pleased, as Chandler made awkward use of a bad roll. He was exposed on two points. An easy triumph, she won his gold-studded belt.

Strip backgammon? Nick asked.

Nah, like I said we got sick of money. He slid the thing out of the loops and Vivienne slung it over her shoulder like a bullet belt.

What's next. See, we're doing categories. It's all very organized.

Yeah, we already did furniture and Vivienne here won the sofa you're sitting on.

Comfy, right?

Nick nodded. They won't welcome you back, Harry.

Listen to the schoolmarm.

Let's do boats, said Vivienne, clapping her hands.

Fine by me, Chandler said. Catamaran?

Vivienne purred, Stake me, Harry?

No boats, he tapped his pockets. What about you, Nicky. You must have a boat or two stashed away.

He did. Nick opened his eyes long enough to say, Boston Whaler. But his tongue was sticking to the roof of his mouth and he tried again.

Perfect! said Vivienne and kissed his hand. Nick sat up for a minute and saw Chandler keeping a vigil on Vivienne's neckline as if waiting for her breast to tumble out of the vee, always a drama. Chandler tracked the movement of her nipples until he took a sip of his drink and that erased the interest. Who goes first? Come on.

Here, Nicky. The glass of champagne in Harry's hand looked refreshing and he took it and drank it down. The coolness woke him up a bit.

You sure about boats, now. What about jewelry? Harry said.

Love it, said Vivienne. She raised her wrist and flashed a slim diamond bangle. In a burst of guilt, Nick had given it to her. She grinned and he reached over and touched her wrist. The strange claw marks were healing mostly well. Vague white and pink lines in the skin made an awkward star now visible only in good light. Right after Thanksgiving he'd tried to end things. They were eating scrambled eggs in her bedsit and she'd scraped at her wrist so savagely with a fork he had to wake up Cecil Bathrick in the middle of the night so he could stitch her up. Nick bought her the bracelet and said it was a bandage and then stopped returning her calls.

Whatcha got, baby, said Harry, and Chandler looked flummoxed. Don't sweat. Here you go. Harry jimmied a gold jewel band, Cartier, off a thick wrist. Nick knew this came from Lionel. A joke, but a serious one. If he lost it, Harry would probably have to steal it back. By the time the doubling cube had been turned twice, Nick was lying back into the deep cushions, then he tipped over sideways and wrapped himself around the back of Vivienne's hips. The charcoal smelled delicious and he dreamed of a sweet summer beach day, the waves high and crashing around him, but he could still stand.

Sometime late in the night the category went to houses. Chandler wrote up a note on crumpled card for a mews house in

Kensington. Free and clear, he said. And sweet as a candy ass. Vivienne's bedsit wouldn't fly, and Harry couldn't put up the Shepherd Market flat as much as he wanted to. Nick woke up just long enough to stake her. In the end he had to offer New Jersey in a scribble on Chandler's folded card because, as Harry pointed out, Grosvenor Square was only a ninety-nine-year lease. Nick dozed off again before Vivienne could kiss him with gratitude. And a little while later, for the first time all night, Chandler found his luck.

The next day Tania was floating on the tops of her toes; Nick could feel her fluttery presence in the doorway to his office and wanted to hurl something. Walk like a human, he said. He needed something for his head, which was remarkably bad. It was already midafternoon and he'd just arrived, barely able to walk here. Maybe Harry had slipped something in his drink. Not beyond him in the least. If only he could figure out the trick to undo it. Maybe not coffee.

What is it, Tania?

A Mr. Richard Howe to see you, sir.

Who?

Richard Howe, of Benson, Howe, and Drury, sir.

What's it about? Nick looked up from his useless coffee and waited for some recognition. He didn't know the name.

He said he's here to organize a title transfer? Mr. Howe estimates approximately twenty minutes initially, provided the documents are readily available. Would you like me to find something for you?

Nick stared for a minute. Oh Christ, he finally said. No, get Mr. Lewis on the line.

Very good.

A minute later, he picked up the phone. Harry, he said, laughing.

I got two minutes, Harry said. More like seconds. The driver here is breaking my luggage. *The handle's right there for godsakes. Just use it.* I'm gonna miss my plane fucking with these guys.

Richard Howe.

Who? *No! The trunk goes freight.* You got to watch every minute here. Every minute.

Harry, who's this lawyer waiting in my office? Howe.

Ask Lionel. I never heard of the guy before.

I don't get it. Nick could feel his chest begin to tighten. Lionel's advising you on title transfers? For what? Chandler didn't know what the dice were for.

Well, Chandler, idiot that he is, won the last round. Did you doze off? I thought you were just being peaceful. You left on your own steam, believe me. Lionel is just helping out. *Put the fucking briefcase down, you moron.*

Lionel's helping Chandler?

You don't want to screw around with this, Nicky. You don't need me to tell you that. Just follow the dots. And who's to say Lionel won't be open to, I don't know, a trade or something. Talk to him. You know he's just trying to get your attention. Ciao, baby. Love to the wifey.

Tania was back in the doorway, waiting for direction. Nick stared at her. This was all very stupid, a stunt. Richard Howe was probably a waiter from Mimmo's in a rented suit. But why would Lionel go after the house? Even as a feint. An easy puzzle to solve. Take what Jean loves most and watch Nick jump. That Clyde had put the house in Nick's name had been a mistake. You're the one pouring in the cash to fix it up Clyde had said. Sounded rational, but very unlike Clyde. Though what wouldn't Nick give to Jean. Anything that was his she could have and more and Clyde knew that. The only thing Clyde had ever liked about him.

Yeah, Nick said to Tania. The file that has all the Jersey stuff, bring that. And maybe some ice water.

Right away.

He felt the the top of his desk. It was a good choice, a sleek pale wood. When it arrived from Italy, four workmen came with it from Milan just to see the screws properly tightened after shipping. It was simple but extraordinary and he could see these things; he could recognize this kind of beauty.

And call Lionel, he said.

Excuse me, sir?

Place a call to my brother, please. And tell Mr. Howe I'll be a few minutes.

Soon Tania was on the intercom. Connected, sir, she said, but it was Kitty who was on the line. Oh, Nicky, we're *sleeping*. Junior howled like the house was on fire *all night long*.

She's psychic.

What's that, Nicky? She's gorgeous, even in tears, but we're all zonked. Lionel walked her up and down Third Avenue until four in the morning!

How are you, Kitty? Isn't your mother still with you?

Yes, but sometimes only Lionel can settle her. Funny, right? I don't know if I can wake him. He just fell asleep.

But she tried and in a few minutes Lionel was on the other end sounding like he'd swallowed knives. Christ, he said.

Who's Richard Howe?

It's still dark here. You ever think—

It's ten o'clock. What's the game here, Lionel? You think I'm going to sign over the house? That's ridiculous.

I'm not the ridiculous one here. Who's staking a stoned-out twat?

Nick smoothed out the wood on the desktop and sighed, changed his tone. It's Jean's house, and Lily's.

Yeah, well. That's very hard.

Just tell me what you want. Why all this crap with Harry. Why do all this. It's stupid.

I don't want anything. What could I possibly want from you. Anyway, nothing you couldn't do in a coma. Just come and talk to me.

I don't think so.

Fine. Walk away. But I mean from all of it.

Nick closed his eyes. It felt like his brain was swelling inside his skull. Harry had certainly put some garbage in his drink.

Sign the note, said Lionel. Right now.

That's not friendly.

Friendly? I tell you what's friendly. Book a flight. Come be godfather to Junior like you promised. So she can finally be fucking baptized. Maybe then she'll stop screaming through the night.

Nick sighed.

Mrs. Ivy will make her famous sour cream coffee cake. It's worth the trip.

Nick didn't answer.

And I'll tell Mr. Howe I've decided to postpone.

Postpone? You hate the Jersey Shore.

Mrs. Ivy spent a lot of happy times there in her youth. Belmar? Spring Lake? I don't know. This is the stuff she tells Junior in the middle of the night. It's like she's got a vision or something.

Nick could picture the house as he'd first seen it, right after the wedding, a stinking dump and Jean's deep, surprising joy. The years she'd spent and all she'd done for the one place she'd deemed essential. London was only a holding pattern; she ached to go back. No, there would be no fresh starts on this. He knew that.

Nick called out to Tania. Will you put Mr. Howe on the telephone with Lionel?

Good boy, said Lionel. Nick put down the receiver.

20

They were counting the minutes until Christmas vacation at the Little Flower and no one cared about meeting a new girl. By her third or fourth day, Lily came home and told her mother it was for backward girls, just like the Clury School, for kids with real problems.

Her mother looked at her for a long time. What can I tell you, Lily.

Lily understood she had humiliated her mother. No amount of explaining about spilled shandies and the need for dry clothes that didn't stink of beer could get through. No one believed her. She scarcely believed herself anymore.

I *can* tell you this much, said her mother. Your father has just about given up on you. She was sitting, as usual, with her legs tucked up beneath her robe, in the near dark, sipping Scotch and smoking, thinking. She didn't have to spell out how ashamed she was of Lily. And Lily's father was apparently beyond shame.

So now she was stuck with twelve silent girls in a cinderblock classroom and an ancient teacher, Sister Ann. The nuns, she was told, lived behind the carved wooden enclosures in the mansion and the boarding students lived in cinder-block cubes just like the schoolroom. She could only go to the convent for chapel and for Friday lunch in the stone dining room. So Lily was surprised to be summoned into the Mother Clarence's study at the end of her first full week.

The convent had once been a Guinness mansion. One of the minor Guinesses, said Emma Hocking. Derek Voose had suggested the Little Flower because a client, Paula Clark, had a daughter there. If that silly cow is for it, began Emma. Then she amended, I'm sure you'll love it, darling heart.

Lily found Mother Clarence's office—a pretty flower-filled sitting room on the second floor—a place for an ideal Victorian mother to rest after tending to all the loved ones. Mother Clarence was standing by the window, contemplating an empty bowl on an elaborate stand.

I'm not sure why we keep it here, she said as Lily entered the room. We never put anything in it. She lifted it up. We've been in this house for twenty years. It was right here when I arrived.

Lily tried to think of a response. I like the blue.

Yes, I do, too. A true lapis lazuli. I like all the colors of this house, even in their faded versions. Hold this. Beware, it's heavy.

She offered the bowl so quickly, Lily had to step forward, tripping a little in her oversized wingtips to catch it.

Extra heavy, said Lily.

It's the lead. Makes it very dense. So, you've been showing yourself to young men I understand.

No, said Lily. The bowl straining her arms. No, Sister, I wasn't. I was changing out of wet overalls because I'd spilled a beer, a shandy, in my lap.

And you spilled it on your friend as well? How old are you? I think thirteen. Your beer?

Mostly lemonade.

I see. I'll take that.

Lily handed back the big lapis bowl; her arms ached with the holding of it.

Maybe we'll let this be, said Mother Clarence. Maybe we'll let it be like the bowl, here, always with us, and heavy, and not clear in its purpose, but not without its beauty. Its grace. Mother Clarence settled the bowl on the filigree stand. She turned back to Lily and didn't smile but somehow rearranged her somber features in a happier mode. Good day, Lily. Someone will show you back to the classroom.

Lily stayed still, confused.

Good-bye, now, dear. That door. She pointed to a high mahogany door different from the one Lily had entered.

Outside, Lily stood blinking on a narrow dark landing of a stairway. A girl with a sharp center part to her blond hair sat on the step opposite chewing on her thumbnail. Ha, there you are, she said. Did she make you hold the bowl?

Lily laughed, but she didn't say yes. Then she started to cry.

Come on, you'll live. The girl gave her a light shove on the arm. Come on. Name's Beven. I'll show you something I dare you to pick up and hold.

She led Lily down the back stairs and through a corridor to a receded wood paneled alcove. You're not going to believe this, said Beven. You're not a screamer, are you?

They'd come into the most cloistered part of the house; Lily could tell by the smell—mildew and incense and vinegar. Everything was dim, only squiggles of light where the heavy purple curtains drew apart. Here. Total, total silence now, said Beven. Don't even breathe. She leaned into a door and opened the knob by tiny degrees and pushed it open slowly to a crack and placed one eye there. Clear, she said. And let the door open wide. Crazy, right?

An old nun was stretched on a table surrounded by thick white lit candles and one small stubby one flickering in front of a gruesome picture of a bleeding Sacred Heart, just beyond her head. The room stank like manure.

Don't gag, said Beven. Use your sleeve. She pulled the cuff of her cardigan over her nose. Take a look.

Lily came closer.

It's Sister Bernadette, the typing teacher, keeled over in class last Friday. She died yesterday while they were all eating lunch. They couldn't get her mouth closed for hours! Had to use a spoon or something.

But why is she here?

They always do this. Homemade undertaking, more religious, maybe?

The smell is horrible, Lily said through her sleeve.

Well, they're not experts. Watch this.

Beven took hold of Sister Bernadette's hand. You can still move it a little. Help me out. Hold this one. She motioned Lily into place. The feeling of the hand was like chilled paper and very light. Lily thought it would weigh a lot more, the way the bowl had. Beven said, I just want to make the rosary into a cat's cradle. I think we can do it really fast. Lily held the hand still, while Beven tangled the rosary into knots around the fingers. Then she led Lily out a different way and took her to her classroom door. What are you waiting for? A kiss? she said. Go in!

* * *

That night, Lily couldn't settle into sleep. Her back felt knobby against the sheet, as if each bone were slightly on fire. She might be getting a flu. She finally slipped out of her own bed and wandered out of the back suite. She began down the long corridor to the front of the apartment, but when she reached the marble floor, she could hear her mother, the click of ice. She wanted to tell her about Beven and Sister Bernadette—did they do that at St. Tom's, too?—but not about the rosary that ended up a thick ball in fingers stiffer than Beven had guessed.

Her mother coughed in a certain way and Lily knew she wasn't welcome. She backtracked past her bathroom and curved into the guest room, as usual. She left the lace bedspread on—something her mother was proud of, an antique lace, soaked in tea to get just the right color—then slipped into the scented sheets and felt the comfort of this bed. As long as she kept the door closed as if the room were at the ready, she was fine. She'd wake up with the soldiers' garbage cans at dawn and find her own bed again, long before Mrs. Veal was in and making trouble.

The sheets soothed her hot back, and she thought of Lawrence and wondered whether he'd gotten her message. She'd called the Dorchester when she got home from school and when his room phone rang his mother answered. How is Lawrence? she tried.

Well, fine, darling. Shipshape, said Mrs. Weatherfield. Are you his new friend?

No, the same friend that you met down in the lobby last month? We discussed art?

Of course, dear heart. I'll tell Lawrence you called. Kelly, is it?

Lily.

Lily, yes, yes, pardon me. All right. Ciao!

Block of cheese, Lawrence had said, but she sounded quite pleasant to Lily. Her voice low in her throat as if she'd been caught singing. Just listening to her would make an average person guess that she was very happy. Lily wondered what her own voice told people.

She was in a half sleep dreaming of Lawrence by the ocean singing to her grandmother in Swedish, and Lily was wading in the water, her legs sandy, the ease of the ocean filling her body, wave rocking, when she woke up to find her father hovering uncertain in the doorway.

Daddy?

What are you doing in here? he said, as if he were speaking not to Lily but to a room of intruders. What's all this crap? He was swaying now into the room, his face lit green by the well lights, a halo of hall light behind him. Who's in here?

Daddy, it's me.

Who put all this garbage in here?

Lily sat up, and now she was ruining the bed. She looked around and it was true, the floor was littered with all her stuff; she thought somehow she'd cleared some of it away. Her father kicked at a pile, a pink bra flipped off the end of his shoe and fell back to the ground; he kicked at the bed. Get up!

What's wrong, Daddy? Though she already knew what was wrong. Get up! Go to your room. You have three for godsake. Not enough for you?

She was up now, wearing an old nightie, something with ducks on it. Stupid and comforting and too small across the chest where her new bosom, tiny buttons of ache, pushed out. She tried to slink past her father but he was blocking the door, and when he kicked her, it was with the same intent as kicking the bra, clearing a mess, making a gesture about the big mess, then he swung wide with his fist, which seemed slow and stupid but hit the side of her head. Oh, she cried and fell backward away from the door, and then he was punching at her shoulders and arms then her chest, her small left breast, and that's what sent her to the ceiling. She'd heard about this, about people floating above their bodies but how surprising to be doing it herself. She hovered in a corner just above where her father had backed her against a wall. He couldn't stop punching at her, though now the punches were light when they landed and often missed, and then just like Lily her mother was floating too. Her mother floated into the doorway and said, Nick? What's happening?

Then her mother floated away and Lily heard the door to the master suite close softy. As if her ears were supersonic and placed right next to her mother's door lock, she heard the quiet *click*. And her father heard the *click*, too. He stopped and wheeled out of the room with a roaring Fuck, and then a choked-off Jesus, Jesus. Then he knocked softly and their bedroom door opened then closed.

When Lily came down off the ceiling she stayed completely still for a long time, then she saw the bib of her blue velvet overalls sticking out from a pile of spent clothes. She yanked them on over her nightie, tied on her wingtips; she couldn't see any socks. In the front foyer her maxicoat lay on the carved bench where it wasn't ever supposed to be, probably her father's first clue to the mayhem she'd caused. Her key was usually in her pocket, but not now; it didn't matter. She let herself out and downstairs she went out the iron and glass door and left it unlocked for all the robbers in London to find. The street smelled like cats. The air was plastic feeling and rubbed her face in an ugly way. She brushed her hands along her cheeks to clear the air and felt the rawness and stopped. All along the shortcut down South Audley the first garbage trucks were making a noise like gunfire, tossing the tins, as if the tidy doorman had never given a single instruction. Everything was slimy about the garbagemen's faces in the lamplight; their eyes were sunk like the devil's. At the Dorchester, the night doorman barely nodded and the elevator man called her Miss and wished her a pleasant sleep. When she knocked on Lawrence's door it was a long wait, and she kept thinking the maid with the hairnet would catch her first and pull her away. But finally the door opened, Lawrence in pajamas with rocket ships like a baby's. Oh, Lily, he said. Are you making bad choices again? And then he let her in and made room under his green satin eiderdown once she'd peeled away the stinking dirty overalls. She lay on her side, back to his front. He spidered one hand toward her breast. But she pulled it in faster, and pressed it down and felt the soreness and shock pour out into his palm.

21

Jean heard a knocking, a cleat against the dock, or maybe something down by the water honking, a goose lost from its mates. She'd left the French door open all night long and now the room felt bone cold and she'd piled all the bedding on top of her, pulled it close to her body. She listened, snuggled down for the knock of cleats, knock of the cleats, echoing out across the water, but then she was awake and it was something else banging softly and her heart sank. She was alone in her London bed, the light from the armory filtering through her ecru curtains, a thudding, banging sound came through the wall. And now she was fully awake and switched on the lamp and rubbed her head. All along the skin of her inner forearm the crumpled sheets had made a complicated impression, like a wing. When Cubbie was small and just barely talking she told him once that a bird had come along and left an impression on her cheek. She'd fallen asleep on a beach towel, strange she'd been that tired, and Louisa had them swimming in the baby pool. He came tottering back just as she was straightening herself out, patting her cheek with the puff of a small compact of powder. He stroked where the towel had left its swirl, frowning as though she were injured and in danger, and she told him it was only the tip of a wing brushed by, or maybe the gill of a fish? And Cubbie said, Me, Mama, his wet salty palm stroking her cheek. She laughed and hugged him close, wet and covered now with blown sand. Let Louisa rinse you off now. Where's your sister? But Cubbie was more interested in her cheek than getting ready to go home. How fortunate she'd been to have this little boy standing sandy and wet stroking her cheek on a sunny windy beach day. Louisa somewhere up by the cabanas wrestling Lily into a dry pair of shorts, and he'd escaped and found her. The thudding was louder now, and immediate. Lily was awake and doing something dopey. She wasn't sure she even wanted to know.

Just like that Jean remembered Claudia and laughed. Cubbie and his Claudia, his true love starting in nursery school. Lily, so superior, already in kindergarten, where she said the boys had desks and the girls lily pods, where the boys wore white coats like doctors when they painted and the girls smocks like aprons. Cubbie said in his school, at Happy Hours, Claudia was boss. And Lily didn't believe him. Claudia can't be the boss, she said. And Cubbie said, But Mommy is. And Lily, stumped—because it was true, Daddy wasn't home enough to be boss, only on weekends—threw a box of crayons at the wall, making a smear of waxy color that took Louisa a week to clean. Lily got a spanking, and a daylight bedtime. It occurred to Jean only after everyone was asleep that Lily's crayons had gone straight at the wall, not to her brother, that Lily never hurt Cubbie in any way; he'd just frustrated her peculiar world order, and she couldn't set him straight. Another bang against the wall. What was she setting straight now? And why was she in the guest room again? They'd talked about this. Her wandering in there whenever she felt like it and leaving a big mess.

She was weary of the daily wrestling with Lily and she couldn't get Nick's attention. Even the disaster at the Working Men's College had failed to grab his notice. Lily pinned to a wall in a basement clubroom by a boy exposed. She was astonished. But Nick only laughed. He's fifteen for godsakes; it's a miracle his pants are ever on. Jean was mystified by this response. What about Lily? But she'd already lost his attention. He had a meeting; he had Billy Byron back in London by the end of the week. Would she be on standby? Billy hated the wives, famously, wouldn't tolerate them except in very controlled circumstances. So far, Nick had no example of the circumstances.

But by chance, Billy Byron had spotted Jean in Harrods lingering at the holiday gift package display and thought she was the pinnacle of something or other. There she is, he'd shouted. Our target. That's who we're aiming for. She's it! Nick looked around, across the vaulted hall that comprised just one part of cosmetics at Harrods. There was Jean taking up a small shopping bag. Her camel coat tied snug, her tall bronze-colored boots, lacy brown stockings. Her hair long and streaky down her slender back. Nothing fake there, just the look we want right now. What are we calling her? asked Billy Byron. Irving, what the fuck are we calling her? You remember.

We can call her Jean Devlin, said Nick, laughing, waving to catch her attention. She's my wife.

Billy looked at him as if he might spit. Irving suppressed a laugh. Not a chance, said Billy.

Nick was confused for a moment. You don't want to meet her?

No, no, thank you, Nick. Irving, get me out of here. Chop-chop. I don't know what we're doing here anyway. Let's go. Right now. Nick, we'll see you later. And Billy was hustling out through the fragrances, Irving straining to catch up. Even so, later on over dinner, Billy leaned into Nick's shoulder and said, Maybe some other time I could get a look at that type again. Nick took a breath. Sure, he said. Then Billy was leaning in the other direction again. So, Jean was on hold for Billy's arrival this weekend, just in case. Who knows, said Nick. Maybe he just wants a restaging of you looking at lipstick.

It's a little crazy, said Jean. She was talking into his back. Isn't it? Though she felt flattered and wondered what to wear for her encore. He's a little nuts, she'd said. But Nick was already breathing the rattling way he did in London, wheezy snores, already deep asleep.

But now where had he gone? And when? His clothes were missing from the chair so he must be out again. More than once in the last few weeks she'd been awakened by an apologetic assistant manager to come to Annabel's or the Curzon House Club or a strange dive in Soho. She half expected the phone to ring, then another soft bang on the wall.

Lily was wrecking the guest room again and that was just intolerable. Jean felt a surge of rage, too familiar these days, and struggled up. She found her robe, her hands so shaky with fury she couldn't tie it. She leaned into the mirror over her dresser until she could bring her face into focus. Just breathe, she said out loud. Just breathe.

Then she opened the door that led to the back corridor and to the guest room. There was Nick standing in the middle of all of Lily's trash. And Lily in the far corner, eyes shut, arms crossed over her chest, like she was acting in a play. Nick? Jean said, but he didn't answer, just kept staring, red-faced, at all the junk on the floor. Fine, she said. Let him take over for once. She slipped back down the hall and quietly closed her door.

The next morning Jean stood at a front window, looking out on the forlorn winter square, sipping Mrs. Veal's appalling coffee. She insisted on having it ready when Jean woke up. Jean was imagining sneaking over to the Europa and having just one decent cup, when she spotted Lily slowly walking down the block, head lowered, shuffling along, bare feet in untied wing tips. Her nightgown was under her unbuttoned coat. Soon she'd be swanning through the lobby. Nearly ten on a Saturday morning, it would be busy. Jean put down her cup and went to meet Lily at the door.

You've really gone the limit, she said as Lily took off her coat. Then Jean took a step back. Lily, you smell! What in the world?

Something had stained the lower part of the nightie and Lily stank like something on a farm, fetid and grassy.

Are you all right? Jean said, worried for a moment.

Lily smiled but strangely Jean thought; her eyes looked a bit hollow.

You can't be doing drugs. You can't be that stupid.

No, no, I'm sorry. I just went to see a friend.

A friend.

Lily nodded.

What time was that.

Early, said Lily, and she looked down at her nightgown as if just realizing she was wearing it. I forgot my overalls, she said.

Jean shook her head. Put up her hands in surrender. I don't know, Lily. I just don't know.

It's okay, Mom.

It's not. And something in Lily's face, some hiding sly glance she barely caught made her want to slap her. Jean forced herself to take a step backward, awkwardly, like they were playing Simon Says. She had such a quick pain in her head, right behind the eyes.

What was all that with your father last night? she finally said.

Nothing.

Nothing, okay. Jean looked toward the drawing room as if she could reinstate herself at the window with the terrible coffee and erase all this.

I'm going to school today, she said, not looking Lily in the eye. Mother Clarence wants to see me.

Lily nodded.

Any clues about why?

No, said Lily. And she must have moved because Jean got a strong whiff of the rotting grass odor she'd smelled before.

Take a bath, Lily. Now.

She was at Selfridges, in the food hall paying a fortune for frozen crab claws—she'd have something nice made on the long shot that Nick brought Billy Byron over for a drink—when Jean remembered Ruby cracking ice trays into the kitchen sink in the middle of the night. So loud she'd been woken up, but it didn't make sense. Ruby in her bathrobe, something dark pink that Jean never liked the smell of, a wisp of foul hair lotion and hand cream. She remembered the smell like Ruby was standing right next to her. When Ruby wore her bathrobe Jean always stepped away to prevent a stray thread from touching her.

Ruby lived off the kitchen then, when Jean was small, before Clyde found her a house among his investments in Red Bank. Ruby wasn't even trying to be quiet. She was crashing every ice tray in the house into the sink and then loading the cubes into a towel, spilling them all over the floor, making a mess. And she was sniffling. She gathered the wet towel up and startled when she saw Jean. Oh Jeanie, now you get yourself back into bed, quiet as a mouse. But Jean didn't know why she had to be quiet when Ruby was making such a racket. Come now, Jeanie, quick as a bunny. And Jean neither bunny nor mouse was offended. Ruby was carrying the towel of ice out toward the front hall and into the dining room where Doris sat still and bent over in a side chair. The front door was wide open even though it was wintertime. Come now, little darling, Ruby whispered, as if Doris were a child. And Doris let Ruby stroke back her hair from her forehead, which was already turning green with a fresh bruise. Her hands wrapped her belly and were strafed on the knuckles. Ruby knelt down and took a washcloth she'd stuck into her bathrobe pocket and took some ice and dabbed along Doris's forehead a bit, and then her hands. Please, said Doris. Oh god. It seemed her stomach was the problem. Hold this close to you, said Ruby. Hug it in tight it will numb everything. Then she put the towel and all its ice carefully onto Doris's lap holding it there so it wouldn't slip away. Soaking, said Doris, attempting a laugh. Soaking wet. Hold it close, said Ruby. Tuck into it now. That's better, said Ruby and for a long time Doris didn't speak. That's better, said Ruby again and this time Doris lifted her head and then smiled just slightly and that's when Clyde came back in the front door and shut it and no one moved. He looked at them all as if they were some unexplained mess in the pristine dining room. Then he climbed the stair and they all heard his own door slam. He must be very upset not to even see her Jean thought.

Jean climbed the stair after him and knocked hard on his door. Daddy? Daddy? Are you all right? But she didn't receive an answer. She went to her own room and cried herself to sleep. What could be so wrong that her father wouldn't see her or answer her. She felt if she had the power Doris and Ruby would be gone when she woke up and she and Daddy could be so happy again, like before. When Doris made a new room for herself—Oh, she said to Jean, I just miss my girlhood room—Jean said to her father, We can find our own house now? But he wasn't listening to her. She remembers that whole year, the year that Doris went back to her childhood room when it was so hard to get her father's attention. And then one day—she remembers this with so much joy, a shot of it like a cool glass laid on her arm on a hot day—in the early summertime, he got used to it. She waved down a taxi and sat in the back with her precious frozen crab. She'd been summoned by the head of Lily's new school. Mother Clarence was expecting her at two. Jean adjusted her skirt, something foraged out of her old clothes from Jersey. A tweed skirt, a button-down cashmere cardigan, a pair of sheer stockings. Her hair in a French twist. Nick would smile to see her. She wished he could see her, because then he'd know how difficult things had become. Just looking at her. She checked her lipstick, paid the driver, and entered through the ponderous front door. All red brick and beveled glass. An eyesore. In the front foyer a short wide stairway led to a window depicting a volcano erupting in colored glass. Light bounced and wriggled in the multiple panes giving the illusion of quick-moving lava. It reminded her of Lionel and his silly skylight. She wished he were looking at this with her; they'd have a good laugh.

Mrs. Devlin? A small slender nun walked toward her with movement so silent she'd completely missed the approach.

Yes, I'm Jean Devlin.

Yes, of course, this way. Jean followed her up the stair to a parlor off the first landing. Funny how these rooms were all the same, down to the bowls on pedestals. She'd been called to a place much like this one for staying out past curfew at Rosemont. Mother Clarence invited Jean to take a seat on the horsehair settee and Jean crossed her legs at the ankle; she saw a glimmer of her shape reflected in the window glass across the room, and thought Nick really would love this performance.

Mrs. Devlin, I won't waste your valuable time. Mother Clarence adjusted a small yellow index card on her ship of a desk, as if cuing herself for the conversation, then she fixed her light blue eyes on Jean. Your Lily seems to have something troubling her. Could you enlighten us?

Jean made a face of surprise. But Lily's just fine, said Jean. She's fine. She's chagrined about all the nonsense at the Working Men's College, embarrassed probably, but I think she fell into the wrong crowd and she's young for her grade. We might even keep her back, if you think it's a good idea.

Mother Clarence stepped out from behind her desk and took a small wooden chair and brought it close. She sat and smoothed the heavy black pleat in her habit. Perhaps it's too soon to say whether she needs to repeat the year. But I did think of something that might help in the meantime. We have a young nun here who seems to have a way with the girls. She's musical and has a delightful sense of humor. I think your Lily might enjoy her. Call it spiritual guidance, or maybe just a little extra support. It might help Lily to succeed here, or anywhere else, I imagine.

Jean felt her jaw go stiff; she could feel the prickle of sweat under the soft wool of her sweater, this preposterous woman. The smell of the cleaning fluid on the black habit. She looked at Mother Clarence's downy cheeks and checked the anger. Tried to because she didn't know what their other options were. There must be other options.

Is that what your index card says, Mother Clarence? More laughter and music for Lily?

Index card? Oh, no, she smiled. No, that's to remind me to shut off the lights when I leave. A note from the housekeeper. I've been running up the electric bill apparently.

Jean gave her a wan smile in return.

I had a twice-a-week visit to Sister Maureen in mind, nothing formal, just a chance to let Lily speak up a bit. She's so quiet!

Lily?

Yes, she is, said Mother Clarence. And now Jean heard just the kind of manufactured compassion she couldn't stand.

Isn't this all a bit progressive? Because we're looking for structure, discipline. She's just blown the free-form quite badly. I'm sorry, Mother Clarence. I don't see the benefit. But if you insist, I'll discuss it with my husband.

Mother Clarence tucked her chin down and watched Jean. Her eyes were not stern or angry, almost sleepy, oddly, as if Jean had tripped into her dream.

Insist, Mrs. Devlin? No, I don't insist. She wrapped her hand around her chin and watched Jean for another moment, then stood. She walked over to a huge and hideous blue bowl balanced on a wooden filigree pedestal. She tapped on the carved leg, made to look like a lettuce leaf perched atop a twisting vine. Amazing these legs can hold even a moth's weight really. Don't you think?

Jean could scarcely listen; she was already telling Nick they needed to find someplace new for Lily. Such a nuisance. But she knew he wouldn't agree. He was high on the nuns, generally. Look at you, he would say. Just look. But she had been a favorite and Lily, so far, was not.

Mother Clarence's gaze turned shrewd. Assessing and not kind. Jean adjusted her skirt.

Let's compromise, said Mother Clarence, her fingers now tracing the rim of the big blue bowl. To Jean, it seemed a sensual gesture, odd, even sexual. She was staring now.

Compromise?

Lily once a week with young Sister Maureen and we'll see if we don't have a star student on our hands by year's end.

Mother Clarence's hands were red-palmed and looked over-warm and Jean felt warm herself and suddenly weary of this wheedling woman. She closed her eyes and sighed. And for the first time since she'd arrived in London she missed Doris. She would call her the moment she got home. She'd been so remiss, so negligent; there was no excuse.

Mrs. Devlin? Are you all right, may I get you something. Some water?

Mother Clarence, why don't I phone you?

Yes, of course. In the meantime, I'll alert Sister Maureen.

Please don't.

I don't understand.

Please don't alert anyone. I'll speak to my husband and will call early next week. Thank you.

Certainly.

Jean stood, and then dizzy, sat back down again. Mother Clarence bent over her and took up her wrist. Jean pulled away as if scorched and leaned back against the itchy settee, nauseated. Oh lord, she said, and vomited all over her tweed skirt and her stockings. She might be sick again. Her shoulders shaking, she clasped her knees and waited.

Somehow she thought Mother Clarence would raise an alarm and she'd be rushed out, possibly to some cloistered infirmary, but instead she stood quiet, a damp washcloth retrieved from a water closet apparently nearby. Jean closed her eyes and tried to calm down her ragged breath. Mother Clarence knelt before her and touched her face with the warm cloth and Jean recoiled. Stop please, I'll— Let me. Please. She took the cloth and wiped her cheeks and mouth. Lipstick and crème blush smeared the overbleached white patch. I'm better, she said. Mother Clarence had a cruet of water; she poured and offered Jean a small glass. Thank you. Yes, she sipped, eyes closed. I think I may be pregnant, said Jean. That must be it. She looked up and thought she detected a headshake as if she were doubted. I am, she said, insisted.

My dear, said Mother Clarence. Let me refresh that, and she took the cloth from Jean's hand. Jean watched, hunched over, and felt a coiling fear, as if this nun had the power of life and death. She felt such a flash of hatred that she vomited all over her skirt again, twice more. This is what happens, she said. This is exactly what happens.

Let me call your doctor.

I don't need a doctor. Can't you see. This is normal. And she wretched once more, now gagging.

Mother Clarence picked up a phone on her desk and dialed a single number. Could you send Maureen, please.

Oh, for chrissake, said Jean. Are you crazy? I said no.

Mother Clarence was holding out a fresh washcloth. And Jean taking it felt the same frustration she'd always felt with Doris, trapped in someone else's stupid ideas, all of them wrong. A young nun came bustling in, fat as a ball with wide blue eyes on alert. Woo-hoo, she said. My goodness. Mrs. Devlin? May I take your hand? Jean stared a warning to back off, but Sister Maureen felt her pulse and soothed her wrist when she was done. We're all right. Nothing racing away from us.

Will you call my husband? Jean said. Her voice croaked; her throat hurt. Please? And she looked at the young round nun as if she would know whether or not Nick could be found, and something in her face let her know this was doubtful. Weeks at a time her father would go off leaving her alone with Doris and Ruby. Weeks, until he came strutting in the door calling for her first and foremost. First and foremost, Huey behind him lugging in whatever box of bribery he'd found in Kentucky or Louisiana. He knew marketing; he needed to go where ignorance prevailed and he could plant some fresh sense about the new way things were going to work now. He was an educator he explained. He was a flimflam man Ruby said once and Doris pretended not to hear her because then she'd have to fire her. Jean was popular with the nuns but never did do well in school. As wrong as Ruby was about her father, Jean got things confused and couldn't believe or listen to her teachers; she was always bored until she met Nick. So bored. And then she was sixteen, almost seventeen and Nick was like some kind of boy she'd never seen before. In her yearbook her friends were already calling her darling and writing about that fabulous man you've snared. She was glamorous and envied but Doris was talking about college.

College? Nick was already a junior at Villanova on the GI bill. What about Rosemont? Doris said. By Christmas, Nick and his older brother, Lionel, were secured for dinner on Christmas Day. They're orphans! cried Jean, when her father wanted to know why strangers would be at the table.

They were men, all grown up and Lionel had been in the European theater, fought in Italy and then Germany at the end. Or so he said. He smoked cigars and drew maps on Doris's damask tablecloth with his thumbnail and Clyde bent to watch the imaginary soldiers taking action. And Nick followed Jean out the back door, down through the cold starry night to the water's edge and sat on the iced bench and listened to the river creak and stretch. Their breath was fogged and sour with bourbon; his mouth pulled her and pulled her. She couldn't stop until his hand was inside her. They were freezing and she pushed into him until he settled her down. We're okay, he said. We're fine. And she took that as something permanent. There's time. He laughed, Lots of time. Lots of time. Then Doris was shouting out into the darkness they'd freeze to death, where are you two? And Nick was already answering, already linking a soothing laughing answer to her chronic distress. We're here. We're coming right in, he called but kept his hands still, one around her shoulder the other, curled around the top of one thigh, until she was buttoned up and calmed down. He pulled her closer. Okay?

Now this fat nun was holding her knees and asking the same thing. Mrs. Devlin? Let's lie you down. Okay?

No. She wouldn't do that. Just get her a taxi. But then her head was lying on a hard needlepoint square and she was flat on the mean settee her legs angled strangely, her bones hurting. If only Nick would come and get her, she'd be fine. Would they call? She heard herself whimpering. Yes, they had called and her housekeeper was already on the way. Not now, said Jean. Excuse me? said Sister Maureen. But Jean didn't explain.

As it turned out that long ago Christmas Lionel had lied to her father, and this was so easy to discover. Lionel never left New Jersey during the war. He was a junior officer in procurement stationed in Harrison. Only friends in very high places got him an honorary discharge. Why would he tell such a stupid lie Jean asked Nick after her father confronted her. Why? Lionel never tells a stupid lie, said Nick. And it was true. From that day on Lionel and Nick were welcome because Clyde felt he had the full compass of them. Jean felt bile rising now and she jutted upright. Gagged and closed her eyes. The fat nun was humming something in her ear, but she refused to listen.

I think I'm pregnant, Jean said, now watching. I think I am.

I think you're very upset, Mrs. Devlin.

Only some notion of dignity got her off the sofa and into a taxi without kicking the fat one out of sight. Late in the afternoon, she was able to see Dr. Cecil Bathrick on Harley Street, the man who came in the middle of the night with the epinephrine shots for Nick.

How's our champ? he asked. As if she and Nick were to be treated like imbeciles just because they were American.

You do know, he *must* ease off a bit, he said. I've told him so. More than once, I'm afraid. It can't go on.

Jean had heard this before, about Nick burning too brightly, which meant he experimented too much, tried too many new things, uppers, downers, but wasn't everyone these days?

Now Cecil Bathrick had done the exam and was drawing a tiny bit of blood. She looked away.

We'll have your answer in a day or two, he said. Sound all right? But by the look of things, I'd say the culprit here is a bit of turned beef. He dabbed at the needle prick with a cotton ball.

I'll ring you when we're certain, he said from the door. And she was left alone to straighten herself out. As promised, he called on Tuesday morning, very pleased to confirm the diagnosis: tummy bug.

22

Nick idled in the bar of the Connaught where Chandler was staying until midnight. Nick could buy him all the drinks he wanted, but Chandler couldn't recall a backgammon game, a man called Harry, or even a mews house in Kensington. Nah. I'm in Leeds when not in the nick, here. All about this album, see. All about the album. Till we get it right, I'm all crammed in.

Chandler was crammed in and Lionel had been crowing, happy the prodigal was returning to New York. Yesterday he'd telexed the office: *Rolling out the red carpet. Will sort all out. Nothing to worry about.* A lengthy telex for Lionel and unusual in its promise. Reading it Nick felt an almost exact mix of relief and disbelief. But when Jack drove Nick to Heathrow early this morning, he couldn't force himself out of the car and onto the plane. Circle round, Jack, he said.

Not easy in this mess, sir.

Do it anyway, please.

It was drizzling and the airport was jammed across every lane. They crawled for a while, edging away from the international departures.

All right. Forget about it, said Nick. Let's go back to the office. Just forget it.

You sure about that, sir. We can still make it.

Nick didn't answer and Jack found the exit lanes.

Around eight in the evening he got a call at the office from Vivienne Vimcreste. I'm in bloody New York. Where the hell are you?

You're talking to me.

I'm at the Sherry fucking Netherland.

How nice.

Prick.

Vivienne.

You fucking slay me, she began and when she wound up into a scream, he put down the phone, gently. He hadn't told her he was going to New York.

He stayed in the office late, half thinking Lionel would call, but knowing he wouldn't now. A telex piped in from Kitty around ten. *Oh Nicky, I'm so, so sorry*, she wrote. And he felt sick to read it. He made himself sit—he still had a job, for the moment—looking over broadsheets of potential ads, a campaign to unseat Mary Quant. Tania had stacked the large-scale prints on the side table. The girls, skinny legs planted too wide apart, purple-rimmed eyes, the lips white, skin pasty, hair too done and frozen-looking. Ugly, he thought. Just ugly. Tomorrow he'd map out a new concept. This played more lampoon than threat.

Four pointless drinks with Chandler, then home. He walked the diagonal across Grosvenor Square listening in the quick new soft snow to the echo of his footsteps. Only a single taxi chugged around the corner, then left the quiet behind. Days still left before Christmas but already places were closing: the Curzon House Club, Annabel's, even Les Ambassadeurs. A dread stuck in his chest, and his breath narrowed down; he dug his pocket for a whiffer, the device. He pumped the thing twice and waited for the calm and the release, then he walked out of the park to the curled ironwork door at number eighteen, smiled at Cyril who held it open wide; on Christmas week the doormen stayed late and Nick didn't know why. He tried his pocket once more for loose bills and handed them over without a word. It's too much, sir!

Merry Christmas. One and all.

Yes, sir.

They rode the tiny lift to the second landing. Quite a night, sir, said Cyril, eyes cast just above the snow-dusted shoulder of Nick's black overcoat. No wind, though.

Nick waited on the landing while Cyril wriggled in the key. There you go, sir. Good night.

He dropped his coat on the ornate bench just inside the door and took a breath, the dish detergent on the old marble slabs. He could see himself down the long foyer framed in all the gilt of the grand empire mirror. A slim tall line in a well-cut suit, Derek Voose's high-nipped waist, sharp shoulders to suggest ease not force, a blade. Nick had dark hair like his father, long behind the ears, and his mother's deep-set gray eyes, her long expressive hands. He watched himself, watched their quick movement straighten the hang of his jacket. First he caught the hem. It slipped away like water; he caught it again. When he pulled the turtleneck high against his throat, he felt the clutch again, but then it was gone. He dragged a light hand over the top of his head, smoothed away something invisible.

He walked the wide hall to the drawing room and in the mirror, meant for someone's castle, saw he was steady on his feet. He had a gait Jean liked to joke about. She could spot him she claimed, across a stadium, a concert hall, any lobby in the world, by the sure steps, long legs crossing with such light confidence. She always knew he'd arrived she said, even before she saw him, because others started to glance up, felt him moving in like a virus. He was solid enough—that's what he saw tonight—though the man at the Connaught poured with a heavy hand. He made his entrance, but she wasn't there.

The lamp still lit by the chair she favored had fooled him. He'd imagined her listening to every step but too pissed off to speak. There was a crush in the downy pillow of the silver sofa, two drinks on the side table, embers nearly extinguished in the fireplace smelling of creosote and old coal centuries thick in the chimney and the pine knots she threw in. There was a pale lick of Scotch in the bottom of one glass and he stood and drank it down, watery. She'd left the Christmas tree lights on, all white, all steady. No gifts beneath, not yet.

He felt a heavy pull to sit, to stop here. But he jimmied the half-crushed box from his trouser pocket, jazzy gilt geometrics, something from the chemists on Bond Street and the bracelet he'd loved and bought on a whim at auction, something spectacular for Jean to cancel out the Vivienne bangle, Harry dragging on him to get the hell out, the party would start without them. But he kept it up, kept the nod going until the others all backed down and Harry convinced them to take a personal check drawn on a U.S. bank just this once. Something Nick would have to take care of soon, something he'd be stupid to put off another day. But he'd pocketed the bracelet—forget the jewel case, they were in a rush!—he just stuck it in his overcoat pocket and left it there like a wish for days. Handed it over to hatcheck girls, and tossed it wherever he pleased until this morning, when he stopped in and found the last cardboard gift box in the bin at Boots and placed his treasure inside.

He could stand straight. Or he could close his eyes and feel the floor rush close. His fingertips were red and pinched, and he was warm in this room; she kept the heat so high he could smell his own aftershave and sweat. The pine scent, the coal grease, the dish soap, and him too warm, all together, all the same. She'd worn her nightie to receive her guest, whoever it was; he'd bet on it. She'd put on the velvet with a front zip and let whatever dope had popped by for a nightcap see her without her face on; she'd curled her legs under her, or she'd pulled aside the opening slit and let her calves show, crossed at the ankles.

He slumped a little against the archway. He could sit in her chair, stretch out on the long silver sofa, or pick one of the low curving couches she'd placed around the fireplace, sit and be swallowed. He was certain he didn't want that. He found his whiffer again, took two more swift inhales, unlocked the fist closing in his chest, then sank to a propped up sit, then tipped. That cool smooth stone on his cheek a relief. He wouldn't sleep, just rest and think.

He awoke to find Jean sitting in a T-shirt against the mirror. Her eye makeup smudged under her eyes made her skin pale; her hair looked even whiter blond and like a frozen whip swirled on top of her head. She'd cut it short. He was opposed, but he didn't have a vote. My god, he'd said. Why chop off your best feature?

I have other features, she'd said, but with a frown. Why did she ever listen to him? The great arbiter of good taste she called him, but often she seemed to believe him. They'd painted white on white streaks in her wheat blond hair and left just enough on top to disguise the clips on a hairpiece. She had options. And she had ballerina legs. She'd spent about forty-five minutes in a dance class in high school and look what she got.

Jean?

Um.

Lily okay?

Sure she is.

He found the gilt box wedged under his hip, tried to plump out the crushed corner, Here, he slid it toward her, across the floor; it crashed like a toy racecar into the squat marble pedestal she sat on.

This for Lily?

No. I have something. It's at the office. I'll bring it.

Now?

Not now. Open it. Please.

She watched him, studied him. What's wrong with your head?

What? Nothing.

You're tilting, to the left. Is something wrong?

You keep asking that.

She plucked the box up and held it close to her belly, as if it were something to warm her. She closed her eyes and rubbed one lid.

It's bad for you, he said. Sleeping in your makeup.

How do I look?

Perfect. He raised himself up against the archway. But it makes some kind of trouble, and erodes your lashes. Eventually.

I'm not worried.

No. Is that my T-shirt?

No.

Looks like it.

It's not.

Never?

She wrapped the hem around his gift. Good night, sweetheart. She stood up, purple panties with a polka-dot frill a little stretched out like something she wore often.

What are those?

What?

Is Lily here?

Where else would she be?

I heard you calling me, he said, rubbing the back of his head against the archway. Taking his knuckles and pressing them into his temples.

What are you talking about?

You called me. I heard you.

Do you need a doctor?

No. He rubbed down the muscles of his thighs.

Numb?

Not really.

A little?

I was at the bar, crowded; you'd be surprised. And I could hear you as if you were standing right next to me.

I wasn't.

Why not? He looked at her, considered the white blond flame of hair, the blue smudge of makeup, the lean long muscles of her limbs for no good reason, the stony look in her eyes, the plum-color sleep mouth turned down, the frilly nylon panties. Her feet were bare.

I'm going to bed; she'll be up early. Jean raised one arm, pushed the other down in a pretty spiral stretch. Her nails half covered in a chipped iridescent blue polish.

He reached for the lower hand. What is this shit?

Mary Quant. It's nice.

It's garbage. Stay. Please.

She bent forward, put her hand on his cheek, his forehead. You're warm.

He held it there, turned, put his mouth against her thumb.

I'm thinking about going home, she said. I'm tired.

I know. I know that.

Soon, she said. I called the tenant today.

He nodded, watching her as she rocked a little side to side, then slid down to sit on her heels, an odd curved squat. He watched her, the sharp intake of breath, round belly tucked inward, breasts against her knees.

You're gorgeous, he said as if stating a fact across a distance, as if she'd already left.

I'm not doing anything. She sat on the floor and let one knee rest against him. She ran her blue-tipped nail along his closest thigh. Feel this?

No.

Now? She pushed down slightly into the muscle.

Yes, there.

She pressed forward and reached to bite his lower lip.

Feel that?

His chest contracted. Um, he said.

She covered his mouth with hers; he thought of a mouse running and his breath went shallow and quick.

She slid a leg across him and the archway molding jabbed into his back. He was wheezing now, but she was fully engaged with his zipper. She shimmied his trousers from his hips, a quick lift off; he could lift her still this way. He could. If he could just catch his breath. She pulled aside the baggy crotch of the purple panties, and deft, she was on him, eyes closed. Who are you, she said, sneaking into my house in the middle of the night. It was quick, quick and he was desperate to breathe, and soon she lay away from him with a cheek to the floor, while he fumbled for his trouser pocket and his whiffer, and pushed down and took a first inhale, again, his head was exploding; he took a second, and forced himself to wait, to let the stuff disperse. A last, a third, he could breathe again, but his hands shook, and his cock lay like something crazed and stupid in his lap.

Cyril was asleep in the vestibule. A red leather chair with a high back, his gray-striped waistcoat unbuttoned just at the top. He had a sputter on the exhale. Nick walked softly past, down the wide stair to the lobby, too cold even with banked fires in both hearths; he'd never get used to the cold here, and the dark. Sir?

He turned round just at the front door, Cyril?

I'm very sorry, sir. It's locked and bolted, you never know who might wander in. Let me retrieve the key.

Of course, Cyril. Yes. Thank you. He watched the old man climb the steps to the key safe and reach up to turn the iron clasp. Everything difficult as if to make it seem more precious. Soon all that strain would be replaced with ease and access, the precious quality reflected only in the purchase price. He could already see it. He was a visionary. Everyone said so.

23

Jean amazed herself by coming to the Clarks' New Year's Day fete all alone. Please, Paula Clark had cooed over the phone. I won't know a soul.

At your own party?

You know what I mean. Be a darling, please. I need you here.

They'd only met once or twice at Derek Voose's big Mount Street parties, but Emma had steered her clear of Paula Clark. Very silly woman, said Emma. Entirely devoted to childish maneuvers. Trust me, she laughed. Back far, far away.

But when Jean saw Paula again at the Little Flower she liked her. Emma wasn't infallible. It was a PTA meeting, though it wasn't called that, more a tea in the old Guinness library for the mothers of ninth graders just before the Christmas break. Most of the tiny class were boarding students, so Paula, Jean, and two women in full veil were the only parents available to accept the rough dry scones with forced smiles.

When Mother Clarence offered Jean her tea it was as if they'd never met before, a surprise and a relief. Jean tried not to wince as the tea hit her tongue; the milk was slightly off. How do they do it? said Paula. I mean it's exactly the same! Immaculate Heart, New Haven, identical acidic tea, flat biscuits I'd swear were baked by the same person.

Jean gave a grateful smile and settled the cup and saucer on her crossed knee. They had that much in common: two East Coast convent girls with daughters in need of grounding. Structure. Discipline. And good lord, a little style, laughed Paula. Her daughter was a hopeless lump she confided, and Jean resisted the temptation to say all she felt about Lily's perplexing appearance. That was private. But to hear Paula's description of plump Beven in a red satin minidress with gold tassels had her weeping with guilty laughter.

Please say you'll come, Paula said offering her invitation. I cannot do it without you.

Jean understood the Clarks had about twelve of these gatherings a year. All the movie people, all the oil people, that's how films get made. Already her husband had credits they could live off for the rest of their lives, Paula said. And we have enough stories, believe me. But what would they do?

She tipped her head toward the old nun stationed by the teapot with a shaking hand, eyes burning with concentration. It's the same for me; a vocation is a vocation. In movies there's immense work and believe me I do my part. The rest is playtime.

Playtime? Jean shrugged.

Well, I know, poor darling.

At this Jean felt a quick sag along her spine. She made herself look up. Paula's face was full of kindness, a simple kindness, all the arch complexity stripped away and she saw a girl she might have gone to school with. For a half moment Jean remembered who she'd been then, full of possibility. Don't say a thing, said Paula, holding up a hand. We won't speak of it again. Jean wondered what she was talking about.

Emma refused to go with Jean to the party. Good lord, she's impossible. See for yourself. And Anna Percy-Flint never went to movie parties on principle. Thieves, charlatans. Jean decided not to invite Nick. She could be independent, too. There were the usual double-parked cars on the quiet square, and the occasional honker who made all the smoking chauffeurs get in and drive the periphery. The Clark door was ajar and lit with luminaria, brown paper sacks cut with shapes of swimming nymphs. Rupert Clark's new project had a fiendish woman with a swimming pool where she lured her victims in broad daylight. She wore a seaweed green bikini with seed pearls stitched along the darts. And here was Paula wearing a preview as a hostess gown. The same bikini, with a diaphanous caftan in pink chiffon, scattered seed pearls clustered near her naval. Cunning, yes? she grinned to Jean, tugging down the front so the pearls glimmered. She smelled so fully of patchouli that Jean had to check her revulsion. Had to refocus her eyes to meet her new friend and offer approval and pleasure, the only possibilities.

Paula Clark's three-year-old scrambled out of the arm hold of Kendra his nanny and slammed into the legs of his approaching father. Oof, cried Rupert and let his long silver hair fly forward as he reached down to straighten the miniature cashmere blazer on his tiny son. Trevor, please, he said. But the invitation was more a please, do it again, as he grinned helplessly at Jean and extended a hand more manicured than her own. Darling? He tilted a chin at Paula but kept his eyes fixed in a corny way on Jean. Is this the new find? Good work!

Hiding in plain sight, I'm afraid. Our daughters are school-mates thanks to Paula. Jean Devlin.

Lucky girls! smiled Rupert. Let's do more for those nuns, Paulie. Really we don't do half our share, he said this while stroking Trevor's head, and the grand sprawl of the other hand played at the seed pearls on Paula's caftan. But this family rhythm was interrupted by a small man in a leopard-skin vest whispering from behind his shoulder. Rupert frowned. Oh good fuck, he said. Tell her it's a party not a crime scene. Vivienne is threatening to leap out the window again. You remember the last time, Paulie. What a bore. Excuse me! More about those needy nuns, you two. Here, Kendra, take him somewhere neutral. Trevor burst into a roar as his nanny wrestled him off through a pocket door beneath the grand front staircase. Shh, sweetie, shh, said Paula, watching them until the door pulled shut. Then she turned and kissed Jean on both cheeks. Welcome to paradise!

He's lovely, said Jean.

No, he's a terror. *You* are lovely. Let's see what you're wearing. Oh! Then she scanned up the stair as if she half expected someone to tumble down on top of them. We better go see, come!

Jean trailed up the stairway after Paula. The caftan had a fish-tail that swept along behind her. She turned to laugh, and Jean couldn't help smiling in return. Paula was good at this. Usually Jean disliked being a bit player in other people's pageants, but with Paula the silliness was charming. The bikini was hilarious, a joke that teased toward very sexy. Jean was reminded of the prim *Vogue* photo of Paula and her daughter, Beven. Liberty blouses and Jaeger skirts on the garden bench. That must have been a good joke. Lily and

Jean were cut from the final project, something about Lily's expression, too distant, no, too *contemplative*. That was the word. What nonsense Jean thought, still irritated. Too sulky was the problem, and she felt that defeat like a raw spot exposed by chance. Then as if Jean had dropped her script, Paula tossed off a cue. And how's our sweet girl?

Jean looked up, unsure.

How's dear Lily? said Paula. Beven worships her.

She loves the Little Flower. And apparently Mother Clarence dyes her hair! You wouldn't think they'd bother, with the habits.

Ah, there she is; there's our monster child. Have you met Vivienne Vimcreste? No? And at this Paula began to giggle. Well brace yourself. Angel? What are you doing? We've just repainted and now you're smudging everything, silly girl. Meet my new discovery. Come down off that sill this instant. I have a treat.

Vivienne Vimcreste turned hollow eyes to her hostess: lids of blue-black eye shadow and matte raspberry lipstick. She lined her narrow back against the deep casement and squinted at Paula through the crowd of her relaxed rescuers. Who is it? she said in plaintive voice of someone being awakened much too early.

It was a handsome room; even the young woman with one leg out the window couldn't keep Jean from looking up at the intricately carved ceiling. Yes, whispered Rupert behind her. She felt his hand on her shoulder light as warm sand. It's a beauty. Did it myself.

No, she turned to look at him.

No, he said. Quite right. No is our watchword.

She blinked, startled, pleased.

You silly cunt, he shouted out. If you don't come down this instant, you won't have your dessert. I'm quite serious. Don't test me, Vivienne.

The girl shivered then, dragged a slim shaking leg back inside and slipped off the sill. Cake? she said mournfully and blinked her large eyes.

Of course, my love, said Paula, and pulled her close, brushed the long angled sleeve of the caftan out of the way and drew the girl in closer. Cake for our safest darling. Paula didn't actually snap her fingers, but gave more of a Balinese twirl of the wrist and soon a caterer's server was standing with a triangle of chocolate mousse cake, gleaming and fragrant. The Vivienne girl accepted it without thanks, then examined the fork for a long time. Spoon, she said. And the server was back, nearly panting.

Vivienne, just eat it, said Paula. It's for you. Your favorite.

Vivienne brought a large mound up under her nose. Stinks like last week's cigarettes doused in water. Why is that, Pooh-lah? What's the secret.

You're jet-lagged, sweetie. It's all the smoke still trapped in your nostrils from the flight.

The flight, sighed Vivienne, patting the cake flatter with her spoon. The flight.

Darling, this is my dear friend Jean Devlin. Say hello like a good girl.

Vivienne looked up, mouth hanging open, chocolate smeared her teeth like lipstick. Jean Devlin?

That's right, said Jean. I think I'll have some of that cake, too. It looks marvelous.

The fuck you will, said Vivienne, and dropped the plate onto the carpet with a splat. She marched out of the drawing room with her arm covering her face.

Christ, now Paula was snapping her fingers, and servers were scooping the cake out of the carpet. She's an infant, said Paula. And of course, she's a garbage can. Whatever crap is floating around, she's taken it. You can count on that.

Before Jean could reply, Vivienne was back pointing a too slender finger. She was a model, Jean realized, now remembering photos in various ads. Cheap ads, for inexpensive booze and panty hose. And then she recalled all of Emma's nonsense about her. You're that stupid bastard's stupid wife, said Vivienne, smiling, head tipped far back, mouth open, a sad hollow stomach stink coming off her breath.

None of that, said Paula slowly, as if telling a private joke, trying not to laugh. You don't know what you're talking about, love. Give me one minute, she said to Jean, taking Vivienne by the arm. Come with me, girlie, right now. And Vivienne collapsed against her and was led like a sleepy child up the vast staircase.

Just after midnight Jean walked out through the cool white quiet blocks of Belgravia to the rush of late-night traffic flying around the circle at Hyde Park Gate. She flagged down a cab and waited while it found a corner for her to climb into the back.

Grosvenor Square, she said.

Right, miss, and up went the flag that set the meter ticking like an egg timer. She sat into the wide flattened leather of the seat, so peaceful, the ticking, the stern, smooth seat, all a comfort.

Darling Jean, take my car. I insist, more, I protest! But she'd escaped Rupert Clark's summoning to anyone who would follow his order.

Please, she'd said, and watched the happy effect her voice had on the contours of his face. His eyes liked her. Found her pleasing. They'd danced and he stroked the curve of her waist and looked with fond frankness down her dress. Damn you with your tricky elastic, he plucked the ribbon on the back that kept her deep neckline close to her body.

The saleswoman at Harrods had objected. An elastic? Are you an old lady? Cut to the South Pole, she said, just as it should be. But in the end she'd tacked in the elastic. This pale aqua was Jean's color, and silk jersey had the right heft for her, better than more flyaway silks. She liked the hang and the weight holding her down.

This is quite nice, Rupert snuggling up in the slow dance, plucked up a gold medallion with amethysts. Like this! he hummed and dropped his lion's head into her shoulder. It was much too heavy; she tried to squirm out from under him. Her legs went stiff and she lost the rhythm.

He pushed his thick fingers into her tailbone. Release, he whispered. No more foolish games, now. You're with me.

With me? The idiocy, the arrogance, she laughed now, sitting back into the mitt of the taxi seat, but her body had caved inward against him, and her legs had gone willowy. Lovely, he said, and she sighed, not wanting to. Home, I think, and soon, she'd said. Pulling away, with a bleary smile, she could feel the vagueness in her own eyes and tried to tighten her focus. Yes. Home is best.

Philip will take you! And that will be convenient because tomorrow, two sharp, he'll pick you up for lunch. Are you listening?

I'm not, she'd laughed and flew down the stairs in search of the clutch she'd left stowed somewhere on the lowboy. But there pressed against the elegant chest was Beven. She was a funny girl, oat-colored hair, split in the middle, two exact curtains hung to her shoulders. Someone's careful layering gave her face a sweet shape. At thirty she'll be doughy, thought Jean. But now, the round cheeks and chin, the round neck, round everything, gave her a milkmaid sweetness even with the frown and the crushed black velvet of her tunic. She was having no part of the beach party.

Beven, will you tell your mother I've slipped out? I'll call her in the morning.

Not the morning, said Beven, examining her rubbed cuff. Jean kept Lily on high alert for this kind of rudeness.

Thank you, dear, said Jean.

He's just an old perv.

It's been a lovely evening, said Jean. She found her purse just behind a small perfect orchid screen.

He's already jacking off somewhere; he won't even remember you. It's all one big wanking operation. Cut.

Good night, Beven. And thank you.

What did it say about her that the favorite part of her life was being alone at night in a taxi. Dark, the red and yellow flashing lights along the park, a swaying turn into her street, and then the wait for the cash. This was heaven. And she knew it.

Inside the lobby, Cyril slept in his closet and she didn't wake him by calling the lift. She slipped off her heels and climbed the stair along the edge to feel the marble treads cool on her insteps. Impossible to know if Nick would be there, likely not. She didn't care now. Such freedom, such heaven. The feel of that heavy awkward hand on her spine, she could summon it and then it would slip away. She put her own hand there, felt the rise and fall of her round hips climbing the stair. Any hand anywhere on her body would be happy. So odd to have that confidence. That was her new deal, dead and confident. Like someone had stolen into her and robbed the fear and confusion that made her feel alive.

In the morning Rupert Clark's driver delivered a note: *Our troubled young friend Vivienne made good on her threat. It's no one's fault, darling, of course not. But we have all the arrangements on our heads now, and good god, the funeral. So, all bets are off, dearest girl. Big hug, R.*

She read the note several times, Rupert's sloppy hand spilling along the thick gray notecard. She thought about the pointed misery on the girl's face when they'd met. The spitting anger. Jean finally understood Paula's private joke and why she'd been invited.

Part III

Winter 1971

24

Patsy in a sterile blue smock swept into Jean's room as though the door had never been shut. Jean opened her eyes in surprise. She had a headache that made the river light bouncing through the window an assault. She squinted to see what she was expected to do now.

I'm not supposed to be here, said Patsy, hovering.

Oh? said Jean.

I just wanted to say don't blame yourself, she whispered. That's all.

For what?

Patsy looked toward the door, then folded down the top sheet and yanked on the blanket. Let's just say I've seen this happen before, more than once. Maybe twice?

Jean frowned, unsure how to answer. Patsy patted her on the wrist.

Have you had babies yourself? Jean tried.

Me? No, thank you!

She looked to be about seventeen or eighteen years old to Jean. More candy striper than nurse. Someone sent around with pamphlets on how to care for the incision. How to clean the baby's ears. This is all very new, said Jean with a small smile. Maybe that's what she wanted.

Even women who have done it a bunch of times freeze up. They just get scared.

I'm sorry?

It's not your fault, that's all. Patsy nodded, smiling.

But she's perfect, said Jean. She's beautiful.

She's lucky!

Jean felt groggy with confusion. What was the girl saying? She edged herself up a little higher on the pillow and read the name tag on the blue smock.

Patsy, I don't know what you're talking about. Jean felt her eyes gray over and a powerful need to sleep.

You stopped your own labor. But it happens all the time! Here at least twice before. Or maybe only once.

You must have something wrong.

Patsy bent in close, a swift odor of too sweet freesia. She plumped Jean's pillows and the bed rocked. It couldn't be right, all this motion. Then Patsy was standing at the end of the bed studying the clipboard attached to the rail. She did a convincing imitation of someone who knew what the numbers meant.

It may feel like you made a decision, like, the heck with this baby? But even if you thought that, and the contractions stopped right then? It still wasn't your fault. Okay?

Patsy, I think—

So you can hold off on any emergency confessions to the padre.

Patsy—

No mortal sins here.

I'm so tired.

Of course you are.

Just dog tired.

Sleep now. You won't even know I'm here.

Jean closed her eyes and her breath felt shallow. Her chest pounding, the blood began to trickle again between her thighs, though the incision on her belly felt too dry, too tight and sore. Everything hurt here. Why couldn't she just go home? Finally Patsy clomped out the door, and the need to shout subsided.

Of course, Jean's father's all-time favorite story had been the birth of Lily. As if the wedding never happened and time leapt ahead to the December morning, the twenty-sixth of December. Everyone hungover from the festivities the day before, and not an ambulance for three counties for love or money, he liked to say. Something had gone wrong between a Bloody Mary with a celery stalk shaped at one end to look like a candle flame, so clever, and the smell of her water breaking, like bracken and clay all mixed together, all over Doris's new slipcovers. A brown thick embarrassing stain seeped from beneath her and the pain shocked her. Just shocked her, as if she'd never heard a word about what this would all be like. Sweetheart, Doris said, actually smiling. Let's get you going! I'll call Nick from the hospital.

Jean insisted she wouldn't go to the hospital without him.

But, honey.

No, Jean said and closed her eyes and groaned. I can't. I can't go without him.

Doris went to the kitchen to make the call and she could hear Jean moaning all the way from there, crying. Her fingers shook so that Ruby took the phone out of her hands and said, Who do you want to dial?

Mr. Clyde, said Doris. Call Mr. Clyde. We know where to find him.

This was a sore spot, Nick's whereabouts, more with her father than with Doris, who accepted everything about him as delightful. Still, it was true. Nick was hard to reach. But Clyde could always be found, just like the sky. A stormy sky, said Ruby. The man was like cloud cover. So within the hour Huey was pulling the Cadillac into the turnaround. Front door! Clyde shouted. Front! Because there was his princess, bundled up, sitting on a folding chair under the portico. What the hell was she doing outside? Ruby dabbing her head with a washcloth. Doris grasping her own hands. Jean looked like she was conscious. Clyde was out of the car before Huey could put on the brake. Get away, both of you. Get away!

Now, Clyde, said Doris. She's all right; this is normal.

What would you know. Get away. I'm warning you. And for the first time since she'd made the horrible smell Jean felt herself. *Go away*, her father shouted one more time. The washcloth fell from her forehead and the air cleared all around her. There was more shouting about the doors, *the doors*, meaning the car doors, and her father had lifted her in his arms, like she was a baby. That he could still carry her seemed a miracle, but he did it, and this was his favorite part. I can barely lift a cigar he liked to add. Normally.

When did Nick get there? Always a confusing part of the story. At the hospital Huey and her father presented Jean at the emergency entrance, Huey running in to announce their arrival and her father carrying her, though losing strength. She can remember the feeling of utter safety, divided by a tiny slit of terror opening black before her eyes that he might drop her and kill them both. She shuddered the idea away. Safety, safety. Her father's love.

No one inside the hospital needed to be told this was urgent. Besides, it was a quiet morning after a busy night. Jean was put on a gurney and wheeled directly to maternity. No foolish questions. Her father would take care of everything.

Tucked loosely into a bed in the prep room, all nice white sheets and green curtains. A sterile ammonia scent in the cool bright masked by something lemony. She remembers the massed green fabric suspended by invisible rods beginning about two feet below the acoustic tile ceiling. Beyond the soft pleats the low moaning of another girl, quiet and muffled, gave Jean the unhappy sense that this most private event wasn't private so far at all, with the saving grace that she was central, that her section of curtains was the most advantageous somehow. Then the piggy bank pink of Dr. Logue's gloves when he came in fully masked to examine her. She smiled to see him. His hands like a pair of toys, she remembers. Deep folding green curtains and pink hands. Looking wonderful, Jean, he said, pulling back one glove to feel her forehead with an exposed wrist, a funny delicate gesture. Nothing to worry about, he said. He stank so strongly of eggnog. She vomited, immediately, all over the pink gloves.

We're in fine shape here, he said, peeling them off at the sink. Everything will be over before you know it, he said, and instructed the nurse to shave her. This is the part that Jean can't think about. Something in this procedure—Standard, said the nurse. And: I'll be careful. And: Don't you worry, now. But do hold still, dear.— convinced Jean she couldn't, wouldn't continue without Nick. She'd wait.

A half hour later when Dr. Logue came back in, frowning, she tried to tell him about her husband and that he was sure to be on his way. But Dr. Logue was looking at her in her terrible state. He'd lifted the paper bib and was patting, poking all around the place she'd just been scraped. She looked away, tears streaming, blocking him out, putting him far away. She said, very loudly, I'll wait.

Jean, dear, he said, tucking the paper bib back around her and lightly placing a new clean sheet. He was even older than her father; soon he'd leave all this and devote himself to birding. Jean, there's no waiting allowed. He was smiling at her as if she were a little girl too sleepy to know her own good. You're afraid; that's normal. But there's nothing to be afraid of. We'll do this gently and then it will all be over. The nurse had alerted him and he was humming all this like a lullaby. He had on new yellow gloves and he'd scrubbed away the eggnog. I'll check back in a little while. Let's make a bet you're in delivery within the hour.

But he was wrong. She would wait. And she did wait, until her contractions slowed down to nothing at all.

It was almost dark outside the green curtains and Nick still hadn't come. Dr. Logue was listening to Jean's heart again, heavy stethoscope pressed cold against her sternum, across her swollen breast at tapping intervals, just as he'd done all day long. Now he said she'd need to make a choice soon. She was in charge he said. Okay? he said. And that was the last time he spoke to her. He'd moved the thick metal piece down her belly and when he couldn't get a steady heartbeat from the baby, he started. Oh good Christ, he said. And made a jerking motion and the nurse brushed a quick swab of something then put a needle, already prepared, into Jean's arm, while he repositioned the stethoscope. There, he said. Right there. And then: Let's go, let's go. Let's go.

Dr. Logue was not at all confident. That's what he said later. Such a sudden shift is a terrible sign. As Jean was wheeled to the operating room, and the anesthesiologist got right to work, Dr. Logue stopped for a minute, as a courtesy to old friends, to tell Clyde Boll and his wife, Doris, to prepare for heartache. Jean's young, he said, as explanation or compensation they couldn't tell, and then he was racing down the hall.

The coldest day, and the electricity was fluctuating and the lights faltered and if he'd been thinking about it, there'd have been hell raised in every department, but the baby was under his hand, he could feel her now and her chest still shivered, he could feel it, the tiniest shiver and he made himself lift her slowly, slowly so not to shock that tiny shiver into stillness. The suction to her mouth, then the blow, delicate, a pat, a second pat, and the lungs cleared and she whimpered. Only a bit of a cry, he kept her close to his chest, as if teaching her heart to keep going. There, little girl, he said over and over until the operating nurse said, She's fine, Dr. Logue; she's a good one.

When she became pregnant again with Cubbie, Dr. Logue watched her like she might jump bail. Every month, sometimes more often, he'd do a full checkup with blood work and take an X-ray just to be safe. She took special vitamins. Let's get this one right, he'd said. And everything went perfectly.

A few weeks before the move to London, she was clearing out a gutter jammed with pine needles over the back door, high up on the ladder when the phone rang. She scrambled down and into the house, panting as she picked up. Hello?

It was a woman who apologized immediately. She was part of a research team, just a secretary she corrected, but one of those making the first calls to the mothers.

Excuse me?

She'd start over. They were doing research on the mothers whose children had died of certain kinds of cancer. Mostly blood and brain. It was a small group affiliated with the Children's Hospital of Philadelphia but if the early findings had merit they'd go nationwide.

What can I do for you? Jean asked. She felt herself begin to tremble, but she had a voice for this, professional, helpful, and she used it.

We're studying the correlation between prenatal radiation exposure and particular cancers.

I see.

And we really have only the one question to begin.

How did you find me?

I'm so sorry! I'm new. That's the first thing on the card. Your son's doctor, Marvin Erlandson? He gave us your name. He said he was sure you'd be happy to help.

Well, he's right, said Jean.

So, there's really only the one question to begin and that is: Did you receive any radiation of any kind during your pregnancy? And if so, how often?

You mean X-rays?

That's right. Even at the shoe store or the dentist. Anywhere.

Only for the baby, to make sure he was all right.

I see. The woman sounded like she was pulling a whole new set of papers across her desk. Excuse me, she said, and then, All right. And would you say that happened more than once?

Several times, said Jean. Oh, at least ten, or maybe twelve, maybe more. There was some worry toward the end he might be breech, so right before the delivery I had two, about five hours apart, but everything was fine, so it was all just precautionary.

Mrs. Devlin?

Yes?

Are you sure about this? I'm just writing down ten to twelve now, possibly more, and you think that's right?

Of course I'm sure.

There was a very long pause. Jean said, Hello?

Yes, said the woman, as if she'd been roused out of a sad dream. Thank you for your time and patience, she said.

Not at all.

After that, Jean couldn't go back up the ladder. Days went by before Doris stopped over and said, What's that ladder doing there? Someone might get hurt.

When Jean came home from London, she arrived quietly, no fanfare. The old airport pickup service from New Jersey met them at JFK. She and Nick were in a flexible moment, that's what she'd called it in the end. You're the flexible one, sweetheart, he'd said. Hardly, she said and booked the flight.

At last, the car crept down the steep driveway. It was still only noon. The sun winter bright on the windows. Lily wanted to see the water and the dock first, no doubt to sneak a cigarette. They'd had twelve uninterrupted hours of each other's company, and Jean let out a deep breath as she paid the driver. She told him to leave the bags in the driveway. That was fine. She'd enter her house alone.

As she pushed wide the back door, something, a bat, dove down at her head. Cringing, Jean forced herself to unwrap her arms away from her face. She'd seen bats before. The house had been empty for weeks now and a window must be cracked or broken somewhere. But when she opened her eyes she saw it was great deal more.

The stove, the refrigerator, the oven were all burned to black and ash. Walls streaked and caked with something dark and fetid, mud and maybe even shit as she looked closer. Her lovely pale violet walls. The cabinets had been set on fire, too. The floor hacked to splinters.

She moved through the house as if pulled by a string. Tiles shattered in the bathrooms, fixtures yanked from the walls, the floor. In the master bath the subfloor had been soaked and had swollen up in waves, creating a smell like cat urine no scrubbing would ever get out. In the living room someone or something *had* pissed on anything that would soak up the odor. Every window that looked out onto the water shattered or missing. Doors ripped off hinges, carpets shredded. The staircase, their beloved staircase, had missing treads. Every other spoke of the banister was broken. In the garage some of the treads, some of the furniture, was piled up high, charred and reeking, as if someone had made several fires drenched with gasoline.

She ran down to the water and told Lily to stay right where she was. Then changed her mind and said she wanted her where she could see her, to just wait in the driveway, while Jean made some calls. She'd had the wit to ask the tenant to keep the phone connected and strangely, given all this, he'd complied. The first person she dialed was Lionel, sobbing, because who else would understand. Lionel said, Angel girl, you broke an agreement; he had a deal. He's angry.

Angry? *Angry?*

Look, you just need to bring in a crew, he said. And presto, everything brand-new. Better than ever. Right?

No, said Jean and put the receiver away from her face when she felt the sobs coming again. She lifted her head and took a long slow breath. She watched Lily through the smashed kitchen window. Lily, arms held wide like a child playing airplane, wandering around the backyard as if nothing had happened. Jean felt a jolt of fury. How could she be so oblivious? This was her home, too. But then she realized she hadn't let her inside.

Look, said Lionel. If you want, I could probably pull a few of the guys from here. How's that? And I'll send Mrs. Ivy along to terrify them into action. Anyway, don't worry. The insurance will cover everything. I've got just the adjuster for you. But let's do it fast. We don't want the place to depreciate.

What are you talking about?

Fuck. Junior's crying.

By the time she dialed Doris she'd collected herself. She told the story almost as a joke. But Doris didn't get it, and said, My god. Come right over here, right now. Just come here. And you stay as long as you like!

Oh, I don't know.

I'll send Ruby.

This is much too much for Ruby.

I mean to pick you two up, now. I'd come myself but I can't at the moment.

Why not? Jean said.

I sprained my good driving ankle. It happened—

Jean stepped closer to the shattered glass of her bay window. Out near the end of the dock, a structure of some sort teetered like a squat unstable totem pole.

Sorry, said Jean. I couldn't hear you. Now Lily was dragging her long coat through the half-thawed mud. All the way across the

Atlantic, she'd been sullen and when Jean did let her in the house, she'd barely said a word besides wow. All right, said Jean. Thank you, send Ruby, and in the meantime I'll call the police.

Hey, Mom? Lily said, banging up the back steps. Mom? Someone's piled all of Cubbie's stuff out behind the garage.

Which meant someone had broken into the locked storage closet in the attic. Ten minutes later Anthony Moldano made a slow awkward reverse down the driveway, lights spinning blue through the trees. He had the window of his cruiser down, his head half out as if he were driving a combine. The radio was still squawking when he parked. He was much fatter than the last time Lily had seen him and when he came into the kitchen he carried the meaty bready smell of a meatball sub.

Hey, little buddy, he said. Welcome home!

Hi.

Jean came in from the dining room still in her coat, carrying a notebook. Mrs. Devlin, now don't you worry about lists. That's our job.

Do you think it could be vandalism and not the angry tenant? I just called him and he says he's shocked.

I'm not ruling anything out just yet, said Anthony, with a wink to Lily. And you shouldn't be calling anyone. Leave that to us. They left the telephone connected? That's interesting. That might be helpful. By the way, have you heard the news?

Jean stared.

It's all true. The old lady is having twins. Anthony grinned and made his fists dance like happy puppets. Not faking you out. Turns out they run on her side of the family? She's got a cousin with twins already, identical, too. They need to actually tie different colored ribbons around their wrists so someone besides the mother can tell who's who. Are you seeing this? Two exact replicas of yours truly?

What? said Lily.

Jean put down her notebook. Lily, sweetheart, get my purse please. It's in the living room.

When she left the room Jean said, I don't think you understand what's happened here.

Anthony nodded toward the scorched cabinets. Pretty wild stuff.

Yes, so, maybe you could make a report and take some photographs?

Got the Polaroid in the vehicle for just that purpose. Really, Mrs. Devlin, no need to worry. Now, who's this approaching? We'll monitor all that for you, any odd comings and goings, starting immediately.

That's Ruby.

You know your floorboards are dodgy here. Anthony bounced the toe of his boot against the wood and it gave. Feels like the joist below is completely shot. Careful how you walk. Jeez, that's a bit dangerous.

Lily, Jean called out. What's taking so long?

I just need to make a phone call.

Not now. Ruby's here. Let's go. We'll be at Doris Boll's, she said to Anthony.

Probably for the best. You just don't know how this is going to fly.

Against her better judgment she called Nick that night after Lily and Doris had gone to sleep. She sat in the wicker rocker she'd had as a teenager, feet on the windowsill, smoking a cigarette, the window cracked an inch, cold air blasting her toes. She could be fifteen, except her bones felt half on fire.

Hello, darling! he said.

Don't even start, she said.

What is it. His voice went cautious and flat, and that was a small relief; she could tell him without giving him any ground. She just needed to tell him. So she talked and talked about every detail, ending with the pile behind the garage, the terrifying, nauseating pile of Cubbie's things. Someone had poured gasoline and lit up what was left of his baby furniture and his toys.

I feel like I'm dying, she whispered.

Nick was quiet for so long she thought she'd lost the connection. Honey? she said, by mistake.

Let me come.

No, absolutely not. She stubbed out the cigarette and shut the window with a slam. Damn, I'm cold. Wait a second. She pulled the eiderdown from the foot of the bed. Doris must have done some emergency laundry the moment Ruby went out to fetch them, because it smelled just like all her linens smelled, washed a moment ago, some mix of ocean and rose in the scent. I'm back, she said. Wrapping the quilt tighter, feeling the knot in her spine give a tiny bit.

I'll fly over in the morning.

She sighed and lit another cigarette, reopened the window.

I know what this is, Nick said.

How could you? But she sat up straight. What could you know about this?

Let me come and see what's going on. I'll call you when I land. Tomorrow.

Jean took a long drag and tried to settle her thoughts, to calm the ramping dread. She didn't think she could do all this alone. She waited another minute before saying, Very flashy. Very hotshot.

Maybe, he said, but sounded relieved. How's Lily?

Impossible.

It's her job.

Well, she's good at it. Jean didn't say good night, just hung up the phone and dragged herself to the bed and fell into a dead sleep.

25

L ily wore her long green London maxicoat, which she made sway like a ball gown as she stepped over the painted rocks that now kept cars from driving down the lane between the courts at the tennis club. Her grandmother insisted she bring a red ski cap and mittens, but she'd stuffed these into her pockets. It was a beautiful coat and when Margaret saw it, she'd want one, too. Lily thought she could just beg her dad to find one for Margaret, but in a different color, then at the Clury School they'd look good. Because Margaret was going there, too. Just like Lily she'd be starting when the new term began.

Tommy answered the phone at the Foley house after breakfast. Lily who? he asked. Tally ho?

He's a turd, said Margaret when she came on the line. You should see his face. It's an emergency zone.

So I saw Anthony Moldano, said Lily. He was at our house.

Who? said Margaret, yawning loudly. Tommy's been sleeping with his face on a cheese grater. Don't touch me. Touch me and I'm telling Mom about her rabbit hat.

Are you okay?

He's in a romantic situation with Mom's hat.

Gross.

Exactly.

What are you doing? asked Lily.

You mean now?

Yes? I think so.

They made a plan to meet at the old beach club by two o'clock. Lily's mother would be at their house all day. Lionel was pressing to send down Mrs. Ivy and the workmen for an assessment, but her mother said no, not until she really saw everything for herself. And Momo agreed, talked about not disturbing the crime scene. But Jean waved her off, as if dismissing what Doris said automatically made things better.

The old schoolyard was empty and full of black ice drifts left in big piles just anywhere. It was the long break now and the Clury School would start even later. They need to dull our pencils so we won't stab each other, said Margaret on the phone. She was still hoping she could get to Star of the Sea by Easter. Margaret's mother said, Why not? But her father was mysterious in his firmness. As far as he was concerned, Margaret could spend the rest of her life at the Clury School, but he wouldn't say why.

Lily fake skated across the tarmac. She looked at the basketball hoop hanging crooked with no net and thought of Russell Crabtree and his beautiful neck. She tried to see him in her mind and could smell his smoky breath almost and feel his hands dropping the pink parka over her face and she held on to that for a moment, but it was Lawrence who she wished might turn up just around the corner. A shocking surprise, he'd come all the way to New Jersey because, because, but she couldn't really carry this dream for long. She knew already that Lawrence had fallen out of her life.

Crossing the bridge, the winds blew sharp on her face and bit her cheeks. She almost put the red cap on but what if Margaret saw her? She did dig out the mittens so her fingers wouldn't freeze right off. The winds lifted the coat away from her body and something in the slap of cold made her feel ashamed, as if she deserved this. Stupid brain.

You don't need to believe every blessed idea that goes through your head, as if God himself planted it there. This was Sister Maureen. You can decide for yourself, dear. What's worth holding on to, and what's just nonsense passing through. We all have a world of silliness and sorrow mixed in all together. You can decide what's true. For yourself. You have that power of discernment.

They'd met the one time by chance. Lily skipping typing class, hiding in the library. And Sister Maureen finding her in the back carrel, as if she just happened to be strolling by. They went to a tiny kitchen that smelled like cooking gas. Sister Maureen gave her biscuits on a flowery saucer. Then she sat down, facing Lily, her knees almost touching and she told a story about her family in Ireland as if she'd been waiting all day for Lily to arrive so she could tell her all about her brother who died in near infancy of nothing that couldn't have been prevented. It was too cold that winter, the house was ticky-tack and useless against the freeze, and he was too little to endure. After he went, and there were many of us, ten in all, it was a frenzy of who was to blame. Who didn't hang the blankets, and who didn't seal the windows shut, and who let the fire bank too low. My mother nearly went mad with the rage of it, did go mad for a while. Sister Maureen smiled at Lily as if this was a memory she was glad to be telling. She nodded. My poor mother. And Lily listened closely, waiting to hear the end. My poor mother, said Sister Maureen. And that was it.

Lily imagined the mother still blocking out the cold wind, as cold as today, as if she could never stop. Never. She wanted to tell Sister Maureen that her own mother wasn't that way. If that was the point of the story, she was wrong. But this was more an idea than a feeling, and the warmth of the kitchen and the dry sweet bite of the biscuits, was what stayed, and Sister Maureen's wide blue eyes looking right at her, then touching her hand and saying, Now here are some typing fingers if ever I saw some. Before she knew it she was back in class and not in trouble for once.

The beach club entrance was boarded up for the winter. The flag-pole shook in the wind like it might be plucked out of the ground someday and fly away out over the ocean. Anthony Moldano had shown them the way to slip through the storm fence on the north side of the old building. Lily wondered if he would be here today. Margaret hadn't said anything on the phone.

Lily stopped and peered through the glass doors into the green and white room with trellises painted on the walls and bamboo chairs stacked in piles and covered by tablecloths past use. When they were tiny their mother played bridge here, until Cubbie got sick and she found it boring. What did they know, these women with nothing more to worry about than a silly game.

Margaret had sounded a little bored too, as if the club and its secret entrances and hideouts had worn out for her. She might already be in one of the cabanas. Lily walked along the boardwalk and the wind whipped at her face, sand sparking her cheeks. She huddled down as she made her way to the line of cabanas at the far end. These were kept by the biggest families.

All were shut down and locked for the winter, but Anthony had taught them how easily they could get inside if they wanted to. Actually Lily had only done this once before. Sat inside a musty cabana on someone's wicker love seat, sharing a stale cigarette with Margaret. The taste so sour on the back of her mouth. When Anthony didn't arrive that day, Margaret told Lily that his penis was blue and curved like a boomerang and he could only father boys. Never a girl. Because of the special shape, and how valuable that was in an Italian family. Any family really when you thought about it. And then she burst into tears.

You know what? I'd pick you instead of Tommy anytime, Lily said. Seriously.

Margaret had sighed and taken the cigarette. It's hard for you to understand because you have some natural drawbacks. It's not your fault. After that Lily wasn't invited back to the closed beach club until today.

In the summertime the cabanas were festive with flowering baskets and pots of sturdy geraniums that held up well in the salt wind. Red, white, and blue. White cabanas, red flowers, blue bathing suits as if everyone were stuck on one holiday. Now a stack of clay pots huddled against each cabana. One pot was turned right side up with a set of sparkling sequined reindeer antlers blooming and this was Lily's clue. Margaret's father wore them every Christmas to midnight Mass. Margaret thought it was funny until the year it became humiliating. Lily pried open the heavy storm door to the cabana and could see the beam of a flashlight lying on a counter. There was a smell inside like the last lobster was still boiling on the electric two burner. And the baby smell of changed diapers. Margaret? she whispered, but couldn't see her.

Early this morning when it was still dark out Lily tried to call her friends in London. She called Beven's house first and her mother answered the phone. Lily? What a surprise! Lily could hear all her beauty rush down the line, opening up in a happy explosion just for Lily. She didn't know what to say and then remembered to ask for Beven. Why, pumpkin, said Beven's mother. Bevvie's in Mykonos. She just loves it.

But what about school? Lily asked and Mrs. Clark snorted a laugh. Well, she said. Entre nous, I don't think we have a brain surgeon on our hands. Do you? But what about you, darling? When will we see you and your fabulous mother?

Lily explained that they had left London and might not be back soon. But Paula Clark had already begun shouting to someone in the room about rancid cream left out overnight on a countertop. Poisoning Britain's best and brightest. A man's voice rumbled and then the line went dead.

Lily sat still for a moment then decided to go ahead and try Geneva. She would find Lawrence. She was ready. She knew how to dial international information. After the long burbling rings an operator answered in French and then switched to English when Lily asked for Lawrence's academy. Shall I connect?

The long rings again and finally Lily could tell the answering voice that she'd like to speak to Lawrence Weatherfield. The man, who sounded as serious as a priest, said young Mr. Weatherfield had already left the school. For vacation? asked Lily.

271

I'm afraid not. We have an excellent chorale society here, said the man. We're quite proud. Sometimes we even tour outside Geneva. We're renowned for Handel's *Messiah*.

Lily tried the Dorchester, though her hands shook a little at the thought of finding Lawrence in London now that she was gone. It was possible she'd be going back and forth a little bit. Her grandmother seemed to think her father had business to finish up there and it would take some time. The operator clicked through a series of pings and then spoke. Yes. The guest has checked out. Will there be anything else, madame?

Lily put down her grandmother's heavy telephone and climbed back upstairs and into bed until the sun rose and Ruby began her normal singing in the kitchen.

Hey, there you are, said Lily, her eyes adjusting to the dark. Margaret stubbed out a cigarette on the top of a beer can and nodded as if Lily had been there all along. I hate Kools, she finally said, but you can have one if you want. She pushed the pack across the glass top of the coffee table along with a bloated pack of matches. They work, she said.

Lily fingered the hat in her pocket. Margaret was wearing a Santa beard slung low across her chin. She moved it higher and pulled another cigarette from the pack. Pass the matches, she said. You look completely different. I wouldn't even recognize you if I just ran into you on the street.

It's just the coat, said Lily.

Yeah, that's a beast, but I think it's your face. You've got something strange happening, like your cheeks are swollen or something.

Lily touched her cheek, maybe the wind had made her face puff up, but it felt normal. Is that your dad's Santa beard? she said.

You remember it?

Just a guess.

Yes, Margaret pulled it off and revealed a constellation of red pimples framing both sides of her mouth. As if something she'd eaten had exploded outward and then stuck there. Lily tried not to stare. She sat on the plastic weave settee, which sagged and cracked under her weight.

Don't break it, Jumbo.

I saw Anthony, said Lily.

So? You already told me.

Lily watched Margaret take a careful drag on the new cigarette. Do you think we'll be in the same class?

Unlikely. I'm fast-track.

I'm probably fast-track, too, said Lily. I wasn't doing *that* badly.

You know what Anthony used to call you? And he wasn't being mean or anything, just offering an adult perspective. He called you Lobo.

What's a lobo?

For lobotomy, like you'd already had one. Or you were a good candidate. He said that's what the Kennedys had to do with a deficient daughter.

Lily just coughed and closed her eyes against the smoke. Anthony had seemed pretty happy about the twins. He probably wasn't thinking much about lobotomies anymore.

Do you even know what deficient means? Margaret asked.

It means disqualified.

Lily looked around the cabana and noticed some old-looking beer cans lined up on the counter and a small rusty thermos, a black sweatshirt caked with sand turned inside out. Does Anthony still come here?

Sure.

Lily looked harder as if to bring her into better focus. The room was dim except for the flashlight, and the wind punched at the boards outside. Margaret's chest seemed to fall inward a bit and her belly even under her pink ski jacket still looked round like it always had. She hadn't changed much really and that made Lily sad as if she understood that Margaret just hadn't grown up fast enough to keep Anthony's friendship, and they had that in common somehow. That need to grow up faster, much faster or everyone they loved would disappear.

Is he coming here today?

Maybe.

Lily nodded. Margaret plucked out a new cigarette and put the Santa beard back on.

Do you want to go to my grandmother's house?

What's there?

Nothing, said Lily.

They didn't bother to clean up the cabana and they left the antlers sticking up out of the clay pot as a sign. Let him worry for once, said Margaret. Lily set them a little higher as if to taunt him and Margaret laughed.

When they got home, Ruby and her grandmother were playing double solitaire at the kitchen table, moving their hands fast and shouting. Pure hell! cried Momo. Ruby gets all the good cards. They gathered the decks and Ruby stood up and put on an apron. Let me get a look at you, Margaret, said Momo. Well, aren't you just a ray of sunshine. The pair of you. She shook her head with delight and smiled.

26

Sticky thighs and an ache in her belly, her old room in Doris's house was hot, but Jean's shoulders when she sat up were soft under her touch, the skin soft and the bones easy as if holding Nick there had made a difference. Holding his chest close to hers. Her hips were bruised feeling, but here at her throat and her shoulders and her breasts she'd opened to him, was still opening to him.

Christ, she said and pulled herself out from the covers and tiptoed across the floor for her cigarettes. She'd come in when Lily and Doris were already asleep. So she didn't need to explain where Nick had gone; she just crept silently up the stairs, an old expertise. Now all she wanted to do was sleep, too.

The moon was a heavy half globe hanging close to the water. No stars visible behind the snow clouds. A cold rush of air came through the seam of the window like a blade along her thighs. And then the phone rang. Nick no doubt, calling from a bar phone in Red Bank to say Lionel could wait until morning. Wouldn't it be better to come back and see Lily first? Spend the night with her at Doris's? As if they hadn't already discussed it. Half an hour and he was already breaking their agreement. She wouldn't answer. Anything more could wait. Until she knew her own mind, until she could think straight, certainly until he'd sorted things out with Lionel. He'd promised her. At least that was how she understood all that had happened at the house, a promise. Now she'd wait and see. But the phone kept ringing, like he was some teenage boy with confidence and a crush. Why did she want to laugh. She picked up the phone saying, You're impossible.

It was the driver who mispronounced her name, Mrs. Devon? he said. She would tell Lionel this later on. Hello?

Mrs. Devlin, she said.

Yes, ma'am. It's Clifford speaking, ma'am. How are you? Clifford?

Yes, ma'am.

Who is this? One of Lily's friends up in the middle of the night making trouble. She'd have his head. Probably one of the boys they saw in Red Bank earlier today, hanging out around the diner. This Clifford sounded colored. How did he get this number?

Mrs. Devlin?

I'd like to speak to your mother or father immediately. Please put one of your parents on the telephone. Right away, please.

Mrs. Devlin? I'm Mr. Byron's driver? Clifford? Mr. Byron said it was a special favor tonight. He sent me to drive Mr. Devlin to New Jersey. That nice house, on the river and all.

I'm sorry?

Yes, I waited mostly in the car, but then took a quick walk around the dock. I hope you don't mind.

Hold on, she said, and got up and clicked closed the door, wrapped the light silky quilt around her; she smiled to see herself in the mirror. Nick's borrowed driver was calling to say Mr. Devlin would like to turn around. She felt the flush on her skin and shook her head. Always the same. Always the same old craziness. But then thought, Well, maybe.

Clifford?

Yes, ma'am, I'm right here.

You can bring Mr. Devlin back. If that's the question.

No, ma'am. I'm calling because we've been here at the Cheesequake service station for quite some time now. And Mr. Devlin won't come out of the men's restroom.

Won't?

I don't want to make trouble.

Jean was quiet for a moment. Have you called out to him? Have you gone in to look?

I can't really do that, ma'am.

Why not?

Clifford was quiet.

All right. But is there someone else?

I think Mr. Byron wouldn't want me to raise a fuss. Make a commotion. If Mr. Devlin just got tired in there and fell asleep. Which is probably the case. He did say he had a headache and wanted a sip of water. But I get someone involved and it becomes a commotion.

A service attendant?

No. That's what Mr. Byron said.

I see. You spoke with him.

Yes, ma'am. But fortunately he was awake, too.

Why had she answered the phone? There must be a way to learn not to answer the phone in the middle of the night. A simple rule. She would enforce it. Soon.

So Mr. Byron thought, if it isn't an inconvenience?

I see, said Jean. All right.

You'll come, Mrs. Devlin?

Yes, I'm on my way. I'll be there in half an hour.

Thank you, Mrs. Devlin. That's good to hear. And if Mr. Devlin chooses to come out of the men's room before then, I'll suggest we not leave until you arrive.

Jean took a breath. Here she was again, running out into the night.

All right, Clifford. Good-bye.

She'd forgotten how dark the parkway could be. No other cars for miles and her headlights made a scant light on the blacktop. She felt herself crawling through sludge though the speedometer read sixty, sometimes more. This car that Doris had lent her, an old Pontiac her father never used but had tuned to a boaty feeling she'd never liked. Silent, plush, slow. Why had Doris kept hold of this car? But then Jean remembered the televisions. How they'd fought and she almost laughed. Nick would laugh harder. Little Goebbels he liked to call her. I just like a little order now and then she'd plead. A little sanity. And here she was, sane Jean, plowing up a black highway, breaking up the dark with some feeble old headlamps set too low to reach a husband making a scene in a pull-off gas stop. Usually he liked a bigger audience than a borrowed driver.

She reminded herself the exit was on the left. She always forgot and she might sail right past and then this night would be truly interminable. But she didn't need the reminder because two fire trucks, four police cars, and an ambulance were all aflame it seemed as she rounded the bend into their brightness. What poor soul, she wondered, as the ambulance pulled away without any lights spinning. She looked for the accident.

And inside, in the men's room Nick was playing a game, but there was no bite in her for him; something was giving inside her, a vicious pain low down. A volunteer in an orange vest flagged her to stop immediately. Signaling fast to roll down her window. Sorry, ma'am. No service. I'll have to guide you back onto the highway. She was about to comply, when she said her name. She didn't know why. Mrs. Nick Devlin, she said. I'm Mrs. Nicholas Devlin. He tilted his head without changing his expression. Over here, Mrs. Devlin, and pointed to a spot near the pumps, away from all the emergency vehicles and their spiraling lights. For a half moment she thought Clifford may have told them to expect her. Right over there, ma'am. She was glad she'd worn shoes. Almost, almost, she'd left the house in ballet slippers, and now she'd need to step around all these big trucks and cars and talk to a lot of men before she got to Nick. She was glad she'd worn shoes. And a jacket. Just a red cotton jacket. She buttoned it up and stepped out of the car and walked to the trooper who took off his hat before he began to speak to her.

27

Nick's plane had left London late, then circled the Eastern Seaboard for over an hour before touching down at Kennedy, then sat on the tarmac for another two until a gate came free. On the other side of a long customs line, he was surprised to see Clifford waiting. Tania must have alerted the New York office. Relieved not to deal with a rental, he sank into the back of the maroon limousine. The leather smelled of orange peel and hair tonic. It was Billy Byron's personal stretch, not from the pool, which was odd.

He stopped to call Jean at Doris's after they crossed into New Jersey. She said go straight to the house. She'd meet him there. At the pull-off, Nick asked Clifford to go all the way down the driveway and then to please wait a moment. He'd find Mrs. Devlin, then Clifford was free to go. One of Clyde's old cars was parked near the garage, so she must be here. The house was completely dark. There was a bright moon over the water half covered by clouds.

Aim the headlights at the door, sir?

I can see, thanks, he said, but actually he couldn't. He felt as if a thick film had formed over his eyes and he blinked to dispel it. His body sagged with weariness against the dip in the seat. Right, he said and forced himself out.

The yard was streaked, all white moonlight and gray shadow, but when he got to the back steps he held on to the rail and stopped. The space before him went black as if the strange film had now canceled his sight completely.

Clifford stepped out of the car. Mr. Devlin? You need help?

Fine, fine. Nick waved him away. I'm fine. Thank you, Clifford. Give me a minute or two.

He felt his way up the railing, and then, like nothing, he was out of the blackness and holding fast to the knob of the back door. A porcelain thing with a painted rose and silver edging. Strange for a kitchen door, but a gift from Jean's father and usually shining.

He stumbled his way through the dark house, calling out, Sweetheart? Jean? But she wouldn't answer. He started up the precarious stair, lit bright by the wide Palladian window on the landing. This is where the ghost sat, Lily always said, right at the turn. Thick white rectangles playing on the damaged treads and up the curved banister. Then all went black again.

He stood and waited. Gripping tight to the old mahogany. What had he taken on the plane? Just some sleeping pills, he thought. Then Clifford gave him something in the car for jet lag, saying that Billy Byron swore by it. Maybe the remedy for this was also in Billy's car stash. His head began to splinter in pain behind his right eye, and that seemed an improvement; it broke up the dark and there, the rectangles of light were back on the wrecked treads and the satiny comforting feel of the banister opened up in his

281

hand again. Yes, better. He climbed the stairs. Jean? he called out. He heard something drop in Lily's room and palmed his way down the dark hallway to the door. Jean?

There she was, crouching down on the floor, feeling along the baseboard, frowning. Her tweed skirt rode up high on her thighs. In the cloudy moonlight, her legs looked pale. Didn't you hear me calling you?

Strange, she said. It's the only untouched place in the whole house. Wait until you see our room. Floors disintegrated. Anthony Moldano and company are guessing some chemical, nothing fancy, but they cut the power. One of them said they were amazed the place hadn't ignited. But nothing in here.

He nodded. Lucky.

She wouldn't look at him. She put her hands on her knees and balanced, watching the floor. In what way are we lucky? she asked, softly, as if curious to hear his answer.

Maybe he should get down on the floor too, pretend that was really why they were meeting in the dark. A surprising possibility. She turned toward him at last.

Her short hair was combed straight back from her face and her eyes were open wide like when he'd first known her. But when she stood up, arms hanging loose, she looked forsaken. He almost didn't know what to say. All the furniture, he said. I can't remember where anything went. Where was the bed?

Right here. Jean walked the shape and then stood where a pillow might have been, facing the corner window. The sky from there looked ruffled with snow clouds, tiny flakes began to spin down here and there. Nick came closer. You okay?

Yes. Yes, fine, she said, moving slightly away.

He touched her shoulder, then reached his arm all the way around, pulling her back against his chest. He kissed the top of her head. She waited a breath, then let herself be held.

Jean, sweetheart, he said, and just stayed holding her. Then finally he said, This is Lionel. I'm sure of it. And it's me, too, in a way. No, wait. Wait. No, don't move, and I'll tell you.

She tried to turn to face him, but he held on to her. I don't get it, she said. I don't understand.

He wants something from me, something in London. Something new.

She shook her head. Oh god.

He sees an opportunity there, and I've been positioned to make it happen. Do you see?

Jean kept still for a very long while. And you said no.

I didn't even say it. Or maybe I did. I did.

A quick bird lift of her chin. Well, why can't you say yes?

He coughed hard, turning away to catch his breath.

You could say yes and then change your mind. Jean unwound herself to face him. Nick tried to smile. Come on.

You could do that, just the first step or two, and then, I don't know, get a proxy? My father never did anything himself, she said.

Sweetheart, I am the proxy.

She watched his face, studied him closely, and her eyes lost the sweetness he'd seen before. Well, that's ridiculous, she said. I don't believe you.

He kept watching her eyes.

You're just saying that because you're stoned. I can't listen to you like this. She shook him off.

She touched the window, ran her fingertips along panes feeling for cracks. The cold was beginning to clear his head.

This room has good morning light, did you know that?

Her face in profile. He loved the long shape of her mouth, the way it curled like a cat's when she was thinking. Tell me, he said. What?

She turned and the curl vanished, and her head seemed a dark unknowable shape. Shifting cloud cover dulled the moonlight.

You know, she said. I think if you try, Lionel may just be receptive to reason.

Nick sighed. You don't understand.

I do understand. Only you need to approach him in the right way. He hates to be ignored. Anything else, he can tolerate, she said. He just wants your attention.

That's what Harry said.

Well, for once Harry and I agree. Just appease him a little.

And then what?

Jean felt along the windowsill. The satiny paint she'd used was still intact.

Aren't you cold? he asked. Where the hell's your coat?

What do you care?

Even in Lily's room the smell of the chemical used to sear the floors seeped in and made his skin feel tight. The stink was twisting deeper now. All right, he said. I'll talk to him. But I can't do the London thing. I'm done with all that, Jean. You have to know that.

You just told me I don't know anything, she said. And then, quieter, Out behind the garage? I can't even begin there. Someone else will have to do it.

Nick nodded. I know.

You'll talk to him?

I will. Yes.

Tonight?

Not tonight.

Let's get this over with, okay?

And then just for a second he could see her eyes light on him as if she'd thought of something tender.

What? he said.

I'll tell you later.

Tell me now.

I was remembering the honey dream.

He smiled. I don't believe you.

Just the part about the honey dripping and I was going to take it in my hand. Remember? She lifted a cupped hand and waved it, smiling slightly.

He watched her. I can't do what he wants, you know. I can't anymore.

She sighed then leaned back against the wall. How about sweater over the head, she said. One pull.

He pulled the sweater up off of her lifted arms. She wore a blue stitched bra he always liked; he touched the strap and she bent to kiss his wrist. You can do anything, she said. You're the king of new, right? Right? He covered her mouth with his to stop her talking, put his hand over her eyes, her throat, then undid the bra. One breast, both, his fingers resting on the cool of her skin. Then he found the zipper on her skirt, yanked on the hook and eye. She reached around and the skirt dropped. His knuckle brushed the scar that divided her belly, both babies born this way; maybe the next would be different. The back of his hand down to the top of her thighs and up again. Lace band bright in the dark, he caught the edge and pulled. Tipped into him, her skin soft, smelling of some ordinary soap, almond, and yes, maybe honey. He wanted to laugh and then remembered Cubbie's odd compliment for his school friend Claudia. He'd drawn a picture of a perfect white square. She's as beautiful as white soap, Cubbie said and now Nick thought finally, he finally got it.

Acknowledgments

Thanks to Elisabeth Schmitz for her luminous and extraordinary editing. Thanks to brilliant Melanie Jackson. Thanks to my beloved aunt Claire Walcovy for her encouragement. Thanks to Katie Raissian, Deb Seager, Charles Rue Woods, Christian Potter Drury, Paula Cooper Hughes, Morgan Entrekin and all the gracious ones at Grove Atlantic. Thanks to Brigid Hughes and Elizabeth Gaffney for taking early looks and to Dick Howe for his essential expertise. Thanks to the Corporation of Yaddo, its wonderful artists and sustaining angels. Thanks to Dana Prescott and Charles Bock for the invitation to glorious Civitella Ranieri. Thanks and love to friends and family: Diana Colbert, Hampton Fancher, C.A.M., Anne Wade, the original loved ones, their devoted writers, the Reillys and the mighty Pod. Above all, deepest thanks, dearest love to Duke Beeson for his oceanic generosity and kindness.